Sue Welfare

Published by Mirror Books,
an imprint of Trinity Mirror plc,
1 Canada Square, London E14 5AP, England

www.mirrorbooks.com twitter.com/themirrorbooks

Mirror Books 2017

ISBN 9781907324888

First paperback edition
Some names and identifying details have been changed.

Typeset by Danny Lyle
DanJLyle@gmail.com

Printed and bound in Great Britain by
CPI Group (UK) Ltd, Croydon, CR0 4YY

Every effort has been made to fulfil requirements with regard to
reproducing copyright material. The author and publisher will be glad to
rectify any omissions at the earliest opportunity.

Dedicated to my precious friend, Kate,
who inspired this story as we drove to
Wales to say one last goodbye.

Acknowledgements

I'd like to thank all the fabulous Beta Readers of Facebook for their thoughts, suggestions, edits and help in getting this book beaten into shape – these include the amazing Fiona Prevett, Lisa Garwood, Cath Duhig, Joanne Flemming and Maria Hartzenberg – although there are lots of others too whose contributions have been invaluable.

Thank You!

I'd also like to thank the very talented women responsible for the nuts and bolts of getting *Losing Leah* ready for publication: Jane Dixon-Smith, Susan Opie for her insightful editing and suggested changes, Maureen Vincent-Northam for her eagle-eyed editing skill and Rebecca Emin. Thank you. I couldn't do it without you.

Chapter One
Losing Leah

THE BREAK

'A missing person: anyone whose whereabouts is unknown whatever the circumstances of their disappearance. They will be considered missing until located and their well-being or otherwise established.' Missing Persons ACPO Guidance 2005.

'Excuse me, you can't be in here, Sir.' She was polite.

The man, who had his back to her, didn't reply. He was crouched, frantically working his way along the room peering under the cubicle doors. He was a not big man perhaps five feet eight or nine at most, and slightly built, dressed in a jacket and casual trousers. He was in his fifties, certainly not young.

'Come on, let's get you out of here.' All business. Val, who had worked security on the early shift at Hoden Gap Services for just over a year spoke clearly, without any kind of edge to her voice, offering no threat, no aggression, nothing to wind the man up, just a clear, crisp instruction – but she was ready

1

for him. Ex-Army, there wasn't much she hadn't seen before. Security officer in a food court and retail area in a fiddling little service station tucked away on the Welsh border was a piece of piss compared to a tour in Basra.

She watched the man make his way along the cubicles, weighing him up as he moved, trying to work out what was going on and how best to deal with him. You didn't have to be a genius to work out that he was looking for someone. There was no indication that he was armed or on anything, although you never could tell, and it didn't pay to make assumptions; sometimes they spat or scratched themselves so they bled, said they'd got HIV or Hep, especially when she'd been working in the big malls in Bristol. But probably not this man – sizing him up, even if he had a knife, Val knew that she could take him if it came to it. He looked like he would snap like a twig. Maybe he was drunk or nuts; she'd seen her share of both over the years.

'Come on, Sir,' she repeated, more firmly this time. Val had a rule of three. It was a personal thing – ask nicely three times before upping the ante.

Still the man didn't respond, instead he carried on searching, lurching from stall to stall, throwing the doors open and banging on those that were locked, ignoring the anxious shrieks from the women inside. He was mumbling something.

The ladies' toilets at Hoden Gap Services were in a long, narrow, rectangular room, painted dark blue and white, with sinks, dryers and mirrors at both ends and cubicles running along both long sides. As the man turned to open a stall door on the far side Val could see he wasn't armed, no knife, no gun. *Here we go*, she thought.

Geno, her partner on the early shift, hung back, staying close to the doorway. There wasn't a door as such just an offset panel so that people couldn't see in. Geno was probably fifteen feet away, maybe more. He didn't say anything or come close enough to give her a hand but he did an exaggerated wink as she caught his eye. Great lazy sack of shite that he was, about as much use as a chocolate fireguard. It hadn't taken her very long to realise that they'd only hired him because he looked the part, that and the fact his dad knew the manager.

Geno nodded towards the man, the implication being that she should hurry up and get on with it. Val looked away; she'd like to snap Geno like a twig.

It was company policy to send a woman in first to handle any trouble, to try and diffuse a situation, the reasoning being that a woman could very often calm things down. Men often saw other men as a threat or a challenge, and adrenaline and testosterone took over, ramping up the chances of something kicking off. Conversely most men, even pissed or off their heads, thought twice before attacking a woman. Not that this man looked as if he was going to attack anyone, but you couldn't be too careful.

Val moved in. He'd had his three chances. She stepped up behind him. The man was stumbling, completely focused on what he was doing. He was also upset, his movements frantic and shambolic. Now she was closer Val could hear what he was saying, 'Where are you? Where are you?' he whimpered over and over again.

Val adjusted her stance, just in case, and then dropped a hand onto his shoulder. 'Who are you looking for? ' she said. 'Maybe I can help.'

Chapter One

Wrapped up in his own thoughts her touch took the man by complete surprise. He swung round, apparently astonished to see her there. Tears were streaming down his face.

'My wife,' he sobbed. 'I can't find my wife.'

*

DI Harry Baker was stretched out in the passenger seat peering out of the window at the spring landscape as it scrolled past us on the motorway.

The day was damp, a pall of heavy grey cloud hanging over everything, cutting away the view of the hills. There were intermittent showers of rain and sleet, and other than the constant stream of traffic in both directions, the landscape had been bleached out by the low cloud and spray, leaving no real colour or signs of life.

'Middle of bloody nowhere,' Baker sighed, picking at a tiny strip of something dark caught in the glass between the closed window and the door panel.

'It's lovely round here. Unspoilt, Sir,' I said, easing the unmarked police car out of the flow of traffic and up onto the off ramp that would take us to Hoden Gap Services.

The call handler who recorded the incoming 999 call from the services earlier that morning had a standard form to complete for the report of a missing person. It covers the bare bones: a missing person's name, age, what they looked like, what they were wearing, where they went missing from and if going missing is out of character, whether they had a vehicle or other means of transport available and finally an assessment of the person making the report, along with their contact details.

Everything has to begin somewhere with something.

The service station duty manager had called it in while security kept the man calm and seated. The missing woman's husband, Chris Hills, was extremely distressed and insisted on talking to the call handler himself. On the recording he sounded upset, angry, deeply frustrated, lost.

'You have to find her,' he repeated over and over again until the duty manager took the phone away from him and even then it was possible to hear him in the background. *You have to find her.*

First responders to the scene were two traffic officers on their way home, about to go off duty, who drew the short straw because they were the closest by miles when the call came through. They had taken down the basic facts and flagged it up, which was why I was driving to the service station with my boss, Harry Baker, to help interview a man being detained by security for losing his wife.

Alongside me, Baker sniffed. 'Personally I prefer my landscape spoilt, shops, houses, nicely manicured lawns, a kebab van here and there, some signs of civilisation.'

I didn't reply. We had been working together for just under a year since Baker's last DS had had a heart attack, decided enough was enough and got himself an allotment.

I'd got the radio turned to Borders FM, a local station, burbling away in the background. Despite the bank of devices we've got screwed to the dashboard, police or no police it's still often the best way to get the latest traffic updates. Coming up to the hour the jingle for the news headlines cut in, and then, 'Reports are just coming in of a missing woman in the Ross-On-Wye area, Mrs Leah Hills, 44, last seen at Hoden Gap Services wearing a camel coat and brown boots. Anyone who–'

'Jesus.' Baker turned towards me, turning down the radio as he did, attention shifting away from the view. 'Anyone issue a statement?'

I shook my head. 'Not us, Sir, not yet. Probably someone at the services phoned it in. It took a while before anyone could get there this morning; there was an accident on the M50.'

Baker sniffed. 'Oh perfect, just what we need. It'll be all over the internet by now. Share this. Tweet that.'

Baker's views on the pros and cons of the internet were well known. 'It was a bloody sight easier when we had some control over who knew what and when they knew it.' He rolled his wrist round to get a look at his watch. 'Where's the husband?'

'Still in the service area at the moment. They're keeping him there till we have chance to talk to him, not that he seems inclined to go anywhere. And the management have given us the use of an empty office to coordinate the search for his wife.'

*

Missing persons cases are unusual because going missing, in itself, isn't a crime. We rank how we deal with each report based on how vulnerable the missing person is, weighed along with the risk they pose either to themselves or to the wider public. The level of risk impacts on the resources that get thrown at it.

Low Risk, low priority – for example a healthy adult who is fed up and walks out of their job, debts, a life they hate – and where the officers, based on what they are told and their assessment of the circumstances, and a few basic enquiries, can decide that no further action is required. People can't be made to stay somewhere they don't want to. Some estimates say that over three hundred thousand people disappear annually in the UK. Over eight hundred every day.

Missing person details are logged onto the Police National Computer and passed on to the Missing Person's Helpline and the case kept under regular review in case things change.

Medium Risk, the missing person is likely to be in some kind of danger or is a threat to themselves or to others. We do all the things we do for the low risk case but take a more active, measured response to trace the person and support whoever it is reported them missing.

The resources made available are ultimately decided by those higher up the food chain based on the information we have available, so how the officer in charge, the SIO, calls it makes a huge amount of difference to what gets thrown at it.

High Risk: the risk is immediate and there are strong reasons to believe the missing person is in danger, either through their own vulnerability, or as a victim of a serious crime, or there are substantial grounds for believing the public is in danger.

There is a checklist of questions applied to each missing persons case and if the answer to any of them is yes then they creep up the scale to high risk.

The list is long but there are some obvious ones, someone is suicidal, depressed, on regular medication and left without it, was the victim of domestic abuse, or a violent crime, or there is reason to believe they were abducted or that they are a danger to others – the list goes on, and officers are allowed a degree of autonomy in how they call it. But no one wants to get it wrong.

So, the higher risk? The more complex it gets, the more resources we can pull in depending on the circumstances, with specialist teams getting involved if we need them.

We're not there yet, but we were already climbing the ladder. Chris Hills was insisting that the disappearance was totally out of character for his wife. According to traffic he said she was steady, shy, and Chris Hills couldn't think of any circumstance where she would have left of her own accord. He was adamant. By the time we arrived a team had already been mobilised on the back of the first responders' report, and Baker assigned as senior investigating officer as we'd come on shift that morning.

*

I slowed down to ride out the speed bumps in the road and then circled round the petrol station into the service area car park.

Baker nodded. 'Who else have we got on site?'

'Charlie Rees is managing the scene, Jack Ledbetter coordinating the search.'

'Safe hands then. Let's just hope she turns up sharpish.' Baker glanced down at the tablet on his knee. 'Leah Hills. Forty-four-year-old florist.'

'Heading off for a weekend away,' I said.

'Where are we with the helicopter?'

'I've put a request in.'

Baker glanced round. 'It would make the search a bloody sight easier.'

On the dashboard my phone, sitting in a cradle, pinged.

Baker raised an eyebrow. 'That must be half a dozen texts you've had since we got in the car, Daley.'

'You're counting?' I said, surprised that he'd noticed.

Baker shrugged. 'The scenery's not much to look at.' He nodded towards the phone. 'Anything we should know about?'

I shook my head. The text alert was distinctive, and personal. 'Not really, Guv, I bought some stuff online a couple of weeks ago and I think they sold my details on.'

'Bloody typical; there should be a government health warning on the internet,' muttered Baker as the phone pinged again. 'Let's get parked up. Can you let Charlie Rees know we've arrived and get an update? I want to take a look around before we talk to the husband. Get a coffee, get the lie of the land.'

I nodded and pulled up alongside a patrol car parked in the staff area. A constable was keeping a log of who was on site. We signed in and I rang Charlie Rees.

'Just to let you know that we're here.' The signal was patchy. I had to move to keep from it breaking up. 'I'll be in, in a little while.'

'Getting the lie of the land, are we?' said Rees dryly.

'That's right,' I said, watching Baker heading over towards the coffee shop. 'What have you got for me?'

'Short answer?' said Rees. 'Bugger all so far, but here we go.'

Chapter One

The area around the service station was colder and a lot bleaker than it looked from the inside of the car. My earlier defence that the surrounding countryside was beautiful and unspoilt was not so persuasive once we were actually out in it. The relentless wind was edged with sleet, the gusts so cold that they took your breath away.

'There are only four possibilities,' said Baker, taking a long pull on his coffee. I wasn't sure whether he was talking to me or just thinking aloud.

He caught my gaze. I decided to bite. 'Which are, Sir?'

'Everyone needs a straight man, Daley, never forget that. Either Leah Hills left here of her own volition, she was abducted, she is still here somewhere or she was never here at all.' He paused. 'This is really good,' he said, waggling the cardboard cup in my direction. 'You should have had one. Warm you up. You look perished.'

I nodded, stuffing my hands deeper into my coat pockets, wishing I'd brought some gloves. 'You're not wrong.'

'Best case scenario Leah Hills turns up in a couple of hours, bit weepy, sorry to have caused all the fuss and we can all go home,' he said.

'And not dead,' I added.

Baker glanced across at me. There was a question in his expression.

'Just seems a weird place to disappear,' I said.

Baker took another pull on his coffee. 'Everyone in transit, people in and out? It makes sense in lots of ways.'

'She's a middle-aged housewife who works in a florist.' I reminded him. In my handbag my phone pinged again. I ignored it.

'And according to Rees, Chris Hills told the first responders that he and his wife were blissfully happy,' I said. 'Soul mates.'

Baker raised his eyebrows. 'Right,' he said grimly, turning round to take in the view.

We were standing on top of a manmade grass bank that was topped with conifers. The bank ran all the way round the services, wrapped around like a protective arm with just a break for the roadway in and out. Between them the trees and the bank did a good job of sheltering the site, but standing up on the top of the bank we were getting the full force of the prevailing wind that swept in across open farmland from the distant hills.

Baker had turned again and was staring out into the car park. 'The report said she was wearing a camel coat?'

I pulled up the notes that had been sent to my phone. 'Uhuh. Nine hundred quid's worth apparently. Her husband bought it for her as a Christmas present. Said this was the first time she had really worn it.'

'And what does that mean exactly?'

'He wasn't sure if she liked it, said he was pleased when she said she was going to bring it with her.'

'Well, let's hope it's waterproof,' Baker said. 'You wouldn't want to go far on foot in this weather.'

I nodded; the wind cut to the bone, I could barely feel my face or my fingers.

The one good thing about being up on the bank was that it did give us a decent view out over the whole site. The food and retail areas were off to our right, low, hunkered down in the landscape and built from red brick, the petrol station, which was situated closer to the motorway, was straight ahead. The car park wrapped around the entire service area, a slatted fence, bins and signage dividing the public car park from an area designated for HGVs. Directly below us, across a stretch of grass and tarmac, a PC, who was watching over the cordoned-off parking bay where Chris Hills' Mercedes was standing, was stamping her feet in an attempt to keep warm. She looked frozen.

'Only four possible solutions. Still here, left by herself, left under duress or she was never here at all.'

'So why would the husband report her missing if she was never here? Doesn't make any sense, drawing attention to yourself. Why would you do it?' It was a stupid question, I'd seen people do all sorts of bizarre things over the years I'd been in the force.

Baker shrugged. 'Maybe Mr Hills is an attention seeker, maybe by reporting it here he's hoping to deflect attention away from somewhere else, his house, his shed, some grim little lock up in a back street somewhere. There are a lot of places to dump a body between here and – where did you say he came from?

'Norfolk, Denham Market.' I paused. 'I grew up near there.'

'Denham Market?'

'Yes, Sir, till I was ten or so. Nice place if you like it flat.'

'Bit of a haul from here.'

I nodded.

'Okay, so plenty of time and lots of opportunity to get rid of a body. Or maybe his wife's left him, or this is a cry for help, or his wife doesn't exist at all, and all this is a figment of his imagination.'

I looked at him. 'Interesting hypothesis.'

Baker snorted. 'Until we've talked to him and seen the CCTV, we won't know, will we? Come on, let's take a look round, and then we'll go and talk to Mr Hills.' He raised the Styrofoam cup. 'You really should have had a coffee.'

I followed him along the top of the bank.

*

In a break room at the back of the services Chris Hills had started to pace anxiously. A PC had taken over from the service station security guard. Hills wanted to know when he could talk to someone more senior. He wanted to know what was being done to find his wife. He wanted to know why it was taking so long for someone senior to arrive. He wanted to know what was going on. He wanted to know why he couldn't join the search. He paced backwards and forwards, unable to sit for more than a few minutes at a time.

*

Hoden Gap Services had nothing to distinguish it from dozens of others like it up and down the country; anonymous, glass fronted, a mix of red brick and wood cladding, laid out to what looked like a standard off the shelf design. Half an hour or so from Ross on Wye it was tucked away off a slip road from the motorway in a pleat of land framed by the rise of the

Malvern Hills. From the top of the bank there were few signs of habitation for miles in any direction. Beyond the carefully maintained grass and trees surrounding the filling station and service area it was mostly scrubland cut with ditches and the odd scatter of fly-tipped rubbish. Signs, faded from being out in the weather too long, read:

> **'Exciting New Development.**
> **Great Investment opportunity**
> **Outline planning for 34 industrial units.**
> **Finance Available. Call us today for details!'**

The invitation was followed by the name of a local estate agent, Thirlings, and their phone number. I made a note.

A couple of hundred yards from the bank, just visible amongst the thin brown grass that had been cut down by the long miserable winter, some optimist had laid out a whole series of roadways, paths, concrete pads and parking bays. Beyond the bare bleached bones of the industrial estate a couple of cars, too far away to pick out their number plates or even their make, were parked up in the lee of a dilapidated shed.

'Can we find out who owns those cars?' asked Baker.

'I'll get uniform to find out,' I said, making another note.

'And can you find out how they got there?' Baker asked, putting his hand up to his eyes to cut out the low sun's glare. 'Presumably there has to be a service road so staff can get in and out without having to go half way up the motorway?'

I nodded and directed his gaze. 'Yes, but by the look of it that's over there on the other side of the petrol station. The service road goes back round… 'I scrolled across to the map on my phone '…to Cudmore, that's the nearest town, which is about three or four miles away.'

Baker nodded. 'So let's find out where they came from,' he said nodding towards the distant cars. 'And how they got there.'

In amongst the rubble, the rubbish and the outlines of the industrial estate, newly arrived uniformed officers had started their search for Leah Hills. Chris Hills' distress and his insistence that her disappearance was completely out of character had already upped the ante.

An organised search always makes me feel uneasy, makes something tighten in the bottom of my belly. It's a potent mix of fear, apprehension, anticipation, and a strange kind of dark and not altogether acceptable excitement. I've never shaken it off and I've never talked to anyone about it, but it's there. I watched them for a moment or two as they worked, willing them not to find a body in amongst the debris. Alongside me Baker zipped up his Barbour and drained the last of his coffee.

'Have they searched the bins?' he asked, indicating a row of industrial wheelie bins and a skip that were partially obscured by the fancy fence that divided the car park from the HGV parking area.

I ran down the notes on the screen. 'They did a visual on the bins and the surrounding area on arrival.' As I ran down the list of what had already been done I was conscious of the guidance for all officers involved with missing persons enquiries. *To ensure that no evidence was lost, no scene compromised, the advice was, if in doubt, think murder.*

Chapter One

I took another look at the officers working in the icy wind making their way across the uneven grass and hoped that this time the advice wouldn't be needed.

'There was nothing obvious or visible; the bins are supposed to be collected later today so they're all brim full. We've requested a temporary hold on collection in case SOCO want to take a closer look, if Leah Hills doesn't turn up.'

'Rather them than me,' said Baker, glancing down at the one closest to us. It was crammed to overflowing with food waste and stained cartons. 'At least the cold and this wind should keep the smell down.'

Baker took one more long slow turn, his gaze travelling around the perimeter of the services, and then he pointed off into the distance. 'See that?'

I looked to where he was pointing. Close to the trees, behind the lorry park, a path had been worn into the grass leading up over the bank, picking out a trail that appeared to go between the conifers and was just visible heading off into scrubland beyond.

'Not everyone can be bothered to go inside to use the facilities in the middle of the night, Sir. We're talking lorry drivers here.'

Baker nodded and then traced a line along the top of the bank. 'There are a couple of ruts along there, can you see? Probably people wanting to stretch their legs, walk the dog, that sort of thing. Can you get someone to check them out too, see if they go anywhere else other than just over the bank.'

I nodded. 'I'll add it to my list.'

'Right, so we've got scrubland, the petrol station, some-where to get a coffee and a burger and the motorway, not exactly very inspiring is it? What sort of CCTV coverage are we talking about?'

'Uniform are on it, but what we've got at the moment is number plate recognition on vehicles coming in and out from the motorway, which also picks up the staff service road.' I pointed with my pen to show him the area covered. 'Cameras are angled to pick up the plates not the occupants. We're busy picking up anything else anyone's got. Chris Hills is pretty sure about the time he and his wife arrived, so Rees has already got someone going through it as it's coming in, and copies of everything are being sent to the station. Uniforms are talking to staff and—'

Baker held up a hand. 'Come on, let's get down off this bank and get inside, Daley, I'm bloody freezing,' he said.

Gratefully I followed him down the slope into the relative shelter of the car park.

*

The retail and food court areas had only one way in and out for members of the general public. There were a clutch of service doors along the back of the buildings, serving the shops, the cleaning staff, and as fire escapes, but according to the notes I'd had from Rees, all of them were fitted with alarms and according to the shop workers and the alarm logs, had not been opened or triggered for at least an hour either side of Leah's disappearance. A series of recent break-ins had made the site owners extra vigilant, both in terms of rear door

Chapter One

CCTV coverage and keeping the logs current. To get in or out staff had to use a swipe card or key in a code. No one who had done either of those things had let any unauthorised person in or out, a fact that could be easily verified by CCTV. Since the break-ins it had become a sackable offence to let any unauthorised person use the rear doors. Work was scarce locally, people wanted to keep their jobs, no one had come in or out who couldn't be accounted for.

The lorry park at the back of the complex could take around twelve rigs, but it looked as if drivers had to walk round and use the main entrance along with Joe Public. Before Baker and I went in to talk to Mr Hills we walked around the outside of the buildings absorbing the details, making notes as we went, trying to get a feel for the place.

Even a superficial recce was making me increasingly doubtful about the CCTV. From where the cameras were placed it didn't take a genius to work out that there were whole areas where there was unlikely to be any decent coverage, if you could see anything at all.

The back doors of the shops and café were well covered, areas where there were likely to be break-ins or the chance of vandalism, the same was true for the HGV parking bays, but beyond that it was hard to tell just how much use it would be.

Back inside the service area people were making their way in and out, oblivious. According to Rees' first reports, none of the staff had seen Leah Hills, not one.

'If she didn't buy anything then it's not likely anyone would have noticed her,' I said to the boss, glancing round the busy concourse.

'Maybe someone saw her in the ladies toilets,' said Baker.

He'd obviously never been in one. 'Before seven in the morning, no queue? The likelihood is unless she did something weird or talked to someone then no one would have noticed her there either.'

'If she made it that far,' Baker said grimly.

'We're organising appeals boards to be put up on the monitors in the main concourse and uniform are tracking down the cleaners. Hopefully the CCTV will turn up something.'

Baker glanced round at the steady stream of travellers. 'Anyone who saw her is probably long gone. We need to get this out to the media as soon as we can and on the website and the rest of it.'

Baker-speak for social media, the thing he loathed the most but which, given the cutbacks, was proving more and more useful.

I nodded.

'We've got a current photo?' he asked.

'Yes, Sir, Rees had it emailed over. You'll have one on your phone.' Baker didn't move, so I got my phone out of my bag.

There were eight messages unread in my inbox, all marked Mr XXXXXX. I ignored them and scrolled down through to my email.

'Chris Hills gave us one from his phone and one of the tech team has pulled another one off the website of the garden centre where Leah Hills works. Here we are—'

I increased the size of the image before handing my phone over. Leah Hills was small, probably no more than five feet two inches tall with long straight dark brown hair tucked behind her ears. She was dressed in the garden centre uniform and looked like a schoolgirl posing for the class photo, with a warm but slightly reticent smile.

'She looks a lot younger than forty-four,' said Baker, handing the phone back. 'When was it taken, do you know?'

I glanced down the details that had come with the photo. 'Last summer. Apparently they do one every year. Her husband told Sergeant Rees that it was a good likeness.'

'Okay, so let's get that out to as many news outlets as we can. Let's get another coffee and then I'll go and talk to the husband, while you work your way through your list.'

I nodded. 'On it.'

As I walked away I scrolled back to the texts. 'RU around 2nite?' said the latest one. 'Yes or no?'

I deleted it, along with all the others and hurried to the office we had been given.

Outside, the sleet was getting heavier and the wind was picking up. I looked out at the worsening weather hoping that wherever she was, Leah Hills had found somewhere warm and dry to shelter.

Chapter Two

Chris Hills

Chris Hills was pacing up and down in the small, cramped staff room at the back of the service area. One wall was stacked with cartons of paper cups and wraps of paper towels, while grey plastic chairs were arranged in a horseshoe around the other three walls. There was a battered coffee table in the centre of the room, littered with cups and plates and leftovers from breakfast, a smell of fried onions and grease lingered in the air. The room was hot and windowless.

Chris Hills had been waiting all morning for a senior officer to arrive, someone he could talk to, someone who would listen and be able to do something about the situation. He was not happy at being kept waiting. He was not happy because he hadn't been allowed to join the search for his wife. He was not happy at being kept out of the information loop. He was not happy.

'Have you found her yet?' he said, swinging round as DI Baker opened the door.

Chapter Two

Baker shook his head. 'I'm afraid not, Mr Hills.'

'Is there any news?'

'Would you like to take a seat.' Baker indicated one of the chairs on the far side of the coffee table, and introduced himself, as he hung up his coat and apologised for keeping him waiting so long. Baker's voice was low and calm, it was a voice that encouraged confidence and co-operation.

'Thank you for being so patient. We need to go over what happened this morning. Would you like anything? A drink, water, before we start?' He glanced at the PC who had been assigned to Chris Hills, well aware that all these offers had already been made.

'I just want to find my wife, I don't want anything else.' Hills said miserably, sliding down onto one of the grey plastic chairs. And then he waved the words away. 'I'm sorry,' he said, eyes bright with tears. 'I don't mean to be rude, but I can't bear this. Really. It's awful – something must have happened, this is not like Leah, not like her at all.'

Baker nodded. 'I do understand and let me assure you we're doing everything we possibly can to find Leah. I just need to ask you a few questions, get a few more details, get straight exactly what happened.'

'I've already told the other policemen. The ones that came first of all. They wrote down every word. Everything.' Hills bit his lip. 'We're wasting precious time here. Leah's been gone hours we need to be out looking—'

Baker nodded. He would have felt much the same if he had been kept hanging around for what must have felt like an eternity with no news. 'I understand that this is really worrying—'

Hills stared at him. 'I don't think you do. How can you possibly understand? I'm worried sick about her.'

'Most people who go missing are back within a few hours,' said Baker. 'My officers are currently combing the area around the service station and the motorway, pictures of Leah are being released to the press. We've got people going through the CCTV. So what I want from you is anything else you can tell us, anything at all that will make the job of finding her easier. I know you've been through it before but it's easy to overlook something small, something that seems trivial.'

'Please don't patronise me. You should be out there trying to find her.' Hills's voice rose as he pointed towards the closed door. A single tear trickled down his face. 'Please,' he begged. 'Please.'

'Tell me what happened this morning,' Baker pressed. His tone as calm and reassuring as before.

Chris Hills stared at Baker, his face was pale, his expression drawn and tense. 'I don't want to *tell* you what happened,' he said. 'We should be looking for her.'

Baker said nothing.

Chris Hills ran his fingers back through his hair. He was a lean man with not an ounce of spare flesh on him, a narrow face and the complexion of someone who spent a lot of his time indoors.

'I could have found her, you know,' Hills said miserably, 'if it hadn't been for the stupid woman dragging me out of the toilets and ringing the police. Ridiculous.'

He looked up at Baker. 'She wouldn't listen to me – the woman, the security guard – she said I had to get out. I knew

23

that obviously, but she wouldn't listen, and then once we were outside she wouldn't let me go, wouldn't let me look for Leah and now it's too late. I'm sure I could have found her.'

Baker nodded. 'We are on the same side, Mr Hills,' he said gently. 'We will do our best to find Leah and the best way you can help us do that is to tell me exactly what happened this morning.'

From outside in the corridor, beyond the closed door, came the sounds of laughter and raised female voices. Chris Hills flinched as if he had been punched.

'Where were the two of you going?' asked Baker, pulling the man's attention back into the room.

Hills clung on to the silence for a moment and then said, 'Wales. We've got a holiday cottage there. We'd been driving a while – three hours or so – we both needed a break, grab a coffee, stretch our legs, use the loo—'

'And where had you driven from?'

'Norfolk, Denham Market.'

Baker nodded. 'And can you tell me exactly where the cottage is in Wales?'

A muscle tightened in Hills' jaw. 'I've already given the other officers the address. And the address of our house in Norfolk. Can you tell me why you wanted my car keys?'

'We need to check the most obvious places first, Mr Hills. It's purely routine,' said Baker.

'Routine? Even though my car was locked? Even though Leah hasn't got a key? Even though I'd already told the other policeman that?'

Baker nodded.

'And did you find Leah in my car?' Hills' tone was weighted with frustration. 'Sitting there, waiting patiently, wondering where I'd got to and what all the police cars were doing here?' He paused, working his fingers into a knot. 'It feels like I'm in the middle of a bad dream. I've been here for hours waiting for you to show up to tell me something and you don't know any more than I do, do you? I can't just sit here.' He lifted his hands to encompass them all. 'How can she have just vanished? She was there one minute.' He gestured as if she was in front of him. 'I saw her. And then she was gone. She hates fuss. She'll hate all this.'

'We're doing everything we can.'

'So everyone keeps telling me.' Chris Hills took a deep breath, any bluster fading. 'I just hope that's it's true,' he said miserably. 'I really do.'

'What were your plans for today?' asked Baker.

'We were heading off for a long weekend. The cottage is near Llandelio. We both love it there. It's quiet, miles from anywhere. Unspoilt. We've been going there for years.' He backhanded away a flurry of tears. 'It's right on the river – it's lovely.'

'And do you always stop here on your way to Wales?'

'Not always but usually. This place is smaller than the big service stations on the M6, and quieter, cleaner, not so many people, which is why we like it. You don't have to pick your way through a maze to get to the toilets, you know, shops selling tat, amusement arcades, fast food places, and the coffee is always good here.'

'So you usually stop here for coffee?'

Hills nodded.

'And how often do you go to the cottage?'

'Three or four times a year. Sometimes more, sometimes less, depends on what we've got on.'

'And what time did you and your wife set off this morning?'

'Around four-ish.'

'An early start,' said Baker.

'We always leave early. That way we miss the worst of the traffic. We expected to arrive at the cottage by ten or eleven. Before lunch anyway. We'd got soup and ham rolls. Leah made them last night, put them in the cool box.' His jaw started to work again, his eyes bright.

Baker was conscious that despite the show of emotion, Chris Hills was watching him closely, his eyes unreadable.

*

Out in the service area, two uniformed constables were canvassing the staff in the shops and café. Although we were taking Chris Hills' concerns seriously Leah Hills was a healthy adult woman. There was a strong likelihood she'd show up safe and sound, or pissed off and angry, teaching someone a lesson for something done or said, real or imagined.

Every police officer had seen it, a row not mentioned to anyone during the interview, the discovery of an affair, overlooked when the husband or wife gave their statement. What had upped our response was that Chris Hills was absolutely adamant that Leah's actions were completely out of character; that he and Leah were happily married and were just off for a long weekend away together, nothing more, but if I'm honest it was the place that did it for me, that was unusual. And I had a strange feeling about the whole thing.

People talk about gut feelings on TV and films and it's dismissed as ridiculous, unscientific, not following the evidence, and all those things are true – in real life it's certainly not encouraged, but as humans we can't help it, mainly because we all have it, that extra sense, that feeling that something isn't right.

I've thought about it a lot and come to the conclusion that it's not any kind of intuition at all, it's about recognising things, little tics, circumstances, that lead us in a particular direction, guiding us to a conclusion subconsciously with little fragments of information that we can't always articulate or even recognise as being clues. It's also equally true that sometimes those gut feelings can be totally wrong – but not always.

While DI Baker was with Chris Hills I went to talk to Sergeant Rees who was co-ordinating the scene from an empty office at the back of the service complex.

Time was already slipping by and along with it the most obvious and simple solutions. Time is precious when you're searching for someone – there is a golden hour – not a literal hour but it is often quoted as a reminder that the longer a medium or high risk individual is missing the more likely they are to have come to harm. After seventy-two hours unless there is strong evidence to the contrary received wisdom is that we'll be looking for a body. The thought hangs over everyone on a missing persons enquiry.

As well as working through the tasks on my list I wanted to get Charlie Rees' thoughts along with an update on what had been done, what needed to be done, if he considered that we needed extra manpower and what was happening to Chris Hills' car so that I could update Baker.

Rees and I are the same rank. He's a bit older than me and easy to get on with. I was glad he was on this one with us. Harry Baker was right, Rees was a safe pair of hands. Charlie looked up as I went into the office.

'Morning, Charlie.'

'Bloody hell, look what the cat dragged in. I wondered where you'd got to. You look perished,' he said.

I nodded. 'Frozen. We've been beating the bounds.'

Rees grinned. 'He's notorious for it, getting a feel for the place, was he? The lie of the land?'

'How did you guess?' I said.

'He's nothing if not predictable.' Charlie nodded towards the constable working a laptop at another desk. 'Go and get me and Sergeant Daley a cup of tea will you, while I get her up to speed.'

*

'How did your wife seem to you this morning?' asked Baker.

'Fine, normal, a bit tired. I don't think Leah slept very well last night, but then she always gets herself a bit het up before we go anywhere.'

'When you say *het up*?' Baker said.

'Nervous, excited, I'm not sure what it is really. She's never been a very good traveller.'

'And is that something new? The nervousness?'

'No, she's always been like that. She gets anxious over the smallest things.' Chris Hills smiled, narrow lips pressed into a thin, upturned line. 'You need to understand that my wife isn't a naturally confident person. She's a bit unworldly, needs me to take care of her. She is always saying that. Which makes all this so out of character; Leah isn't the sort of person who would just wander off. Something's happened to her. None of this makes sense otherwise.'

Baker nodded.

'We've been together a long time. Soul mates, I've always thought that, right from the start. Right from when we first met.' He paused, gnawing miserably at his lip.

'And how long have you been together?'

'Twenty-five years this June. Seems like yesterday.'

Baker nodded again, expression in neutral.

*

The photographs we had of Leah Hills had been printed off and copies pinned to the board above the desk Rees was using. Both were high-resolution images, sharp. She was slimly built and finely made, with tiny elfin features, big dark eyes and shoulder length dark brown hair, that – in the photo from her husband's phone – she had pulled back in a half ponytail.

In this image Leah was wearing a long-sleeved, black tee shirt and narrow, cropped cream trousers with ballet flats; she was caught in three-quarter profile and although she was smiling, it looked as if she had been caught unawares. There was something vulnerable in her expression, and Baker was right, she looked a lot younger than forty-four.

The two photos we had had been sent to the mobile phones of all the officers on site, and Rees had arranged with the service station management to have them up on the bank of information and CCTV screens in the main foyer with a scrolling banner underneath that read, 'Have you seen this woman?' along with a number to call if anyone had.

Rees had already passed the images and a brief statement on to the media officers so they could get something out on the lunch time news, but so far there had been no comeback, no one had recognised Leah, not in the coffee shop, or the burger bar or the newsagents, nor in the shop selling jackets and gloves. The cleaners hadn't seen her, the man in charge of security in the back office had taken a long hard look but had to admit he'd seen no one like Leah either on the CCTV or in person, but had pulled the footage for the last few hours. It wasn't altogether unexpected, most people in the service station were in transit and unless someone did something notable or unusual then to the staff they were just another anonymous face amongst a steady stream of anonymous faces.

The tea was warm, strong and very welcome.

'What about Chris Hills' car?' I asked Rees. 'Anything interesting.'

He took a look at the screen of his laptop. 'One of the first places uniform looked when we got here, nothing and no one in the passenger compartment, popped the boot, just luggage inside.'

'Hers too?' I asked, cradling the cup to help thaw my fingers.

'Apparently. We've taken some initial photos and shown them to the husband and he said that he thought everything was the same as when he last saw it when they left home this morning, nothing obvious missing, nothing extra or unexpected that he could see.'

I took a look through the handwritten notes that were on Rees' desk.

'Anyone look in the cases?'

Rees' eyes moved back to the screen to double check.

'No. She wasn't in the car and if we needed to search it later then it would still be there, nothing's compromised.'

I nodded, it made sense. 'Did anyone pick them up? The cases?'

Rees hesitated. 'I don't think so, I think they just looked, but I see where you're going with this. The cases could easily look the same but someone could have had another bag inside a case and lifted out the contents.' He paused.

'Or be the contents?' I said grimly.

'I'll get the keys,' said Rees.

*

In the break room Baker glanced down at the notes he'd been given by the first responders. 'And your wife is—'

'Forty-four,' said Chris Hills. 'Leah was seventeen when we first started going out together, although we waited a couple of years before we got married.' Answering a question that he hadn't been asked.

'And you, how old are you, Sir?'

'Fifty-seven. I'm a bit older than Leah, not that it's ever been an issue or made any difference.'

'And did you and Leah share the driving on the trip here?'

'No. No, Leah doesn't drive. But I don't mind that. I enjoy driving, I always have, and if I feel tired we just stop and take a break. That's why we stopped this morning.'

'You were feeling tired?'

'No. I just wanted a coffee, that was all.' He glanced towards the door. 'Where do you think she is?'

He swallowed down a sob. Baker gave him a second or two to compose himself, keeping his own expression in neutral.

'Has anything out of the ordinary happened recently, before you left home or on the way here? Anything that may have made your wife distressed or upset?'

'You mean like a row? No, Leah and I don't row, we never have. I know what you're thinking. I know that sounds corny, I mean neither of us is perfect, we have our ups and downs, disagreements about things but we can usually sort them out without an argument. Like I said Leah is a lot younger than me; she has always looked up to me, and I've always taken care of her, looked out for her. I can't imagine how she's feeling at the moment; she depends on me.'

Baker glanced across at the PC. His expression was also impressively deadpan.

'Not necessarily an argument, just something, anything that might have upset your wife. Something at work maybe. Has anything out of the ordinary happened recently?' asked Baker.

Hills shook his head. 'We were both looking forward to having a few days off. I know it's early in the year but we've both been busy–'

'You're an accountant, Mr Hills, is that right?'

He nodded, looking more confident now he was back on safe ground. 'That's right, with Forth & Row. They're a software development company based in Cambridge, on the Research Park. They're an international company, but that's where they have their European headquarters.'

Baker made a note.

*

Outside in the car park Charlie Rees and I pulled on latex gloves. Rees clicked the remote for Chris Hills' Mercedes; the side and brake lights flashed and there was a soft clunk as the central locking released the doors. He looked up at me and nodded.

'You want to start with the boot?'

I shook my head. 'Let's go over it all, shall we?'

He grinned. 'We've not done this in a while, Daley. You want the driver's side or the passenger's?

*

'And what about your wife? You said that she works?' said Baker.

'Yes, Leah's a florist. In Denham where we live. We were grabbing a few days between Valentine's and Mother's Day and the end of the tax year. A long weekend – travel to Wales on Thursday morning come back Monday afternoon. It's the first time we've been to the cottage this year. It was meant to be a treat.'

Baker nodded. 'And you said that your wife was tired? Would you say more tired than usual?'

'It's her job. I keep telling her that she ought to go part time, but she's worried about letting people down. They put on her a bit at work.' Hills laughed and shook his head. 'Typical Leah; she worries about everything. Treats floristry like it's some kind of religious calling. I keep telling her no one's going to die if she isn't there to stick a few more bits of greenery into a table decoration for some woman with more money than sense.' He stopped, reddening. 'I'm sorry, that sounds harsh, but I'm only teasing. She knows that. She loves her job. Always has.'

'And so what time did you get to the service station this morning?' asked Baker.

'Just before seven, ten to, quarter to – something like that.'

'And what did you do when you arrived? As best as you can remember?'

Chris Hills sighed as if it was tedious to repeat what he had already told the first responders.

*

'Passenger,' I said.

Charlie nodded. 'Right you are.'

When I first joined Mercia Police, Charlie Rees and I used to work together regularly and had a well-rehearsed procedure when it came to searching, and without a word we fell back into the same routine. We took a side of the car, each working through the glove compartments, visor, roof lining, the door pockets, central storage areas and under the seats, before moving on to the rear seats, door pockets and the pockets on the rear of the front seats, the foot well and the parcel shelf, looking for anything that might help us find Leah.

Every police officer is aware of the risks of contamination, so we worked carefully and systematically, and the search would be recorded so that later other officers could check who had been where and what they had done, which prevented duplication but also in the event of this becoming more than a missing persons enquiry would help prevent cross contamination and accidental transference of evidence between scenes. We worked in silence.

The front seats and foot wells appeared empty with nothing under either seat. There was a quantity of grit and soil on the slip mats in both sides of the foot wells, which we left for forensics to collect if they needed to.

On the back seat was a plastic box of groceries packed with tea and cereals, pasta – dried foods – as well as a small holdall that contained books, magazines and a DAB radio. On the floor standing in the foot well behind the passenger seat was a cool box with a packed lunch inside.

*

'We came in off the motorway. Leah got her coat from the back seat,' said Chris Hills. 'She hates the cold, always has done. Anyway it got caught on something and she was tugging at it.' He mimed pulling something from behind him. 'I was worried that she might tear the lining.' He reddened. 'I may have snapped at her – seems ridiculous now – but anyway she finally got her coat and insisted on trying to put it on in the car. I told her it would be better if she just waited till we stopped but she wouldn't listen.' He paused. 'I should have been more patient. I wonder if I upset her. You don't think she went because of the thing with the coat?'

Baker's expression remained fixed. 'Is your wife usually impulsive or easily upset?'

Hills frowned. 'No, not at all. Not usually but just recently–' he stopped.

'Recently?' Baker pressed, but Hills was still focusing on the coat and the car.

'A couple more minutes and it would have been simple and she was struggling to get it on. Pulling it round over her shoulders–' His words faded into silence.

Baker glanced down at the notes taken by the two traffic policemen going off shift who had caught the 999 call. He'd circle back to Hills' comment about her recent state of mind.

'And your wife's coat is brown, is that correct?'

'It's a camel coat,' snapped Chris. 'Beautiful. Nine hundred pounds worth from Higgins and Hill in Cambridge. I bought it for her last Christmas. It's got this big fold-over collar, like a cowl.' He mimed again. 'To keep her neck warm. And a half belt.' He hesitated. 'Oh and she was wearing black leather boots. Camel skirt, black sweater. I don't think I told the other officers that.' His tone was clipped, the details precise.

'You seem very sure. Mr Hills,' said Baker.

He nodded. 'I am. I've always taken an interest in what Leah wears,' he said. 'I like her to look nice. If it was down to her she'd be in jeans and a jumper all the time.'

'So what happened then?' prompted Baker.

'I parked up close to the front doors of the service area, by the fence, by the kerb there. I'd barely stopped the car before she got out. I thought she needed to go to the loo. She finished putting her coat on, doing it up. She's got one of those handbags that goes across her body, like a satchel – not much more than a glorified purse really. She always brings that on holiday with her.'

'And Leah had that with her when she got out of the car?'

'I remember seeing her put it on over her shoulder, oh and she had gloves on – leather, but they're fine, you know not great thick things.'

'Can you remember what colour?'

'Black and her bag is black as well. *Osprey*. That's the make.'

The PC alongside Baker made another note.

'And did you say anything, either of you?'

'I'm not sure now. I think I asked her if she wanted a drink. And she said no. She likes tea but the tea here tastes – well, they just throw a bag into hot water and hope, is what she always says. Then I asked if she wanted a hot chocolate, to warm her up and she said yes–' Hills paused as if trying to piece it together, moment by moment. 'Then she closed the car door and went inside.'

'And you're certain that you saw her go into the service area?'

Hills frowned. 'I keep going over and over it in my head. I'm absolutely certain I saw her in the rear-view mirror. It was still quite dark and she had got her coat all bunched up round her face, trying to keep the cold out.'

'And was there sleet then?' said Baker.

'No, no the sleet hadn't really started then, it was more rain. Cold though.'

'But still dark?'

Hills nodded. 'Yes, although the car park was pretty well lit.'

'You told the officer you spoke to earlier that the car was in the shadows where you were parked?'

'Yes, but I only parked there because it was closer to the doors.'

'And what about you? Presumably you got out too?' asked Baker.

'I'd been driving in my shirt-sleeves and a jumper. It was bitterly cold once out of the car. I turned the engine off, the lights, checked I'd got my wallet, and then took my jacket out from the back seat, locked the car, and followed Leah inside.'

'And how long did that take approximately, do you think?'

Hills pulled a face. 'I don't know. How long do those things take? Two, three minutes, maybe five at the most, not long, I didn't hang about. It was freezing, and I wanted a coffee.'

'Did you say anything to Leah about meeting up before she went inside?'

'I might have said, "I'll see you by the coffee stand or meet you in the foyer, or see you in a minute," something like that. I don't remember precisely, but it's not a big place and we've been here lots of times before. It wasn't likely we would miss each other. I went to get a coffee. There were a couple of other people in the queue, someone else waiting to pick up their order, I think – so I waited. They're always quite quick in there, which is another reason why we stop here, so I told the girl behind the counter what I wanted, paid for it and then nipped off to the gents.'

'And you didn't see Leah?'

Chris Hills shook his head. 'No.'

'And how long do you think you were gone for?'

He sighed thoughtfully. 'Four or five minutes. It's hard to tell. When I got back the coffee wasn't ready so I waited at the far end of the counter till they'd finished making it.'

'And kept an eye out for Leah?'

Hills nodded. 'All the time.'

'Okay. So all in all it had probably been ten minutes or twelve minutes since you'd parked up and your wife went inside.'

Hills nodded again. 'Something like that.'

'And she wasn't in the foyer when you came out of the men's toilets?'

'No.'

'And you didn't see her while you were waiting for your coffee?'

'No. I thought maybe she had got caught up in a queue in the ladies. She was always complaining about having to queue.'

'Then you got your coffee?' prompted Baker.

'Yes, and then a crowd of people, a coach party or some- thing turned up. The girl at the stand asked me if there was anything else I wanted, and I realised I'd forgotten Leah's drink so I paid for that and while she was making it I went outside to see if I could find Leah.'

Chapter Two

'What made you go and look then?'

He pulled a face. 'I'm not sure. I suppose she seemed to have been gone a long while. It's not like her to be long.'

'Can you remember what it was that made you notice the coach party?'

'The noise, I think. The place had been fairly quiet and empty up until then and then suddenly there seemed to be lots of people milling about, and the noise level went up.'

'Okay and when you say you went *outside*, do you mean into the car park?'

'No, just out of the coffee shop.'

'In amongst the coach party?'

Hills nodded.

'So *not* outside into the car park?'

'I just said that, didn't I?' snapped Hills. 'Sorry, sorry.' He held up his hands in a show of apology. 'Look, do we have to keep going over this? I'd got no reason to go outside. Leah and I always meet up inside. And as far as I'm aware there is only one way in and out.'

'And you say the entrance area was quite busy by then?'

'Yes. It was packed.'

'And was it possible that Leah could have slipped outside without you seeing her?'

Chris Hills sighed. 'I suppose so, but why would she? Where would she go? I've got the car keys, she doesn't drive. We're in the middle of nowhere.'

'And you didn't see your wife?'

'No,' said Hills, his exasperation growing. 'No, I didn't. Look, can we just stop this now?'

'Please if you could just stay focused, we'll get through this as quickly as we can.'

Chris Hills looked at him, his expression unreadable and then he said, 'And then do what?'

Baker said nothing, just waited.

'I went outside to look for her,' said Hills after a few seconds.

'To the car?'

'Yes, to the car.'

'And Leah wasn't there?'

'No. I've already told you – she doesn't drive, she hates the cold – I didn't think she would be there. I can't imagine Leah going outside voluntarily in this weather.'

'Did you look round?'

'A minute or two, not for long. It was still dark, cold. I came back in and rang her mobile. The call went straight to voicemail. I thought maybe she was taking a call and that was what was keeping her, why she hadn't come back.'

'Was Leah expecting a call?'

'Not that I knew of. To be honest I was getting annoyed by then. I wondered what was so important that she couldn't at least let me know where she was, you know, come and find me, point to the handset and roll her eyes. It would be just like her to take a call from work. And why the hell were they ringing her anyway? She is supposed to be on holiday.'

'It's a bit early for work, isn't it?'

'You'd like to think so, wouldn't you, but it wouldn't be the first time. Delivery drivers sometimes ring her if the garden centre is locked up and they can't get hold of anyone else.'

'So you thought she might be on the phone?'

'I'm not sure what I thought, by then I was beginning to get worried, and a phone call made sense. If she was talking on the phone maybe she was still in the toilets or in one of the shops. I went back to the coffee stand, assuming she would show up. And that was when I thought I saw her heading out to the car.'

Baker looked up. 'Leah?'

Chris Hills nodded.

'What made you think it was her?'

'The coat. From the back it looked just like her. Same build. She was going out into the car park, I couldn't see her really well. She'd got a cake box in one hand and I wondered if she had bought something for us to have with the drinks. I wondered if that was what had taken her so long. There were other people making their way out, so I called her and when she didn't respond I ran over and grabbed her arm.'

Chris Hills paused, his gaze fixed on a point in the middle distance, staring at something that neither Baker nor the constable could see. When he spoke again all the energy had drained out of his voice. 'I knew it wasn't Leah the minute I touched her. The coat wasn't right, it was cheap, thin material and there was a button missing on the cuff. The woman in the coat swung round, and pulled her arm away. I thought for a moment that she was going to hit me.' He paused. 'She did look a bit like Leah. At least superficially.'

'But it wasn't her.' There was no question in Baker's tone, just a statement, even so Hills looked at Baker and snorted.

'Would we be here if it was? I told her I was sorry, that I thought she was someone else. But she wasn't having any of it; she shook me off and was gone before I could explain.'

Baker nodded. 'Was your wife on any kind of medication?'

Hills shook his head. 'No.' He paused for a second or two. 'Well at least, not now.'

*

The interior of Chris Hills' car had revealed nothing obvious. No signs of a struggle, nothing broken, no obvious blood stains, no visible fibres or hair, no weapons, just the smell of lemon air freshener with an underlying hint of leather as if it had been freshly valeted. Rees glanced at me and nodded towards the boot. We closed the car doors and moved to the back of the car. I popped the button on the fob that opened the boot and we both peered inside.

Uniform were right; the whole space was full, packed with matching black hard shell suitcases and a large holdall. At first glance there was nothing that caught the eye. One by one we lifted them, moving them carefully, hefting the weight, considering if they were unduly heavy or light; nothing on the face of it looked suspicious. Rees pulled out a torch and moved the holdall aside so he could move the suitcases forward and take a look into the voids around the luggage.

*

'Are you saying Leah was taking medication some time recently?'

Chris Hills looked uncomfortable, as if he was breaking a confidence. 'Leah stopped taking her tablets a couple of months ago, maybe longer. When I say stopped what I mean is she'd finished the course and decided she could manage on her own. The GP knew all about her coming off them, you have to reduce the dose slowly. She thought it might be the start of the change, you know mood swings, one day up, one down, crying, not herself.' He looked uncomfortable, as if caught out. 'It was me who insisted that Leah go to see the doctor but she didn't like to bother anyone. In the end I said if she didn't go I'd take her.'

'And what sort of tablets was Leah taking, Mr Hills?'

'Antidepressants. Although,' he said hastily. 'I wouldn't say she was depressed per se, you know, not really, just hormonal. It was getting us both down.'

Baker nodded. 'I know this is difficult but is there anything Leah said that made you think she might harm herself?'

Hills stared at him. 'No, of course not,' he said, shaking his head emphatically. 'No, I can see where you're going with this, but no, not Leah. No, she is full of life, always smiling – always busy. It's what made the mood swings all the more noticeable.'

Baker nodded again. He needed to let the rest of the team know that Leah Hills had recently been treated for depression. It was another weight on the scale, another marker that increased the likelihood of her being at risk. He wondered why Hills hadn't mentioned it before.

*

I looked on as very carefully, disturbing the interior as little as possible, Charlie Rees worked his way around the boot space, leaning in over the suitcases, looking down along the sides and then the back – into the spaces created by the luggage.

'Here we go,' he said quietly, glancing back at me. 'Take a look.'

I stepped up beside him and peered over his shoulder.

'See it?'

I nodded.

'I'll go and let Baker know,' I said. 'Close it up.'

Rees nodded and pressed the boot lid shut before locking the car with the fob. We both headed back inside while the officer who had been watching Hills' car looked on wordlessly.

*

In the break room at the back of Hoden Gap Services, Chris Hills was getting more restive.

'So what happens now?' he asked. The interview felt as if they were getting close to its conclusion.

'I'll have one of my colleagues take you to the police station as soon as we can,' said DI Baker. 'We'll make arrangements for you to stay locally if necessary.'

Hills' eyes widened, the implication hitting him.

'Can't I go to the cottage and wait there?'

Baker shook his head. 'I'm afraid not.'

'But what if Leah goes there?'

'We have already got officers going out to check on the cottage. You're helping your wife a lot more by being here helping us.'

Chris Hills didn't look convinced.

*

45

Chapter Two

I was very aware as I made my way back out of the cold that I was walking the same route that Chris Hills said Leah had followed — along the path by the side of his car and then in through the main doors — but where to then? Had she come inside at all? Had she even been there? The main doors opened automatically onto the bright well-lit entrance way. I hesitated for a second before I stepped inside. Where had she gone? Where was Leah?

Once you were inside the options were pretty limited. There was a café and burger bar taking up most of the left hand side of the building, facing out onto the shops on the far side — a newsagents, the coffee shop, a place selling coats and kites and over-priced designer label walking gear. Beyond that was a corridor leading towards the back of the building, towards the toilets, a small shower block and the back offices and service areas for businesses.

Nothing caught my eye or my attention, except the bank of monitors above the area that led into the toilets; the screens were showing live footage from the CCTV cameras across the site and two, front and centre, had pictures of Leah on them, asking if anyone had seen her.

I glanced around at the faces, the families, the couples, the travellers, in case by some miracle Leah was amongst the people making their way in and out of the foyer. No one gave the screens a second glance.

I needed to talk to Baker so that we could get the go ahead to call in the Scene of Crime officers to do a proper search of the car, the area around it, and also go through the suitcases.

*

In the break room Chris Hills said, 'I don't understand why you haven't found her yet? She can't have gone far. She can't drive–' He gnawed anxiously at something on the side of his thumb. 'Do you think someone took her? Is that what you think?'

Baker shook his head. 'We've got no evidence to suggest that's the case.'

'It doesn't mean that it didn't happen, does it? Is that why you don't want me to leave? Do you think whoever it is will contact me – is that why you wanted my phone?'

'We've got nothing that indicates that your wife has been abducted, Mr Hills. There's nothing you can do here that isn't already being done. Now is there anything you need?'

'My wife,' said Hills grudgingly.

'What happened after you followed the woman in the coat?' asked Baker.

'I just told you it wasn't Leah.'

'I know but I meant what happened after that?'

'I phoned Leah again. It went straight to voice mail like before. So I went through each of the shops in turn and then I spotted a woman going into the ladies toilets. And it occurred to me that she might still be in there. She could be ill, she could have fallen over, fainted, anything. So I opened the door and called her name.'

He paused, taking a breath. 'I thought there was a chance that she might have collapsed. It's not impossible.'

'So you went inside?'

Chapter Two

Hills began to speak more quickly now, sounding anxious and fraught. 'Yes, I was calling her name, "Leah, Leah".'

For a moment there was silence in the little break room, because everyone knew what had happened next, but before any of them could speak again there was a knock at the door. The constable who had been taking notes got to his feet and opened the door a fraction. DS Mel Daley was standing out in the corridor. She nodded towards her boss.

'Excuse me, I'm sorry to interrupt, but I need a word with DI Baker,' she said.

Baker turned at the sound of her voice and nodded, and then, turning back to Chris Hills, asked, 'Would you like to take a break, Mr Hills? My officer could get you a coffee or something if you'd like?'

Hills shook his head. 'I don't want to take a break I just want this to be over.'

*

Closing the door and moving a few steps away to ensure we were out of earshot, Baker said, 'So, what is it, Daley?'

'Charlie Rees and I had a closer look at Hills' car. We found her coat in the boot.'

'You're certain?'

I took out my phone and found the images I'd taken before locking the car.

'Maybe he made a mistake about what his wife was wearing?' I said.

Baker shook his head. 'He's absolutely adamant.'

I glanced across at Baker. 'Wouldn't be the first time a witness made a mistake.'

He nodded. 'Or maybe he didn't think we'd bother searching the car?' said Baker.

I handed him the phone; in the light from the Charlie Rees torch it was easy to pick out an expensive-looking camel coat, tucked down behind the cases. It had been folded or fallen so that the lining was facing outwards; the lining was dark brown silk, edged by the camel fabric of the coat. It had been rolled so that the long edge bearing the label: 'Higgins and Hill, size 10' was clearly visible.

'Well spotted,' Baker said, grimly.' Let's get SOCO down here asap and make sure you don't let anyone take the bins away before they have been over them.'

I nodded.

Chapter Three

The Camel Coat

Before Baker went back in to talk to Chris Hills he and I went to see Charlie Rees.

The general consensus was that we needed more bodies on the ground, needed to get Chris Hills back to the station and needed to sort out the issue with the coat. We would also continue with questioning Hills. He might be upset and distressed but we were all well aware that almost half the women killed in the UK every year are killed by a partner or ex-partner, two women a week killed by someone they were linked with romantically.

Makes you think about relationships in a whole different way, because however sexist, unreasonable or unfair it seems, husbands and partners are almost inevitably suspects. Not that we had a body, not that we had a crime, but we all knew the mantra, when in doubt, think murder.

When Chris Hills spoke to the first responders he was ad- amant that his wife had been wearing the coat Charlie Rees had found in the boot, as he was when he spoke to DI Baker, despite the obvious evidence to the contrary. He could be mistaken, he could be lying, we needed to unpick it and find out which it was.

The other problem we were having was that no one besides Chris Hills appeared to have seen Leah in the service station at all. Not one. The nature of the place meant that any would-be witnesses were probably long gone and half way to god knows where. We were hoping the news bulletin and the press release would help with that.

Leah Hills having recently been treated for depression increased concern and escalated the degree to which we thought she might be at risk. It meant DI Baker could call in the extra manpower and increase the resources we had available. Finding her coat had been a surprise but it wasn't that big a deal in the great scheme of things. People under stress made mistakes; police officers see it all the time. Chris Hills could have easily made a mistake about the coat and be clinging to his raft of certainty in the midst of the chaos in which he found himself.

Scene of crime officers – SOCOs – would start collecting the forensic evidence. We needed to sift through the interviews – currently still ongoing with service station staff, go through what CCTV footage we had already collected as well as chase any more that was available, and most important of all we needed to find out who had been the last person to see Leah Hills before she disappeared.

There is a book – a written procedure – on how to deal with missing persons and we follow it as closely as we can, step by step, to ensure that nothing gets missed, nothing lost or overlooked.

Chapter Three

*

Baker went back to the break room.

Hills was on his feet as soon as the door opened. 'Did you find her? Where is she? Is she all right?' he demanded as Baker stepped into the room.

Baker shook his head. 'I'm afraid not, Mr Hills, but there are a couple of things I'd like to clarify with you.'

Hills dropped back into his chair as if he had been shot. 'More questions? No – no, look I've already told you everything I can remember about this morning.'

Baker made a show of picking up the notes that he had been using earlier, and apologising if the questions seemed pointless or repetitious. While he read a woman came in wearing gloves and an overall, carrying a rubbish bag, and cleared the coffee table in the break room. It would join the material being sifted and sorted by the SOCO team, just in case Chris Hills had discarded something important in amongst the debris. It wouldn't be the first time.

Baker glanced across at Hills. He was narrow shouldered, with a pale, triangular-shaped face, and a neat, greying, schoolboy haircut, swept over to one side. A man who would, under usual circumstances, just melt into the background. While he had the pallor of a man who spent a lot of time inside, he was dressed for the country, for walking or fishing; Lovat green corduroy trousers, a checked Viyella shirt and a pale creamy brown v-necked sweater, and brogues – none of them were new, but they appeared to be good quality and well looked after. Chris Hills was a neat, tucked up and tidy sort, a man who you could pass every day and barely notice. But Baker couldn't help the thought that it was the most perfect disguise. Despite what the tabloids said, and their choices of the least flattering images, the cruellest of people seldom if ever looked like monsters; their trick was to look just like the rest of us.

'You mentioned to my sergeant that Leah wasn't a good traveller. Was she especially anxious today?'

'No, if anything quite the reverse. In lots of ways things are getting easier for us.' Hills paused and smiled. 'I'm taking early retirement, at the beginning of the summer. June probably, we're just sorting out the fine print and running through the paperwork, you know what these things are like. I've got a good pension, some investments, savings. I'm looking forward to us having more time together.'

'I?' said Baker.

'*We, we* are looking forward to having more time together,' corrected Chris Hills crisply.

'And how does Leah feel about you retiring?' asked Baker. 'Presumably it'll be a big change for both of you.'

'She's really supportive. Always telling me I work too hard.' Hills shook his head and smiled. 'Says I bring my work home with me. You know how it is; I can't always switch off when I get in. It'll be nice to have the time to do some of the things we've had planned.'

'Such as?' asked Baker, still with one eye on the notes in front of him. Alongside him the PC was still adding to the record of the interview. Baker had thumbed through to the notes on what Leah had been wearing. Hills had mentioned the coat at least half a dozen times in the earlier interview.

'Travel, home improvements, all the usual things, nothing too drastic. And I'd got a surprise planned for her.'

Baker's quiet, respectful almost deferential approach appeared to be working on Chris Hills. He was opening up, practically chatty.

'A surprise?'

'Yes, although it seems trivial now under the circumstances. We've been going on holiday to the cottage in Wales for years, since we first got together, not every holiday obviously, but at least once or twice a year, more often three or four. Leah doesn't like to fly and neither of us really ever fancied a cruise, so we've explored a lot of Britain together. But anyway, I was planning to tell Leah that now I'm going to retire that we could finally move to Wales permanently. I suppose we've always planned that that was what we were going to do, just never really talked about it, certainly never thought it would happen so early. The cottage needs a bit of work doing to it, but nothing that we can't sort out and better to get it done now while I'm still working.' He paused, voice cracking. 'It was going to be a surprise. Something for us both to look forward to. A new start.' His bottom lip started to tremble as he tried to keep it together.

'And you were going to tell her when?' said Baker, gently, pushing on past the emotion.

'Over the weekend. I'm not sure exactly when. I was going to pick my moment, you know, when the time was right. I wanted to start making plans for what we need to do to the cottage. Renovations, some basic improvements. I thought it would be good to make a start now while we're not living there.'

'And what about Leah's job?'

Chris Hills frowned. 'What do you mean, Leah's job? What about it?'

'Well, if you move presumably Leah would have to give up her job. Do you know how she would feel about that?'

Hills frowned again, as if it was an odd question. 'I don't think she'd mind. It's just for pin money really. Something to keep her busy while I'm working, and she wouldn't need it if I was at home. She certainly wouldn't need the money – but if she wants to carry on working I'm sure she could find something else.'

Baker nodded, imagining what his wife, Joanne would have to say if he casually announced she should quit her job at the school and traipse halfway across England without a word of discussion because he fancied taking early retirement.

*

DI Baker had asked me to give him a few minutes before joining him in the interview with Hills. While I was waiting we photographed the coat in situ before taking it out of the car and logging it in to evidence so that the chain of custody wasn't broken. Charlie Rees had gone through the pockets, which were empty, then bagged and tagged the coat while I called the station to ask them to request a trace on Leah Hills' mobile phone. The permission would need signing off higher up the food chain.

*

Chapter Three

Baker glanced back at the notes, adding the information about Chris Hills' retirement while DS Daley slipped back into the room, carrying a cardboard box, and sat down alongside Baker.

'We obviously need to ask you if you have got any idea where your wife might be? Anywhere she might go? Any friends? Relatives? Someone she might go and stay with?' asked Baker.

Hills shook his head. 'No, none at all.'

He glanced across at Daley, anxiously.

'Like I said before we're in the middle of nowhere here. Where would she go? We only stopped to get a coffee. *A coffee.* Why on earth would she go anywhere?'

Baker nodded. 'So, no family or any friends you can think of?'

Hills shook his head. 'You have to understand that Leah and I have always been really, really close, right from the first time we got together. I suppose you could call us antisocial but neither of us is much for friends. Leah was an only child. Her dad cleared off before she was born and her mum used to drink. Her mother lived in sheltered housing in Wisbech – died a couple of years ago. I don't know the last time the two of them actually spoke. When we first got together Leah was looking for security, I knew that, I've always known that.'

'And so what about you, Chris, what about your family?'

'My sister, Helen. But we're not particularly close.' His gaze slid towards Daley, his glance appraising and curious, and then back to Baker, who stayed silent.

Baker smiled and looked at him, but said nothing, creating an unspoken question, waiting for more.

Hills waited out the silence for a minute or two and then said, 'Helen and I fell out a few years ago.' His tone was sharp, the words coming out fast. 'She upset Leah, it was over something and nothing but when I went round to try and sort it out my sister went for me. I mean really flew for me, she's always had a temper. It wasn't pretty and I said some things that couldn't be unsaid. We both did. I don't think she had ever liked Leah, that was very clear. We've never made it up. We don't see each other or talk.' There was a hint of defiance in his expression.

'So you don't think Leah would have gone there?'

Hills snorted. 'No, not in a million years, and how could she? Helen lives in Norfolk, Leah doesn't drive.'

'And what about Leah's friends?' pressed Baker.

Hills shrugged. 'I don't think she has any, not really. Like I said we've always had each other. There were some people at work, but I wouldn't really describe them as friends, not really. There were Christmas parties and birthdays occasionally. Mostly we'd go together, Leah and me. She's always been a bit of a homebody, she's nervous around strangers and people she doesn't know very well. It was me that encouraged her to get a job in the first place – to build her confidence.

'When we first got together she was at home, then I found her a job at a florist in town. She's always been artistic, creative, and she really took to it, went to college on day release and everything.' He looked up at Baker. 'I've had to encourage her every step of the way. Every step. I don't think she would have stuck with it if I hadn't persuaded her that it was a good idea.'

'Which makes her disappearance all the more unlikely?' prompted Baker.

Hills nodded.

'So no friends then?'

'Her closest friend – I suppose our closest friend really, died about eighteen months ago. They'd worked together for years. Looking back, I do wonder if that was what triggered Leah's depression, first losing her mum and then Elise. The two then were close in age too, Leah and Elise. It really shook us both up.' He paused. 'Elise was only a couple of years older than Leah.'

'I'm sorry,' Baker said in an undertone.

'She had ovarian cancer, by the time they diagnosed it there was nothing they could do. Leah was devastated. We both were. The sister she'd never had, that was what Leah called Elise. Two peas in a pod really those two. Silent killer they call it. Ovarian cancer.' He paused. 'It really shook Leah up. And I think it worried her, seeing Elise go like that, that she might lose me as well. She had already lost her mum, so there was just the two of us. Me and her against the world.' He smiled. 'I keep telling her that I'm not going anywhere, but like I said there is a quite an age gap. Plays on her mind. And I suppose actually neither of us are ones for many friends. We've always had each other.'

'So no one springs to mind? Someone she might turn to if she was stressed or depressed or unhappy?'

Hills shook his head. 'No. Leah has always turned to me. Always. From the very first.'

'Anyone else in your family?'

'No, my dad died when I was in my teens, mum when I was in my twenties. So, both dead. And like I said, I've got one sister, Helen, who might as well be. She's a couple of years older.'

Baker nodded, alongside him Daley sat poker faced, balancing the box on her knees. Baker wished that he could have the benefit of her thoughts on Chris Hills, as it was Daley was totally unreadable. He glanced at her and she took the cue. She smiled.

'Hello, Mr Hills. I'm DS Mel Daley. I'm part of the team helping to find your wife. You mentioned to the officers and Detective Inspector Baker that your wife was wearing a camel coat when she got out of the car this morning?'

Hills nodded. 'Yes, that's right. I bought it for her for Christmas.'

'And you're sure that she was wearing it?'

He hesitated, a flurry of emotions crossed his face, and then he stiffened. 'Yes, I'm certain, why? Why are you asking about her coat?' His colour drained. 'Oh my god, have you found it? Have you found Leah? Is she all right? Where is she?' He was on his feet now, being propelled towards the door by instinct alone. 'You have to let me see her.'

DS Daley stood up and held out a hand to steady him.

'It's all right, Mr Hills, please sit down,' she said gently but firmly. 'We haven't found Leah yet. I just needed to check with you, give you time to think about what you saw, maybe reconsider – it's easy to make a mistake – the light wasn't good, you weren't really paying attention, after all why should you?'

Hills' jaw worked itself into a knot as he slumped back into the seat. 'I didn't make a mistake,' he said. 'I know what I saw.'

Chapter Three

'I appreciate that.' Daley spoke in the same calm voice. 'I just wanted to check whether your wife packed any other coats to take with her. For your holiday?'

He nodded. 'Yes, she had a walking jacket with a fleece inner and a little fold up waterproof thing in a zipper bag. We've both got one. Navy blue. Folds down to nothing.'

Daley nodded. 'And Leah didn't put either of those on when she was getting out of the car this morning?' she asked.

'No. I already explained. She had a camel coat on, it was on the back seat. I'd bought it for her for Christmas.' He spoke slowly as if there was some chance that Mel Daley was finding the words hard to follow.

Baker said nothing, wanting to watch Hills' reaction.

'And you're sure about that?' asked Daley.

'Of course I'm sure.' Chris Hills' earlier affability was slowly evaporating.

'The thing is, Mr Hills, while searching your vehicle we found a camel coat in the boot.' Daley opened up the box on her lap and from inside took out a coat, safely sealed inside an evidence bag, and set it down on the coffee table between them. It was still folded exactly as they had found it so the label was on the outside, clearly visible.

'Is this your wife's coat?' asked Daley.

Hills stared down at the bag and its contents. He looked as if someone had punched him.

'That's not possible,' he said, looking from face to face. 'It can't be her coat, that's Leah's, I saw her put it on. I saw her in it. I know I did. She was wearing it this morning.'

Daley waited until he was quiet. 'Did your wife have another beige wool coat with her?'

Hills flashed her a furious look. 'Of course she bloody doesn't. She has only got one camel coat. I saw her put it on. It can't have been in the boot of the car. I saw her in it. I saw her. This is nuts, you shouldn't be in here questioning me, you should be out there looking for Leah.' He stabbed his finger angrily towards the closed door. 'I saw her put that coat on and walk into the service station, and no, she didn't have two. It was nine hundred pounds – Leah doesn't have that kind of money to spend on a coat. I thought she would love it – I thought–'

At which point Chris Hills stopped as if gathering himself together and then he slumped forward in the chair and burst into tears.

*

Outside, the area around the Mercedes was being processed in preparation for it being put onto a low loader so it could be taken in for forensics to go over it. DI Baker explained to Hills that he was going to be taken to Hereford police station by one of the uniformed officers and they would sort out accommodation for him to stay in the area while the search was ongoing and a Family Liaison Officer appointed to support him while they continued to look for his wife. This time Chris Hills didn't protest.

*

Chapter Three

I drove back to the station, Baker in the passenger seat as usual staring out of the window. The weather hadn't improved any, the visibility down to bugger all in places, not that it stopped other cars careering past us, tail lights flashing in the murk.

'I wouldn't want to be out in this,' said Baker, as I turned up the wipers to full speed.

'Maybe she's not,' I said, braking hard to let in some numpty in a Range Rover who had just seen that the outside lane ahead was closed and had a fifty-mile an hour average speed limit on it.

'What do you make of him?'

'Chris Hills? He's under pressure, we never see people at their best.'

Baker laughed. 'Not like you not to have an opinion.'

'It's hard to weigh him up. He seems genuinely upset and worried about her, but there's something else going on there.'

'You think?' I could feel Baker's gaze on me, encouraging me to go on, waiting for more.

'I read the report from Traffic, all that *she can't manage without me, we're soul mates*, stuff. Bit creepy if you ask me. Maybe fine when you're teenagers, but not at their age.'

Baker nodded.

'When we get back I want you to get onto the garden centre where Leah Hills works, see if they knew she was going away and get onto the Norfolk lot and get them to send a couple of uniforms round to check out Hills' home address, the neighbours. The usual roll call. Let's get the time line started, who saw her last, where and when and schedule a briefing.'

'Chris Hills is the last one we have currently?' I offered.

'Anyone one besides Mr Hills.'

'He is upset.'

Baker nodded. 'He's something all right. I'm always suspicious of people with no friends and you're right, the whole *we only need each other*, soul mate stuff is a bit suspect.'

I glanced across at him and shook my head.

'What?' demanded Baker.

'I had you down as one of life's natural-born romantics, Sir.'

Baker snorted. Outside, the sleet smeared the windows. 'Let's get back to the station, all this unspoilt countryside is getting on my nerves.'

I nodded. 'Yes, Sir.'

Ahead of us the traffic had unexpectedly slowed to a crawl. I glanced in the rear view mirror hoping the cars hurtling up behind us could see the tail back and slow down. I wasn't ready to end up as a motorway statistic.

'The coat thing is bloody odd,' said Baker thoughtfully. 'Surely if he put it in there he knew we'd find it.'

'Maybe he *did* make a mistake, maybe she was wearing something else,' I said, my attention fixed on the road. The average speed limit was now on both carriageways as we met another stretch of road works.

'Have uniform picked up all the CCTV from the service station?'

I nodded. 'Rees is on it, they'll pick up as much as they can find on site. I'll check on progress as soon as we get back. And see how we're progressing with her phone.'

'Let's hope we get something else from both. We need to have eyes on her. And I want to go over Chris Hills' account with him again. '

Chapter Three

I had watched Baker in action lots of times questioning witnesses, victims and suspects. He was a big man, maybe six four, with broad shoulders and was a big presence in any room, but despite his size he always spoke quietly, barely above a whisper at times, and had a manner that made people feel at ease and encouraged confidence. Good guys or bad, nothing about the way he carried himself unsettled people, quite the reverse, people told Baker things that they wouldn't tell other people, and always had. Watching him in action was an education.

I also knew that going back over and over a story that they had already told was the thing that most people hated the most, the telling and the retelling was wearing and frustrating and emotionally exhausting, but often it was then – when they couldn't believe that they had to tell their story one more time – that the truth slipped out. Whether it was genuinely overlooked or carefully hidden, it all came out under Baker's persistent questioning – the row they'd had, the affair, the jealousy, the drug habit, the shop lifting, the one moment of madness, the regret, the panic, the grim little secrets that almost everybody has, the resentments, the gambling, the trouble at work, the drink problem, the other man, the other woman, the one mistake, the error of judgement. Baker had a gift for uncovering that stuff.

Things were revealed during those sessions with DI Baker and his quiet relentless manner that would never usually see the light of day and people fought very hard to conceal. The hidden things that when they got too much made people lie, steal, cheat, disappear or sometimes worse, much, much worse. I didn't envy Chris Hills one little bit.

Chapter Four

Asking the Right Questions

Back at the station one of the civilian staff had arranged for Chris Hills to have something to eat and drink and make any phone calls that he wanted. He said he had no one that he wanted to ring.

An incident room had been set up on the first floor and the techies had set up computers on the desks on the far side of the room, along with additional phone lines. While Hills was being settled in, a team was moved into the incident room to deal with and log the statements and information coming in, collating and indexing it so it was available to everyone involved.

I made the first of the phone calls to Charlotte's Garden, where Leah Hills worked, to have it confirmed that she had taken a few days' holiday, had left on Wednesday evening at 5.30pm and wasn't expected to be back in until the following Tuesday morning.

Chapter Four

Then I rang Norfolk Crime Unit requesting their assistance and asking if local uniformed officers could be sent round to check out Chris and Leah Hills' residence and talk to their neighbours. Finally, having updated the information I uploaded what data I had to the National Missing Persons Database, and filed missing persons reports so that what we knew and what information we had was available nationwide, and then I went in search of the results from the first batch of CCTV footage that had been collected from Hoden Gap. There would be more coming in from around the immediate area in which Leah had gone missing over the next few hours and days if we couldn't locate her before then.

CCTV footage from the scene was very often the best way to get a quick steer on what had happened and where the missing individual had gone, and we always tried to get it picked up or downloaded as quickly as possible as lots of places didn't store it for long before overwriting the disk, the tape or files. The problem with it was there was no narrative, no real way of knowing what was important and what was not; the cameras recorded everything, the only way to access what it had for you was to watch it, more often than not hours and hours and hours of it: cars coming and going, people walking past oblivious to the fact they were being watched and recorded.

In the incident room two constables were updating the log both on paper and on the computer so that everyone involved both locally and nationally could see what had been done, what was planned and what had been discovered, what was actioned, while Baker went off to talk to the DCI about letting us have more manpower.

A full-scale search hadn't been triggered at that stage – we were focused on the service station, the area immediately around it and the roads to and from. If Leah wasn't back within a few hours, a specialist search team would be mobilised, but meanwhile there were civilian staff under the direction of Charlie Rees, who were bringing in and logging films and witness reports and keeping track of what was where, an essential job on any case. On the wall of the incident room, marked up on a white board, someone had already drawn out a timeline relating to Leah's disappearance.

I added in the date and time that Leah was last seen at work and realised that other than Chris Hills, that was the last time anyone else had seen her alive, which made me think about Baker's comment when we had been up on the bank: there were a lot of places to get rid of a body between Hoden Gap Services and Norfolk.

The phone in my bag trilled again. At some point I was going to have to answer it, but not now. There were a lot of other things to do and even if there weren't, my instinct was to keep on ignoring it.

In the room a few doors down the corridor in the media suite some of the station's civilian technicians was going through the first CCTV footage we'd managed to get hold of.

Inside, people were watching monitors, head-phones on in some cases. By the door Sheila Hastings, the team leader, was working a mouse back and forwards across the desk, concentration fixed firmly on the screen in front of her.

I knew from Charlie Rees that she was working on our footage.

'How're you doing?' I asked. 'Got anything yet?

She didn't look up. Sheila Hastings is tall with dark, wavy hair, muscular broad shoulders and not an ounce of fat, and looks more like a field athlete or a farmer than a geek, and is considered one of the best we have when it comes to trawling through hours and hours of grainy film and pulling together a narrative from what she finds. Her desk is almost always bare except for a monitor, keyboard, a note pad and an empty in-tray.

'And there was me thinking you'd brought me coffee and a muffin,' she said, her gaze fixed firmly on the screen.

'Next time,' I said.

'How many times have I heard that,' she said with a sigh.

'So what have you got?'

'Bugger all so far. Some of this stuff we're getting in is really shoddy. We've got some footage that's still on old VCR tape. I'm having it digitised so we can re-run it; the tapes are so fragile they're likely to split or jam if we play and replay them.'

I nodded. 'Do you mind if I sit down?'

'Help yourself, although I'm not sure what I've got so far will help you.'

I pulled up a stool.

Sheila sat back a little so that I could see an image of the road into the service station that was caught in a frozen frame.

'We're using the picture of Leah Hills pulled from the website of the Garden Centre where she works for comparison, and they've emailed over a list of employees,' she said indicating a page in the notebook alongside her. Sheila clicked through onto another screen. 'I've had Carol over there trawling social media, Leah Hills isn't signed up to anything as far as we can tell so far, but Charlotte's Garden where she works is on Facebook, Twitter, Instagram and has a couple of things up on *Youtube*, so we're concentrating on those at the moment, looking to see if she was tagged in anything anywhere. See if we can identify any of her friends or places she might frequent – all the usual.'

I nodded. The truth was, despite Baker's attitude to the internet, everyone was everywhere these days, a Google search and some time spent on Facebook could yield an amazing amount of information, and save hours of old-fashioned footwork, but as DI Baker was always keen to point out to me whenever I mentioned it, it was important not to get blindsided by the bright shiny things in life – not everything could be sorted out from behind a screen or from a keyboard.

'What about the footage from Hoden Gap?' I asked as she clicked her way out of the Charlotte's Garden website.

Sheila Hastings frowned. 'It's a bit frustrating if I'm honest. So far we haven't found her on any of the footage, so at the moment we've got nothing to show that Leah Hills was ever there.'

I stared at her. 'Are you sure?' Leah having never been there was one of Baker's four possibilities, and the one that I thought we would most rapidly be able to knock off the list.

'So far, nada,' said Sheila apologetically. 'Look, let me show you what I've got at the moment, and I have to say it is only a first pass on the most readily available footage.' She clicked back onto the first screen I'd seen where the footage had been stopped, and with a keystroke ran the images forward.

'Here we are. We've got Chris Hills pulling into the service station at six forty-six this morning. His car gets picked up on the automatic number plate recognition on entry to the service station. Then it disappears as he drives round to the retail and food area.'

I nodded watching the dark Mercedes move across the footage; between screens. 'The car reappears here as he's parking up. There.' She pointed to a shiny black square in the top lefthand corner of the monitor that was barely recognisable as a car, let alone Chris Hills' car.

I screwed up my eyes and peered at the screen. 'Can you actually *see* that?' I asked.

Sheila grinned. 'It's not great, is it? But that's where Chris Hills said he was parked, and then it's being coned off in later footage, and it doesn't move until our guys show up with the low loader, so I'd say I'm pretty damn certain it's his.'

'Okay, so we've got his car parked on the far side over by the fence?'

'He's a long way from the security cameras that they've got monitoring the front apron, and being so close to the fence, the bins and the bank and the trees make it pretty tricky to pick out any real details,' said Sheila, fiddling with the keyboard and mouse to try and sharpen the image. 'There's a light behind there that causes all the objects, the fence, the bins to cast a shadow just where we want to look.'

'Could that be deliberate?' I said, narrowing my eyes to try and pick out the details; god only knew how someone spent all day looking at this stuff and didn't go blind.

'It could be, there are lots of other, better-lit parking spaces between the entrance to the car park and the service area, but it's also the closest available spot to the door so it makes sense to park there, given the weather was so awful.' Sheila moved forward a few frames. 'The image quality on this footage is really poor. I've tried to clean it up as best I can. The passenger side of the car is in shadow and too far from the main doors to be picked out by the interior lights from the retail area. If anything, what light there is makes it worse. See, the interior lights create an area of glare and any images flare so you can't really see what's going on. Anyway, despite that–'

Her fingers worked over the keyboard again, clicking on the mouse, making an attempt to zoom in on what looked like a figure, barely visible on the edge of the screen, moving past what they knew to be Hills' car. 'Can you see that?' she said, indicating the screen.

I leaned in closer, squinting to try and make sense of the image. 'Yes, just about. Any way we can make that a bit clearer?' I asked.

Sheila pulled a face. 'Probably, but not here. I mean, I've tried the best I can with our equipment, but it's a long way off and like I said, the images weren't that great to begin with. We'd need a specialist lab. I can't even say for certain that that person actually got out of Chris Hills' car.' She ran it back again, more slowly this time, not quite frame by frame but almost. 'What do you think?'

I shook my head. 'Me neither.'

They could have walked across from the petrol station, and come along that path there, or come round from the HGV park at the rear,' said Sheila, pointing as she spoke. 'The camera wouldn't have picked them up till they had rounded the fence.'

'Okay, so have you got anything else? Another angle?'

Chapter Four

'Not of that section of the car park at the moment, but we live in hope. Then we have this from the interior of the service area.'

Sheila clicked between screens. The next piece of footage showed the main central automatic doors at the entrance to the retail and food area, the cameras were pointing front and centre from the foyer. They showed the doors that I had walked through earlier that day when I came back out of the cold from searching Chris Hills' car.

'I've checked the time stamps and rolled the footage back by half an hour just in case they were off, although they appear to be more or less in sync and I'm planning to go back further once I've got time, just to double check,' Sheila said, her gaze still firmly fixed on the screen. 'Here we go.'

The images moved past quickly, faster than normal speed although people were clearly identifiable, the picture quality much better than the footage from the car park.

'People in, people out,' said Sheila, as the clock on the bottom right hand corner rapidly churned out the passing seconds, minutes and hours. 'But no sign of Leah Hills. I've been through it three or four times now and I just can't see her. Here's her husband coming in.' She slowed the film down and rewound it. Chris Hills walked in through the central doors, still fiddling with the zip on his jacket. He looked round, paused for a moment or two, apparently checking his pockets, and then headed towards the area where I knew from my visit that there was a coffee shop.

Sheila set the footage back to fast forward; people hurried in and out. 'Here he is again on the phone,' she said. 'Then he goes outside, comes back in.'

I watched the events unfold, just as Chris Hills had told us in his statement; nothing about the way he moved suggested he was aware he was being filmed or that his movements were contrived or self-conscious, his body language consistent with the things he had told both the traffic officers and Baker during his interview. At the end of the sequence Hills came back into shot, almost running.

He hurried towards the doors and grabbed a woman who was about to leave. As his hand made contact she swung round, almost as if she was intending to hit him. Even on CCTV his shock and surprise was palpable. He had quite obviously thought it was Leah and from his reaction, had been astonished when it wasn't.

He backed away from the woman and for an instant the camera caught his expression. He looked totally stunned.

Sheila looked up at me and sighed. 'I've been through the rest of the footage until traffic show up, after Mr Hills got picked up by security, and I'm obviously still going through it, just in case his wife was hiding somewhere and left after he got picked up, but so far, nada.'

I looked at the screen, staring at Chris Hills' horrified expression, frozen in the single frame, wondering where this left us and what the hell was going on. I needed to talk to Baker and talk to Hills again. Was all this a hoax after all, and if so why?

'So we haven't got anything at all that suggests that Leah Hills ever went in, in the first place?'

'Not at the moment, but we've still got a lot to go through, shop footage, burger bar, coffee shop,' said Sheila.

Chapter Four

I nodded, knowing that wasn't the real problem. 'The trouble is there is only one way in and one way out of the public areas,' I said.

I stared at the picture of the automatic double doors behind Chris Hills.

'Maybe she went in another way? Round the back. We've got CCTV footage of all sorts of fire doors, we just haven't found Leah Hills coming in or out of any of them yet,' said Sheila.

'Hills told the first responders and DI Baker that he saw her go in the main entrance.'

Sheila shrugged. 'In that case I can't explain it. The angles from the interior of the shops looking out into the main entrance are pretty rubbish. I've had a quick flick through on the right time stamp, and have got people going back over it now, but so far we've come up dry.'

'Okay well thanks, keep looking and let me know if you find anything,' I said.

Sheila grinned. 'You're first on the list.' And with that she turned her full attention back to the screen.

I knocked on the door of the suite we used for informal interviews, and waited till Baker called me in. After a moment or two the door opened. 'Excuse me can I just have a word, Sir?' I said.

Hills glanced up as the door opened, and caught my eye, his expression was expectant. He was in his shirtsleeves; he looked anxious and tired, and something else. In front of him was a glass of water, which he picked up, holding my gaze.

'It's always you, isn't it?' he said grimly. 'Have you found her?'

I shook my head. 'Not yet, Mr Hills. But we've got good people out looking for her.'

'You said that before,' he said, but didn't look convinced.

Out in the corridor I told Baker what I had seen on the CCTV footage and what Hastings had told me.

'Okay – in that case we need to establish where and when Mrs Hills was last seen alive,' said Baker.

I glanced down at the notes I'd taken while talking to the owner of Charlotte's Garden. 'Wednesday evening half past five is the best I can manage so far.'

Baker rolled his eyes. 'Let's see if we can place Leah Hills in the car with her husband this morning.'

I headed back to my desk.

The UK has the highest amount of CCTV and public surveillance devices per person in the world; we are constantly being watched. I just needed to work out where to begin looking for Leah Hills.

*

Baker stepped back into the interview room. Hills looked up. 'What's going on?' he asked.

Baker took a seat. 'We've encountered a problem.'

Chris Hills stared at him. 'What sort of a problem?'

'It would appear that we're unable to find your wife on any of the CCTV footage from Hoden Gap.' Baker paused, his voice becoming quieter. 'I have to ask you this again, are you certain that your wife was with you at the service station this morning, Chris? We need to try and understand what's going on here and at the moment it doesn't make much sense. Are you sure Leah was with you?'

For a few seconds Chris Hills held his gaze, looking bemused and completely wrong footed, and then it occurred to him what Baker was implying.

'What do you mean *am I sure Leah was with me*? Do you think I made all this up? That I invented my wife? Of course I'm sure. I'd just spent three bloody hours in the car with her.' He was on his feet now, white faced and rapidly losing his cool.

'Do you think I'm crazy? Deluded? Some sort of loony? Leah went into the service station this morning, I saw her go in. And now she is missing. Do you understand? *My wife is missing*, do you think I'd make something like that up? *Do you?*' He ran his fingers through his hair and began to pace. 'I can't believe this is bloody happening. I'm going to wake up in a minute. How come you can't find her? Are you even fucking looking?'

'Perhaps she stayed at home? Perhaps you dropped her off somewhere else? Where is Leah, Chris?' said Baker, his voice level and encouraging.

Chris stared at him as if he didn't understand what Baker was saying.

'I don't know,' he said. 'I. Don't. Know. Is that clear enough for you? She went into the service station. I saw her go in. Look. I need to get out of here – if you can't find her then I will.'

'Where would you start?' asked Baker.

Hills snorted. 'Is this some kind of sick trick question? I'd go back to the service station. I'd go to the cottage in Wales; she has to be somewhere.'

Baker nodded. 'We've got both those places covered. We just don't understand why no one saw her at Hoden Gap.'

Chris shook his head, 'I don't know, I can only tell you what I saw. I saw her. She got out of the car, she put her coat on. You have to believe me.'

Baker changed tack. 'Can you think of anyone who might want to hurt Leah? Or you?'

Chris Hills pulled a face. 'You mean you think someone took her? Like kidnapped?' He paused. 'You said that there was no reason to think she'd been taken by someone?'

Baker said nothing, and instead he waited while the thought took hold. After a second or two Hills shook his head.

'I can't think of anyone or any reason why anyone would want to take Leah. Leah's not anyone, not anyone important, not special.' He stopped, reddening. 'I mean me neither, we're just ordinary people,' he added hastily.

'What about something connected to your work? You said you work for a tech company, in finance.'

Again Hills paused for long enough to consider what Baker had said. 'No. I work in the finance department but not on anything particularly high powered. I can't draw down money from the company account for example or make transfers for major purchases without permission.'

'And what about Leah?'

He stared at Baker and laughed grimly. 'She's a florist,' he said slowly. '*A florist*, not a nuclear physicist or a politician. She arranges flowers for a living.'

Baker nodded, scratch the surface of Chris Hills and what lay beneath was far more bitter, far less affable than what was on the surface.

'Please, I know this is frustrating but we have to explore every avenue. I'd appreciate it if we could have your mobile, please?'

'Why?'

'We'd like to be able to monitor any calls. If Leah has been abducted or if she rings in—'

Hills already had his hands in his pocket. 'Here,' he said slapping his phone down on the table, 'Take it. I've got nothing to hide and you can do anything, go anywhere, have anything you want that can help find my wife.'

He pulled out two sets of keys. 'The house in Norfolk, and those for the cottage in Wales. Go where you like.'

Chapter Five

Team Briefing

'So let's go through what we know, then we've got an update from the search team, and Sergeant Rees.' Baker was standing in front of the white board in the incident room. The timeline was as empty as it had been when I went in earlier.

Leah, dressed in her florist uniform looked out nervously from a glossy 8 x 10 that was pinned to the board, at the gathered officers. Baker gave everyone a resume of the chain of events as reported by Chris Hills, and then some of the issues thrown up by the lack of CCTV corroboration.

'So far we've got a missing person report for Leah Hills, and no trace of her whatsoever in the area where she was supposed to have vanished. Or come to that, nothing to prove she was ever there in the first place. The search team have put in a request for helicopter support but I'm reluctant to authorise it without some solid evidence that Leah Hills was at Hoden Gap.'

There was a murmur in the office. 'So you reckon it's a hoax, Guv?' said one of the younger DCs, Jonathon Andrews, who was perched on a desk.

'Mrs Hills' whereabouts is still unknown – she has to be somewhere – so at the moment we're treating it as a genuine missing persons enquiry although we'll obviously update that as and when we have more. The picture Mr Hills paints of his wife suggests that she is emotionally vulnerable.'

I heard someone at the back mutter *nutjob*; for some people no amount of sensitivity training was going to make a ha'pporth of difference. I was standing alongside Baker and, ignoring the comment, picked up the thread with what I knew.

'The CCTV footage for Hoden Gap is lousy. And there is a possibility that her husband could be mistaken, she might not have gone inside the service area at all,' I said. 'But even given that, so far we've not been able to place her definitively at the services, so we have to consider that she may not have been there at all and therefore, obviously that she is elsewhere. We've actioned a search from the Norfolk Police of where the Hills live and are currently waiting an update on that, and also officers are searching the cottage the Hills own in Wales.'

'If there is any chance that the heli will help I'd like to get it here,' said Baker. 'As you can see from the description, Leah Hills is small, emotionally fragile and it's blowing a bloody hoolie out there. We need to find her. There is a danger in just assuming that the technology is infallible.' He turned towards the reports and interviews that had already come in and were piled on the desk just inside the door waiting to be gone through by support staff so the information could be collated, recorded, and hopefully give the team something tangible to go on.

'One thing Chris Hills is absolutely adamant about is that Leah Hills isn't the kind of woman who would just disappear. She's recently been treated for depression and was unsettled or uneasy last night. We are all agreed that she's vulnerable and at risk. Let's find her before it's too late.'

My gaze went back to the piles of paper. The truth was the answers we were seeking could easily be buried inside. I'd long ago discovered that police work was more often about paperwork than car chases.

'Despite our lack of current information Superintendent Gresham agreed that we will be classing Leah Hills as being at high risk, until or if circumstances change,' said Baker. 'And I'll be reviewing the decision on the helicopter hour by hour.'

I waited. There was a subtle shift in the atmosphere in the room.

'So to recap, from what her husband said about her general demeanour, and her recent treatment she may well not be in a great state.' Baker paused. 'Certainly disappearing is completely out of character. And we have to be aware that she may not wish to be found. Her husband is concerned she might be having some kind of breakdown. We need to find out where she was seen last, with whom and when.

'We need to track down friends, relatives, work colleagues. Sergeant Rees has drawn up an action plan and will be allocating manpower and roles. Her husband is of the opinion that they're soul mates, so let's see if we can find someone with a more objective view of their relationship. Be aware we could be dealing with a potential suicide. But remember we could also be dealing with a murder.'

There was a moment when no one said a word. We were all aware that Leah Hills had been missing for over six hours. Time was rapidly moving on. She hadn't been found in the Service area or on the wasteland or wandering along the motorway verge. The simplest solutions for her disappearance had already passed.

'We've assigned Robbie Halliday as liaison officer to Chris Hills.' He paused. 'Halliday will be moving Mr Hills out to a hotel in the next hour or so. Local radio have been on the phone and we've had a call from someone at Mercia TV asking if we'd like a slot on their news roundup tonight. Media Liaison plan to put out an updated press release within the next half hour and we'll need to give them something meatier later today if Leah Hills hasn't turned up by then,' said Baker.

'Have we got anything meatier?' asked one of the team who would be dealing with the mound of paperwork.

'Not yet,' said Baker. 'But the Superintendent is keen for Chris Hills to do an appeal. Sergeant Kelly Frost will be running the media campaign but let me make this absolutely crystal, I don't want any of you talking to her or anyone else about that case without clearance, everything goes through me first. Is that clear?'

I made another note. Kelly Frost would help put the appeal together and, along with Robbie Halliday, support Chris Hills through the process of dealing with the media. She was good and Robbie Halliday was calm and unflappable under fire.

The same officer pulled a face. 'Have we got the resources to deal with the calls, Sir?'

Baker nodded. 'Superintendent Gresham has signed off on the extra manpower. Given how many people go through Hoden Gap in the course of a day it'll be our best chance of finding someone who actually saw Leah Hills there this morning.'

It was a good question, though. Back when I was in uniform I'd helped work the phones during more than one missing persons enquiry after a TV appeal. It had been a real eye opener. People rung in, in droves with ideas, theories, psychic visions, or just plain attention seeking, as well as phoning in possible sightings, ninety-nine percent of which had proved incorrect, a case of mistaken identity, or just plain wrong, and had tied up manpower that otherwise might be out searching.

But, and it was a big but, just one call, just one tiny piece information could also lead to the person being found. So, on balance, it helped, but the experience of being on the phones had coloured my judgement.

'Leah's picture is on our *Twitter* and *Facebook* page,' said one of the younger officers, sitting at the front 'And we've already had a good number of shares and retweets.'

Baker nodded. 'Good. I know it's got an amazing reach but I've never quite got my head round all that sharing and liking.'

There is no one size fits all in missing persons investigations, but there are a set of basic principles that did fit almost every case – where to start, who to talk to, and a paper trail – now duplicated as an electronic record – that would ensure everyone investigating has access to the same information and worked in a measured and logical way that in a perfect world covered all the bases. As senior investigating officer Baker would decide on the strategy, and the officers assigned to the case would work their way through it, implementing the plan, reporting back at every stage.

'And what have we got back from Norfolk?' asked Baker.

I picked up the thread. 'Officers are currently checking the house out and canvassing the neighbours. Denham Market is not a very big place, everyone knows everyone else.'

Behind me on the white board an image from Google Earth, showing an aerial shot of Hills' home clicked up.

Backer glanced at me. 'Your old stomping ground, Daley?'

I laughed. 'Hardly, Guv, I think I was about ten when I left but it's not very big, a little rural market town. The street the Hills live in is in the older part, in a nice area close to the High School.'

'Dormer town?' suggested Rees, who was sitting at the front.

I hesitated. I knew what he was asking. Did everyone leave at seven in the morning and not roll home till after six, in which case what were the chances anyone would have seen Leah? Truth was I didn't really know, but that wasn't how I remembered it.

'It's years since I've been back. But no, I wouldn't say so – I'll do an update as soon as we've heard back from Norfolk. And similarly with the Hills' cottage in Wales.'

Behind me the white board flickered and pixelated before clearing to show a sea of green, cut through by a narrow river. 'Rurally isolated, no near neighbours. The local force despatched officers as soon as we called it in and have said that there is nothing to indicate that Leah Hills has been there, although obviously it's early days and there is still time for her to show up. They have an officer assigned to monitor the cottage – although given their resources they're not sure how long that will be possible.'

'Which takes us back to possible abduction,' said Baker. 'No one we've spoken to so far saw a struggle and we found no evidence of one. Although obviously she could have been lured or forced into a vehicle.'

All in all we were working pretty much in the dark. We didn't know which way to call it, all we could do was keep searching, keep looking for something that would lead us to Leah.

'From what we've had in so far kidnap seems unlikely,' I said. 'But obviously at the moment it's not ruled out.'

'We're also going through the database to see if there has been anything nationally with a similar M.O. We've requested financials for Leah and Chris Hills, and put in a request for phone records,' I said, working my way through the checklist I had in my notes.

'Chris Hills has told us that he's nothing very special at Forth & Row but we'll need to confirm that,' said Baker. 'They're a software company based in Cambridge. I want to see what we can find out about them and him.' Baker paused. 'We've nothing on the timeline after Wednesday evening verified by anyone other than her husband. Realistically Leah's got to be somewhere. Let's see if we can find out why the hell Leah Hills would disappear from her perfect marriage without her soul mate.' His tone was dry and clipped.

He glanced across the room at Sergeant Rees, back from Hoden Gap to collate and control the flow of information.

Baker nodded. 'All right I think that's all we've got at the moment and I don't have to tell you that it's not enough,' he said, winding the meeting up. 'I'll leave you to the tender mercies of Sergeant Rees. Let's get out there and find her.'

At that point Rees came forward and led the officers through who should do what, dotting i's and crossing t's in case anyone was in any doubt. The search, the CCTV, a widened sweep, the Welsh cottage, the Hills' Norfolk home.

*

Just as we got to the door of Baker's office a uniformed officer appeared round the corner, holding a sheet of paper.

'S'cuse me,' he said. 'Leah Hills?'

I nodded. 'Thanks, what have you got?' I asked. He handed me the paper.

'We just had this in from her phone provider.'

I glanced down at the information. The surprise must have shown in my face.

'What is it?' Baker asked.

'According to this Leah Hills' phone never left Norfolk. From the triangulation it doesn't look as if it's ever left her house,' I said.

Baker paused for a second and then said, 'You need to get yourself to Norfolk, Daley. You're okay with going?'

I nodded. 'I'll be going home, Sir, of course I'll be all right.'

Baker pulled a face. 'Norfolk. Long way–'

I laughed. 'You make it sound like Siberia.'

'Have you still got family there?' he asked.

'Hoping to save on the hotel bill, were you, Sir?' I said.

He grinned. 'The thought had crossed my mind,' he said, opening the door to his office.

Chapter Six
The First Pass

LEAH'S HOUSE

I keep a go bag on top of the wardrobe in my bedroom. It's stocked with a few basic essentials and a couple of books that I've always planned to read but never have, so it doesn't take me long to get ready to go anywhere.

My flat is on the first floor of a purpose-built block in Greytree Street. It's close enough to the town centre that I can walk if I want to and far enough away so as to be less noisy. There are nine flats spread over three buildings built in an open- mouthed square around a stretch of grass set with silver birches, benches and tubs of flowers, the closest thing I've got to a garden.

It's not fashionable or trendy, but it's near to work and the shops. I bought it with the money my dad left me, as a stopgap till I could find something better, bigger, more me, further out of town with a garden, maybe bought when I found Mr Right, all the while thinking how grown-up it made me, having a place of my own and how proud my dad would be. He was always saying that property was the only decent long-term investment for the ordinary man, or in my case, woman.

I took out my keys, let myself into the shared lobby, checked my post box and then climbed the stairs. Truth was the last thing I fancied was a drive to Norfolk at that time of the day; it would take four, probably closer to five hours in the dark and the wet, but we needed to find out what was going on with Leah Hills, and Norfolk had been where it started. A part of me hoped that it hadn't ended there. The information that had come back from the local force was that there were no signs of Leah after a visit from uniform. A living Leah. How did we want to proceed?

Given there was some chance that Leah was still in the house and given that Chris Hills had already given us permission to enter the premises, a locksmith had been called in to open the front door and uniform had performed a room by room search and turned up nothing. The fact Leah's phone was there didn't mean that she was. The officers had been unable to locate it, but the reality was that she may have left it home deliberately, or forgotten it, but it did seem unusual – one of the first things most people take when they leave the house is their phone. So, that was me off to Norfolk then.

When I unlocked the front door to my flat there was a postcard on the doormat waiting for me, with a picture of a cat on it.

I picked it up, turned it over, and smiled. It was a standing joke between me and my neighbour, Fiona, who lived in the flat downstairs. Ending up as crazy old cat ladies seemed to be woven into both our futures. Fiona was a tax inspector, me a copper, you could see how that could pan out.

A couple of times a month we would try to get together and go out for a drink or supper or go to a film or a play or a club, always in another town, and told any men we met that we worked in retail. A tax inspector and a police sergeant on the pull wasn't a winning combination.

The card read: 'Friday?' in Fiona's neat boxy handwriting.

I pulled out my phone and ignoring all the other texts tapped in a message to her. 'Not sure yet. Off on a job. But yes, if I'm back, M xx'

A message pinged back straight away. 'Anywhere nice?'

'Norfolk.'

'Good luck. BTW I've found a fabulous ginger Tom with your name on. Neutered and good to go.'

I laughed, and stood the postcard up on the mantelpiece along with all the others, and then checked my house phone for voicemail.

'You have one new message,' said the metallic voice at the end of the line. The phone clicked and burred a little as if whoever it was, was calling from inside a sewing machine.

'Hello, it's me,' said a male voice. 'I know you don't like me ringing you at home, but you aren't answering my messages. I might be able to get away on Friday and I reckon I could get away this evening – if you wanted to see me, too, that is. If you hurry. Where have you been all day? I've been trying to let you know. So tonight? Not for long, but long enough.' He laughed. 'Text me and let me know how you're fixed.'

The First Pass

I deleted the message and went into the bedroom to finish off my packing. How come he just couldn't take a hint and leave well alone? Sooner or later I was going to have to tell him I'd rather roll naked over broken glass than see him again. The problem was the sound of his voice still made my heart do that fluttery back flip thing that hearts do, and it was no good my head telling me that it was crazy and totally wrong, it wasn't my head doing the thinking.

Fifteen minutes later I'd folded a couple of day's worth of clean clothes into the bag, made sure everywhere was locked up, confirmed with the hotel that they were okay with a late check-in and was back in my car. It was just after six, with any luck I would be there by ten, although Norfolk felt a long, long way from home these days.

It rained all the way there.

*

It felt strange as I got closer and closer to Denham Market, driving in on half-familiar roads that took me past towns and villages I'd known as a teenager, and it was worse still as I drove in from the A10 heading towards the hotel, making my way through streets that evoked memories from my childhood, catching glimpses of places I recognised and some part of me still knew. It was far more unsettling than I'd expected. It had been nearly twenty years since I'd left Norfolk but still there was an odd feeling akin to relief that I was finally coming home.

Although I had grown up in a village a couple of miles along the A10 from Denham Market, it was the main market town for the area, it was where I had gone to High School, where our family did their main weekly shop, the place where I had had my first kiss up on the playing field with some boy called Charlie when I had come to stay with my dad for a week in the summer. It had to have been after my parents split up and my mum had followed Ken to Hereford. Maybe the first summer. The second – I couldn't quite remember how long those turn and turnabout holidays went on for.

But Charlie and that fumbling, unsettling, awkward kiss? The thought took me by surprise. Where the hell did that come from? Creeping around an unfamiliar one-way system – I hadn't been able to drive the last time I'd been there – I could see where I needed to be but couldn't work out how to get there. The hotel, the Royal Oak, was tucked away, back from the main road, under a Georgian archway. It was a classic coaching hotel with mullioned windows and wood panelling, and a place my mum took me as a child for afternoon tea.

I watched it sail by again. The rain carried on falling.

Finally after the third or fourth pass round the block I found the turning into the hotel car park. I hoped, as I swung into a parking bay behind the Royal Oak that Leah Hills had found herself somewhere warm and dry to sleep or better still had been found and was back safe and sound at home, although even as I thought it, I knew that if that was the case I would have heard from the station, and if she had shown up I wondered about the life she had with Chris Hills. Despite his polite, deferential manner there was something about him that was unsettling, but what it was exactly was impossible to put my finger on.

The First Pass

Inside, the hotel was almost exactly as I remembered, it even smelt the same, old wood, and log fires mingled with floor polish. The reception desk was discreetly tucked away in a corner of a panelled hallway that wouldn't have looked out of place in an old manor house. The receptionist looked up as I opened the door. 'Sergeant Daley?' she said with a smile. I nodded, feeling the same sense of having come home that had haunted me all the way down A10. 'I'll show you to your room,' she said. 'The kitchen's closed but I can rustle you up some sandwiches if you'd like?'

I nodded gratefully. 'Sounds fabulous.'

Up in my room I called in to let Charlie Rees know I had arrived, caught up on my emails, and read the summary of the searches carried out in Wales and Norfolk. There were the messages on my phone that I really should answer; something else besides Leah that really needed sorting out, but I ignored them.

I kept thinking about Leah and the drab, miserable isolation of the service station. An email from Charlie confirmed that as of twenty-two hundred they still hadn't found her. Press releases had gone out on the six pm, nine pm, and ten pm news slots and calls were coming in, but nothing that we didn't already know and currently nothing else that looked promising.

So, Leah wasn't safely tucked up out of the rain, she was still lost.

Exhausted from the day, and the drive, I climbed into bed, pulled the duvet up over my head and lay in the dark, listening to the rain and wind outside the window, tapping like fingers on the little lead panes.

I dreamt that I was walking around the bank at Hoden Gap Services, anxiously searching in the grass for a lost button. I couldn't remember where I had seen it, or where I had lost it, and then I was running through the newly mown grass on the playing field at Denham Market. Someone was chasing me and although I couldn't be sure I knew in my heart that it was Chris Hills.

*

I woke up well before it was light; almost as tired as when I'd gone to bed. I took my time in the shower, thinking about what we knew. The scant outline of a life. Leah's picture was on the breakfast news. It helped a lot that she was pretty in a non-threatening girl next door way and didn't look her age. The photo made her look vulnerable. I'd imagine the phones were ringing off the hooks. Meanwhile, on screen, our media liaison officer Kelly gave a rundown on where we were with the search and appealed for anyone who had any details or information to come forward.

By the time they got on to the Nasdaq and the FTSE One hundred I had dried my hair, pulled on clean clothes, made a cup of tea and was ready to head down to the car.

I'd arranged to meet local officers at the Hills' house.

I parked up by the kerb and glanced at the little huddle of men waiting for me, two in uniform, and one taller and lankier wearing a battered Barbour over jeans. It was just before eight in the morning. The rain had stopped finally. I got out of the car and buttoned my coat. The day had turned out cold and bright, with an edge on the wind that appeared to have followed me across country. I had arrived a couple of minutes earlier than agreed so I had no reason to apologise but even so found myself doing it anyway.

'Morning, sorry to keep you waiting. You must be DS Carlton,' I said, extending a hand. 'I'm DS Mel Daley. We spoke yesterday on the phone.'

'Mike, please,' he said with a smile. He was in his thirties, nicely made, broad shoulders, a gym bunny by the look of it. 'And you're fine, we only just got here.' He rubbed his hands together and blew on them. 'Uniform started canvassing the neighbours yesterday and are on it again today. They went in last night after your call about the mobile, did a search, room to room and the garage and shed—'

'Anything?' I asked, hopefully.

Mike Carlton shook his head and turned to introduce the two uniformed officers who had been waiting with him.

'Constables Fuller and Browning.' He grinned. 'Best we could do at short notice.'

The older of the two men raised an eyebrow.

I nodded my hellos. 'Were you the officers who went in last night?'

The older of the two nodded.

'Anything strike you as odd or interesting?'

'Not really, I mean you'll see for yourself, the place is like a show home, nothing out of place. Although the shed outside is different again.'

'Different how?'

'It's full of art,' the man said, in a matter of fact voice. 'Nothing else like it in the house.'

Chapter Six

I nodded. 'Okay and no sign of the phone?'

'Not so far.'

'Thanks for the help; let's see if we can track it down today,' I said. I had spoken to Mike Carlton on the phone the previous day – everyone was up to speed on Leah Hills' disappearance and despite our best efforts and a widening search it seemed that nothing had changed significantly overnight. Which was not good. The longer Leah was gone the less likelihood of a positive outcome.

'So, we all set?' I asked.

Mike nodded. 'We are. You got the key? I've got the locksmith on speed dial if not. He carded the Yale last night – in, in one.'

I smiled and pulled on latex gloves before taking out a key fob from inside a polythene bag I'd got tucked in my shoulder bag. 'No need. Courtesy of Mr Hills. "Nothing to hide," he said. And I'm obviously taking him at his word.'

I stepped up, unlocked the front door of number 34, Fieldview Road and pushed. The door was tight in the frame and resisted for a second or two, making a scraping noise as it finally cleared the woodwork. The air inside was warm and smelt of something slightly lemony, maybe polish or an air freshener. It reminded me of the smell in Chris Hills' car.

Number thirty-four was within walking distance of the town centre, a modest Edwardian semi on a curving terrace amongst a dozen other similar pairs of houses, which now, a hundred years after they had been built with a view out over open fields and farmland, were surrounded on all sides by infill housing and 1960s bungalows.

At the far end of the road was a path leading into the playing field. I traced the path in my mind's eye down to the end where it vanished through a gap in a neatly trimmed privet hedge. I had completely forgotten about the footpath. Maybe if there was time I'd go and take a walk down that way, take a look, for old times' sake.

'You think she's still here?' asked Mike Carlton, peering past me into the hall.

Snapping back into the present, I shook my head. 'I genuinely don't know. Usually by now we've got something, CCTV, or someone's seen something. Going missing from a service station doesn't help, people in, people out, but although I'd have thought if she was there the cameras would have picked her up – we've got people tracing vehicles, going back to interview staff, trawling through the CCTV. You know what it's like. Leah Hills has got to be somewhere.'

'Between here and Wales?'

I nodded.

He pulled a face. 'A lot of ground.'

I nodded.

He pulled a pair of paper boot covers out of his jacket pocket. 'Little present for you,' he said, and handed them to me before taking out another pair for himself.

I smiled at him. 'I was going to offer you the same,' I said, unzipping my handbag. 'And gloves as well.'

'Thanks, but I'm fine.' He tore open the wrapping on the boot covers. 'Me, I hate camping out in hotels. Anything else you need?' he asked, as we both peered into the hallway.

Chapter Six

I shook my head. 'World peace, comfy shoes, and to be back home. This is the other side of the known universe for me.'

Carlton laughed. 'I thought you said you used to live round here?'

'I did. But that was a long time ago; things change. I'd forgotten what it was like.'

'Not enough hills for you now then?'

'You could say that. And the hotel staff here are way too cheery in the mornings.'

I glanced across at the two officers who were waiting for instructions and then turned back to Carlton. 'How do you want to do this?'

'Your case, your call,' he said, indicating the open door.

'Okay, let's take a quick look around first, get the lie of the land, and then if uniform can start downstairs, we'll take upstairs. We also need to collect items for DNA comparison.'

Carlton nodded. 'Righty-oh. And what are we looking for, besides Leah Hills?'

'The phone as a first priority, and then anything that might help. Usual stuff. Diaries, notebooks, laptop, letters, bills−' We stepped inside, DS Carlton letting me take the lead.

The hallway was painted magnolia with what looked like the original black and white chequer board tiled floor. To the left, a flight of stairs with a brown wooden handrail and cream finials led up to the first floor. On the right hand side of the hall were two stripped wooden doors that looked as if they were original to the house, with a third facing us at the far end of the corridor. The hall was bare except for a coir doormat and a period hallstand and mirror. No coats, no pictures, no flowers or knickknacks, nothing that gave anything away about the people who lived in the house.

Carlton opened up the first door on our left, which revealed a sitting room with a view of the hedge and gravelled front garden. The walls were magnolia, the furniture – a shabby-chic three piece in burnt orange – was arranged around an original tiled fireplace, and a blue and orange rug set on bare, dark-wood boards. There were built-in cupboards in the alcoves that flanked the chimney breast and a flat screen TV on a cantilevered arm that was screwed to the wall. No pictures, no ornaments, just a single basket of cream and orange silk flowers tucked into the empty hearth.

'So what do we think?' said Carlton, as we both surveyed the room's interior.

'That the whole place is crying out for a makeover.'

Carlton nodded, 'We've stopped doing that, we kept getting complaints. Anything else?'

'Well, according to the husband one minute Leah Hills was in Hoden Gap Services, heading inside for a pit stop, and the next there she was – gone. Except that her phone is in the house somewhere, and the coat she was supposedly wearing when she disappeared was in the boot of his car.'

Mike Carlton sniffed. 'So what you're saying is that you think there's a good chance she's still here somewhere?'

From the tone of his voice we both knew Mike Carlton meant dead rather than alive. 'I don't know, but yes, I reckon there's a fair chance,' I said.

I took my phone out of my bag and dialled Leah's mobile number. 'Straight to voicemail,' I said, grimly.

'It must be switched on for it to ping the tower.'

'Okay, well it's here somewhere. Let's start down here please, gentleman,' I said to the uniformed officers who were waiting out in the hallway. 'And please be aware we're looking for a mobile so it could be slipped in anywhere. I'd like to find it before the battery drains if we can.'

'Doesn't exactly scream welcome does it?' said Carlton, still walking slowly round the bare sitting room.

I glanced at the thermostat on the wall above the light switch just inside the sitting room door. 'Set to seventeen, so not exactly toasty warm either. Chris Hills told us that his wife hated the cold.'

'They could have turned it down while they were away.'

'I'd believe you if it weren't for the fact someone's marked the surround with a felt tip and taped it in place.' I looked back into the room. 'No photos, no pictures, nothing personal.'

I let my gaze move slowly around the walls – working with Baker was rubbing off on me – and then walked over to a side-board that stood against the wall behind the sofa and opened the top drawer with a fingertip. It was empty. 'Who has drawers with nothing in them?' I asked, lifting the lining paper to check underneath. 'Did you find anything on Chris Hills?'

'Not a thing, I took a good look before you arrived, nothing came up, although we've not had everything digitised yet, he's clean back to the late eighties.'

'And Leah Hills?'

'Invisible. Not so much as a parking ticket. What's in the other drawer?'

I slid it open. 'A chess set and a packet of playing cards.'

With nothing under the lining paper.

I bent down to open the cupboards with a gloved finger. 'Sherry, scotch, advocaat, lemonade, glasses. Jar of cherries in syrup.'

Carlton grinned. 'Sounds like Christmas to me.'

'If you live in the dark ages maybe. Or is it a Norfolk thing?'

'There's bugger all in here,' said Mike lifting his hand to encompass the room. 'Hard to imagine anyone settling down round the telly for the night with a box set and takeaway.'

I had to agree with him.

I went back out into the hallway. The uniformed officers had already started on the kitchen, which was through the door at the far end of the hall. It had oak units with cream granite tops, there was nothing on the work surfaces bar a stainless steel kettle and a toaster; the room was as featureless, faceless and impersonal as the sitting room.

Mike Carlton came in behind me. 'Do you think they were maybe getting ready to sell up?' he asked.

'I don't think so. He didn't mention it.'

A wide rectangular window behind the sink overlooked a tidy paved and gravelled garden and a long wooden shed. 'We'll need to check that too,' I said. One of the PCs nodded. 'We checked it out last night. One of them is using it for a studio.'

'The art,' I said.

He nodded.

I nodded, remembering that in his statement Chris Hills had mentioned Leah being artistic.

The final door in the hall led into a home office, which I assume at some stage had been the dining room. There were the usual things inside, a desk, computer, printer, filing cabinets, and then, more unusually on two walls there were shelves from floor to ceiling, full of box files and plastic storage boxes. Everything was carefully labelled in precise block capitals; the box files were arranged in lines of ten, all numbered but without names, the storage boxes were labelled with combinations of letters that made it impossible to guess what was inside.

Mike Carlton opened a desk drawer – inside, all the contents were slotted into a moulded plastic holder, pens, pencils, scissors, staplers all the usual contents of an office drawer, meticulously arranged and lined up like soldiers on parade. 'Nice and tidy,' he murmured.

'Bit of an understatement,' I said. I went across to the shelving and pulled out a box at random. Inside were a neat stack of electricity bills going back to the 90s, all in order, all carefully clipped together with a payment date written on the top right-hand corner in the same anonymous block capitals. I dropped the bills back into the box and replaced it on the shelf.

'Right, okay let's get upstairs and make a start. If we can't find the phone up there we'll make a start in here. It's going to be a marathon sorting through all this lot. We're going to need more bodies.'

Carlton nodded and stepped aside as I led the way. We were about to climb the stairs when there was a knock on the front door. As I was the closest I opened it.

Outside an elderly man in a cardigan was standing on the doorstep. He looked the two of us up and down, taking in the blue paper booties and latex gloves and then said, 'Good morning, I'm Ivan Craddock, I live next door I just came round to see if there was any news? One of your officers came round yesterday. Dreadful business. Have you found Leah yet?'

'I'm afraid not,' I said gently. 'I'm really sorry but I can't say any more at the moment.' And with that I made to close the door. There was meant to be a uniform on the gate keeping people out but looking across I could see that Craddock had nipped through a small gate in the hedge, bypassing the constable, and made a note to pass the information on.

'I told the officer yesterday that they're a lovely couple,' said the man hastily. 'Chris in particular; he would do anything for anybody. The constable yesterday said that if I remembered anything, anything at all that I was to get in touch. He left his card, but as you were here.' The man let the words hang in the air between us. He was peering past me trying to see what was going on inside.

I nodded. 'Why don't I come outside and we can have a chat,' I said, peeling off my gloves.

'You could come next door and have a cup of tea if you wanted? I'm sure mother wouldn't mind.'

I shook my head. 'That's very kind but we're busy at the moment; I'd prefer to talk out here unless it is something sensitive?'

'Oh no,' said the man shaking his head. 'No, nothing like that.'

I peeled off my booties and stepped back out into the sunshine, pulling the door behind me.

Ivan couldn't quite hide his disappointment.

'The thing is I heard your car door closing when you arrived this morning and then I saw your car parked out here, and I suddenly remembered that I'd heard them leave. Yesterday. Leah and Chris. At around four yesterday morning. I mean, I don't keep tabs on them or anything but I don't sleep well.' He stopped, reddening slightly. 'I'm often awake at night; mother sleeps very lightly, slightest sound and she's awake and wanting to know what's up. It's a strain sometimes—'

'And you're saying you saw Leah getting into the car?'

Ivan nodded. 'Yes. Yes, I saw them both.'

'And how did Leah seem?'

'Right as ninepence.'

'I don't suppose you remember if she was wearing a coat?'

The old man pulled a face, a study in concentration and after a second or two's consideration said, 'No, I don't think she was. You can see almost everything, because of the street light.' He pointed back towards the road. 'I quite like it, means I've not got to keep a light on, on the landing, but I think Chris said he's had to put up those blackout curtains in their room – anyway the thing is I thought I'd heard them go out earlier, before that. Out here on the drive. I heard the front door open and then the car door or the boot, it disturbed me enough to make me get up, go to the bathroom; anyway when I looked out of the window a little bit later their car was still there, which surprised me.'

'So you think you heard someone going to the car before they left at four?'

The man nodded. 'I'm certain of it.' He pointed to the front door. 'It makes a very distinctive noise.'

Right on cue Mike Carlton opened the door. Ivan Craddock was right, even half closed it still caught on the frame.

'And like I said I don't sleep very well,' Ivan said. 'I'm certain I heard it open. It was what woke me.'

'And do you know what time that was?' asked Mike.

'Around three-ish. I glanced at the clock on the landing.'

'Maybe they were loading the car?' I suggested.

The older man nodded. 'I suppose they could have been but they usually do that the night before. Chris likes to have everything packed and ready for the off. Be prepared, just so, you know that kind of thing. They always leave early.' He paused, looking embarrassed. 'Not that I'm spying on them or anything but they've lived here years, you get used to people's little ways.'

I nodded. 'Thank you, that's really helpful. Did you happen to look outside and see anyone the first time the door opened?' I took out my pad to make a note. I wasn't sure what it meant, if anything, but sometimes it was the tiniest detail that made all the difference.

'No, I mean I don't look out at every noise but I remember it distinctly – actually it was more that when I looked out later at four-ish and they were still there that it stuck in my mind.'

'And you are friends with the Hills?'

The man nodded. 'Have been since they moved in. I mean we're not in each others' pockets or anything, but I keep an eye on the place when they go away, take the post in, take the bins out.' He smiled. 'That was the very last thing Chris said to me Thursday night, you know, before he left, he popped round to say they'd be away until Tuesday, and then he said, "Don't forget to put the bins out, will you, Ivan?" Like I'd forget.'

I glanced across at Mike Carlton who nodded. 'I'm on it,' he said.

Chapter Seven

Riverside Cottage, Wales

DI Harry Baker stretched as he climbed out of the car, feeling things in his neck and spine crackle and click back into place. Looking out across the raised pad that had been hacked into the side of the sloping valley side, he wondered exactly why anyone in their right mind would want to live at Riverside Cottage. It was miles from anywhere, without a sign of any other habitation in any direction. The flat area around the cottage had been topped off with coarse granite chippings creating a stark, functional driveway and parking area. The views might be amazing but Chris Hills' holiday home was most certainly not beautiful.

Even the term *cottage* was a complete misnomer. Riverside Cottage was a grim little 1960s bungalow, with narrow, metal-framed windows and an air of decay and neglect. It was square, practical and looked totally at odds with the surrounding rolling hills. Before he arrived Baker had imagined whitewashed walls and maybe thatch, with dormer windows and climbing roses growing around the front door. He stared again at the squat, ugly little structure. Baker couldn't imagine a worst place to spend your retirement, no pub, no places to eat, no shops, no village, nothing to look at but hills and trees and the tumbling river, which, even this far away from the water you could hear rushing over the rocks and boulders.

Baker checked his phone and wasn't at all surprised to find that there wasn't a signal. He had had to turn off what passed for the main road in this neck of the woods, and drive for maybe a mile or so along a narrow, rutted single track lined on both sides with dense stands of commercial forestry to find the damned place, which was tucked away in amongst scrubby conifers on a narrow terraced shelf perched above the fiercely flowing river, which according to *Google* and Chris Hills was a tributary of the Cothi. Baker wandered over to the verge and peered down at the rushing water. As far as he was concerned one river looked very much like another.

Joanne, his wife, would have had plenty to say if he suddenly announced that they were going to up sticks and move to the middle of nowhere. He considered the idea for a minute or two; Jo was about the same age as Leah, give or take a year or two, but there was no way they would consider making a move like that without a lot of discussion. Hours and hours of discussion, possibly more discussion than Baker could cope with. No, it wouldn't work for them, and it niggled away at Baker that Chris Hills thought that it was going to be a surprise to Leah.

Despite everything Chris Hills had told him, he couldn't quite get his head around the fact that Leah didn't know or hadn't guessed what her husband had got in mind. Jo knew what Baker was thinking even before he did. There is no way she wouldn't have guessed that he was up to something. So was that the key to what was going on that Baker was looking for? Had Leah known what Chris Hills had got planned? Was that why she had vanished? Was it that she didn't want to move to Wales, give up her job, to be stuck out in the middle of nowhere with her soul mate? Or was the answer less attractive, darker?

As he was considering the state of the Hills' marriage a marked police car drew up and parked behind his Audi, which reminded him for the umpteenth time that he would have preferred to have come to Riverside Cottage with Daley. Besides being an excellent police officer Mel Daley drove like a dream, there is no way she would have bottomed his car out three times on the mile-long track, and she was good with people.

'DI Baker?'

Baker lifted a hand in greeting as a uniformed sergeant headed towards him. He was a big man whose size looked as if it owed as much to beer and appetite as genetics.

'Sergeant Bill Williams, pleased to meet you, Sir,' said the sergeant, offering Baker his hand. He paused a beat and then smiled. 'Yes, William Williams, my parents had a warped sense of humour.'

Baker smiled. 'Good to see you, Sergeant. Thanks for coming out. This your patch?'

'Twenty years man and boy, and we couldn't have you out here on your own, poking about, getting up to god only knows what, now could we?'

Baker nodded. 'So, what do you reckon?'

The sergeant turned towards the house.

'Well, we came out here yesterday, me and my constable, after your lot rang, and took a good look round. The bungalow appears to be empty as far as we could tell, and the garage, too.' He pointed to the long, low, ugly structure that ran along the back of the bungalow, parallel to the back wall of the bungalow and conservatory.

'We went right round the house, down to the river, checked the orchard over there behind the conifers. There's a couple of sheds right at the bottom there, in a little dip, but they're more or less derelict, not weather tight but we had a quick look anyway. There was no sign of Mrs Hills.'

'Do you know anything about the Hills?'

The sergeant shook his head. 'Not a lot really. They use the place for holidays a few times a year, keep themselves to themselves apparently. Local woman cleans for them.'

Baker pulled his notebook out of his pocket. 'Is that Irenee Jacklin? Chris Hills said he had someone keep an eye on the cottage for them while they're away.'

Williams nodded. 'That's right, lives just up the road.'

Baker lifted an eyebrow.

The sergeant grinned. 'All right, maybe four or five miles up the road, but it's not that far. She's the local answer to Google, knows everything and everybody, if you know what I mean. And then her husband and son do any heavy work that needs doing about the place. Last year a couple of trees blew down in one of those big storms. They came over and cleared them and then cut them up for logs. They cut the grass up by the bungalow, keep the orchard tidy and mowed, that sort of thing. I think Mr Hills lets them have the fruit. I'm not sure that they have any use for it above the odd pie and bowl of apples but it's the thought that counts, and Irenee often has a trust stall outside her bungalow and sells the odd bag here and there. Earns herself a few quid extra, better than letting it all rot.'

Baker nodded. 'I'm planning to go and talk with Mrs Jacklin after we've done here. Do you want to come with me?'

'Anything we can do to help.'

'Appreciated,' said Baker. 'I'd like to take a look around here first.'

'Certainly, although we did have a pretty thorough go round yesterday.'

'I don't doubt it,' said Baker. 'Just humour me. Did you go inside?'

Williams shook his head. 'No, but we didn't see any signs of entry. There was frost here on the roadway first thing yesterday morning, none of the ice on the puddles had been broken on the trackway in.'

'So you're saying that no one had driven in?'

'Certainly didn't look like it.'

'And if anyone had walked up?'

'I'm not saying conclusively that someone didn't walk up here, but this is a bit of a frost pocket, by the time we came to look the frost hadn't cleared completely and there were no signs any footprints around the house on the concrete paths or on the grass.'

Baker was impressed. 'Good work.'

William's nodded. 'It's not conclusive mind.'

'No, I appreciate that.' He paused. 'Would you want to retire here?' Baker said thoughtfully, looking round at the bungalow and the view out over the valley beyond.

Chapter Seven

'Be all right if it was tidied up a bit, and they did something about that track. The fishing's really good along this stretch of the river,' said Williams indicating the stream below the house. 'Sea trout, brown trout, even the odd salmon. Maybe the two of them hankered to live in the middle of nowhere, you know, people do, enjoying the peace and quiet. Back to nature and all that good life stuff.'

Baker thought about the picture of Leah Hills that they had pulled off the website of the garden centre where she worked. She looked tiny, almost fragile. 'She hates the cold,' he said.

Williams looked at him. 'In that case, then I wouldn't have thought so. I mean look at the state of those windows, single glazed, metal framed, let every breath of wind in. And it looks damp to me.'

'Let's have a look round,' said Baker. 'See if we can find any signs of the elusive Mrs Hills.'

The bungalow had been built onto a shelf of rock that had been cut into the hillside that must, once upon a time, have run straight down to the river. The broad gravel strip to the side of the house extended round to the front, one side meant for parking and the other to ensure the front garden was as low maintenance as possible, Baker suspected. To the front of the house, beyond the gravel, was an uneven unkempt sloping lawn, made up of rough grass and the ghost of what once might have been flower beds, framed with shrubs and a row of stunted trees, which gave way to a steep bank, the last of the hillside, cut with steps that led down to the riverside.

A washing line with a few pegs on it swayed in the breeze on what passed for a lawn, beyond that under the row of wind sculpted trees, clumps of snowdrops clustered at the foot of a few of them and were the only signs of life.

Baker looked over the valley and then back towards the cottage. The front windows had a good view out over the river, the inner frames made of metal were peeling, the outer wooden ones were rotten in places, here and there tiles had lifted on the roof. Hills was right about it needing some work.

To the rear of the bungalow was a glass and wooden conservatory furnished with a faded cane table and chairs, the table covered in sun-bleached floral cloth. The whole place looked tired, neglected, shabby and unlived in.

'Quite the little love nest,' said Baker grimly.

'It could be nice,' said Williams. 'If you'd got a few quid to spend on it, some new windows, a coat of paint. And they only use it a few weeks a year. Shame really, it would make a nice home for someone.

'For them apparently,' said Baker. 'They were planning to retire here.' As he spoke he handed Williams a pair of latex gloves before pulling on a pair himself, and then he reached up into a strip of guttering fixed above the conservatory door and fished out a key fob, with three keys on it chained to a tennis ball. 'Here we go, just where Mr Hills said it would be. Presumably his wife would know where it was as well.'

'Didn't she have her own key?' asked Williams.

'Not according to Chris Hills. He'd got a set with him. There are these left here in case he loses his – but apparently they always came here together, she doesn't drive, so she didn't need one.'

Williams frowned. 'My missus wouldn't wear that.'

Chapter Seven

'Mine neither,' said Baker

He chose a key at random from the fob and slipped it into the lock. By some stroke of luck he picked the right key on his first attempt though oddly it didn't cheer him, instead it felt like a bad omen. The conservatory door resisted at first, Baker put his shoulder to it and grudgingly the door gave way. The conservatory was warmer by several degrees than outside, though the air was stale and dusty. A second key opened the inner back door.

'Has Irenee Jacklin got keys or does she use these?' Baker asked, holding up the tennis ball.

'No, she'll have her own. Little woman, she is, barely five foot tall, she'd never reach that gutter without a step ladder.'

Baker nodded and pushed the back door open. The inside of the bungalow was noticeable chillier than the conservatory, and was as depressing as the outside of the house. It smelt of bleach and damp and something wet and decaying, and had the feel of a seaside beach house that Baker remembered from his childhood. It was furnished with a grim collection of cheap mismatched furniture all of which, though spotlessly clean, had seen better days.

The back door led directly into the kitchen, which appeared to still have the original blue and cream Formica units that had to have been put in when the house was built, along with a matching table and two chairs, set in the middle of the room. One wall was dominated by a large cream enamelled range. There was a bag of kindling, logs and coal in a basket alongside it. On the opposite wall was an ancient cooker, and under a run of battered blue worktops were a washing machine and fridge, both with their doors open.

A quick recce of the kitchen cupboards turned up nothing but the sparsest of equipment and a few staples tucked down into jars, presumably to deter vermin, along with a selection of tins and bottles.

The kitchen door opened up into a central hallway leading to the front door with doors off on either side.

Both men had fallen silent, walking from room to room. While Williams checked the bathroom, Baker checked the cupboard in the hall, which contained nothing but a hoover, a brush and dustpan and an ironing board, and the electricity meter tucked away in the corner, slowing winking its red Cyclops eye.

The bathroom was even colder than the rest of the house, despite housing the airing cupboard. Baker glanced inside – the immersion heater was off and the slatted cupboard was bare except for a pile of towels on the centre shelf and a couple of blankets folded and stacked on the top shelf.

There were plain white tiles above the sink and around the bath, but no curtains at the tiny opaque window, which added to the room's bleak appearance. There were traces of black mould under the sill and up the wall around the bath and in the grout round the tiles. Some patches had been scrubbed but were still painfully obvious in the pale blue emulsion, which Baker thought probably explained the smell of bleach. In a little mirrored cupboard above the sink were two toothbrushes, a disposable razor and two new bars of soap still in their wrappers. Obviously the Hills didn't leave much there between visits.

Chapter Seven

Back in the hall Baker found a hook to unfasten the loft hatch, which on closer inspection revealed nothing more than a water tank, which blessedly contained nothing more than icy cold water.

At the front of the bungalow was the sitting room with its view out over the river. There was an armchair either side of the hearth, and a sofa pushed back up under the window, an old fashioned TV and VCR on a little coffee table stood in one corner, with a selection of board games and videos tucked underneath it. There were shabby rugs on a patterned carpet, and a scuttle full of coal and sticks, but not hide nor hair of Leah Hills.

Across the hallway were two bedrooms, one was more or less the same size as the sitting room, and also overlooking the river. The main bedroom had a king-sized bed, made up with fresh, sharply ironed blue and white bed linen, there was a bare dressing table with a trifold mirror, matching wardrobe and bedside cabinets. All empty.

Next door in the smaller of the two bedrooms were a set of bunks and a single bed. Baker stared thoughtfully at the single beds, which were all made up with matching floral throws that had long faded out to pastels.

Baker turned back the cover on the single bed, underneath was a duvet and a pillow in matching blue covers. It looked like the linen had been on the bed a long time. The bed felt damp and there was a starburst of black mould on the pillow and the sheet that covered the mattress.

'Have the Hills got a family?' Williams asked; he was standing behind Baker in the doorway.

Baker shook his head. 'No, there are just the two of them, according to Chris Hills.'

Williams joined him, looking round the smaller bedroom. 'Maybe they rent it out. Like I said, the fishing is good here and this is a prime spot. Nice and quiet if you're a fisherman, or fancy a boys' weekend away.'

Baker raised his eyebrows. 'These beds haven't been slept in for years by the look of it. Would you come somewhere like this for your holidays?' He dropped the bed cover back into place.

Bill Williams pulled a face. 'Oh I don't know. Some people don't mind where they stay as long as it's warm and dry, and I reckon once that range is going in the kitchen and the fire's lit it'd warm up pretty quick.'

Baker raised an eyebrow. It was obvious from the smell and the mould that Riverside Cottage was neither warm nor dry. 'And what do you make of those?' said Baker, pointing up to a pelmet that ran across the bedroom window. Sitting on top of it was a collection of soft toys and a doll, a faded teddy bear and a train.

Williams shrugged. 'Maybe they have family who come to stay once in awhile? Or maybe they're childhood treasures, my missus has still got her first teddy bear, keeps it on the dressing table.'

Baker nodded. 'Maybe their cleaner can shed some light on it.' He paused and took another look around the room. The whole place gave him the creeps. 'Three beds seems odd.'

'Odd?'

'Strikes me as strange, that's all.' Baker stood for moment or two considering what it was that the house told him about

Chris and Leah Hills, and the truth was that rather than making things clearer it made things muddier.

'Right,' he said after a second or two more. 'Well, Leah's not here. Let's take a quick look round the outside and then go and see Irenee Jacklin.'

Outside the sunshine was finally cutting its way through the last of the frost, burning off the remaining dew that clung to the grass. Baker was glad to be back outside in the daylight.

The two men made their way around the open yard that wrapped itself all the way around the house, taking in the views and Baker's need to get the lie of the land.

At the back of the terrace, and running parallel to the conservatory was the long, narrow utilitarian garage, with a concrete and gravel path between the two. The garage took up almost all the space available at the back of the bungalow before the land, covered with stunted trees and scrub rose again.

The garage would have easily housed two cars nose to tail. None of the keys Chris Hills had given Baker or told him about fitted the lock, and the gutter yielded nothing more, so they were confined to peering in through the windows. There wasn't that much to look at – a bare, chipped concrete floor, along with oddments of outdoor furniture and a parasol stacked up in one corner. The far end wall was clad with painted tongue and groove board, and studded with an array of hooks from which were hanging a coiled garden hose, odds and ends of gardening equipment and a selection of tools.

Baker and Williams walked all the way around the garage. On the back end someone had added an open-fronted lean-to woodshed, maybe six foot deep and the whole width of the garage, which was full to the eaves with seasoned logs and stacked timber, piled around and alongside an old fashioned concrete coal bunker full to the brim with coal, but there was no sign at all of Leah Hills.

Baker walked back to the front garden followed by Sergeant Williams. The two men stood side by side and looked out over the valley. At the front of the house, with its view out over the river, Baker could pick out the distinct outline of what had once upon a time been proper flowerbeds and a formal lawn, but now just the bare bones remained, a rough outline ghosted in the grass. Beyond that lay the rough grass and the row of gnarled conifers with their clumps of snowdrops, marking out the boundary where the garden broke in a wilder, rougher, unkempt landscape.

Beyond what remained of the front garden was the flight of steps made from slabs of rock that led down to the riverbank, and then down on the bank, threading its way between the conifers and outcrops of rock was a narrow well-trodden path heading upstream.

'Okay?' asked Baker.

Williams nodded and they made their way down the steps with Baker in the lead, and then in single file along the pathway. When they got beyond the conifers the land flattened and spread out in a broad V shape – the whole area was planted with ancient fruit trees in formal rows. The grass was cut back and there were scatterings here and there of rotted fruit, above them some still clung on determinedly to the bare branches. The whole of the orchard, which stretched off and away to a natural rise in the distance, was surrounded by a windbreak of conifers, which made it feel like a place apart.

Baker suppressed a shudder. 'Lot of land, you'd think they'd do something with it,' he said.

Williams sniffed. 'I suppose they're not here long enough over a course of a year. Nice lots of trees though, plums, apples, pears. Seems a waste just to let it all rot.'

Just off the main path was a tyre swing, peppered green with moss, perished and full of water, it hung low on a thick wire rope from the branch of one of the ancient apple trees.

Baker pointed it out to Williams. 'Kids again,' he said thoughtfully.

'And the Hills haven't got any children?'

Baker shook his head. 'Not as far as I know.' He put his hand up to shade his eyes. 'There has to be another way in if someone is coming in and mowing all this.'

Williams nodded. 'You're right. Did you notice the spur as you came in? On the left, runs off the main track.'

Baker said nothing, not wanting to admit that most of his attention and efforts had been focused on trying to keep his car out of the bigger ruts and potholes. William took his silence to mean that he had.

'Well, that goes round the back of that ridge, behind the house, right round to those derelict sheds down the bottom that I was telling you about. I'm assuming that that's how Irenee Jacklin's husband gets the mower in. Sit and ride job like a little tractor, more than likely he brings it up on a trailer. We took a drive down that way yesterday when we had checked out the rest of the place but didn't see any sign of anybody and nothing that looked out of the way, if you know what I mean.'

Baker thought about the manpower it would take to search the whole site properly. 'No ice on the puddles broken, is that what you're saying?'

Williams nodded. 'Nothing had driven down that way before us. And I had Andy, my constable, walk both sides to check the verges.'

'Okay, we need to think about bringing in a search team if she doesn't show up soon. Let's go and have a talk to the Hills' cleaner,' said Baker.

'Right you are. I'll be glad of a cup of tea,' he said. 'Have you any idea what's happened to her? Leah?' he asked, as the two of them turned back towards the river path and the bungalow.

Baker shook his head. Neither man said a word; it didn't augur well that twenty-four hours after Leah Hills had disappeared they had nothing to work on that gave any indication of where she might be or what had happened to her.

*

Mrs Irenee Jacklin was a woman who, Baker suspected, had been aching to talk to someone about the Hills for a long, long time, although there was probably a lot of people Irenee would like to dish the dirt on given half a chance. She was small and plump with a crisp perm and lips that over the years had pulled themselves up like the tightly gathered top of a drawstring bag.

Chapter Seven

Baker had followed Williams to Mrs Jacklin's bungalow and Williams was now cheerfully making himself at home, drinking tea and eating a fruit scone at the dropleaf table in the sitting room. Baker had declined Mrs Jacklin's offer of refreshments.

Irenee Jacklin lived in a pin-neat bungalow just outside Llandeilo, the very first one on the edge of a little purpose-built estate that had been angled so that it faced the local shop and post office and the doctors' surgery opposite. DI Baker guessed that it was as close to heaven as someone like Mrs Jacklin could get. All the time they were speaking the elderly woman's eyes were on the move, flicking up to check on the activity outside the window, the comings and goings, and who was talking to who and for how long.

'So have you found Leah yet?' she asked.

'No, not yet, but we're doing everything we can to find her,' said Baker.

'I thought not. You wouldn't be here if you had, I suppose. She is always so nice, Leah, always leaves me a card and a little thank you note when they've been to stay up at the cottage, never misses. All these years. Not once forgotten.'

As she spoke, Baker took out his mobile phone and set it down on the arm of the chair. Irenee glanced at it. 'You'll be lucky to get a signal here. Drops in and out. Been all over the local papers, people complaining. You can use the house phone if you want, if it's urgent. We've got this call plan, my boy set it up, many calls as you like – not abroad obviously – but all included.'

Baker smiled. 'Thank you. I'm fine.'

'You're sure? It's no bother.'

Baker nodded. 'When was the last time you saw Leah?'

Irenee Jacklin took a moment or two to consider. 'October, I think. I could check my calendar if you'd like, if it's important. Early on it was, first or second week. The weather was really lovely here then, warm, really sunny, proper Indian summer.'

'And how long did they stay for?'

'A week I think – I can't be sure but I can check for you. It's all written down, my boy puts it on my laptop for me, keeps all my appointments on there now, hairdressers, doctors, he's set it up so it sends me a text, clever – if you can get a signal obviously.'

Baker nodded. 'Thank you, that would be good. And do they come here a lot? Regularly?'

'Chris and Leah? Not really, depends on what Chris has on workwise I think, but they always come in the spring, never ever miss, middle of February. Chris always says it's his favourite time of the year, all that new life, the snowdrops out. I think it's a bit bleak myself but he seems to love it. Are you sure I can't offer you anything. A cup of tea, coffee? It would be no trouble.'

Baker politely declined while across the table Williams started on his second scone.

'Right, and so that's what, about four months, maybe four and half ago you last saw her?' asked Baker, making a note.

'Yes, about that.'

'And how did Mrs Hills seem to you then?'

'All right. Although I thought she'd lost weight. Looked tired. You know, a bit peaky. They'd arrived a bit earlier than

I expected and I was just finishing off making the bed up when they drove up to the cottage. I wondered who it was. I don't usually see much of them while they're staying there. My Barry was just bringing the coal in, gave us both a start, made us both jump. They keep themselves to themselves, Chris and Leah.'

She glanced up, nodding towards the window at the street. 'Although they use the shop and the post office while they're here, and I sometimes have a word with them then, if I catch them.'

'And what did you talk about? In October?'

Irenee pulled a face. 'Hard to say now. I mean it was months ago. I can barely remember what I said last week. Nothing very much, the weather, I suspect, if I thought it was going to get colder, if I thought the good weather would last. You know, just chit-chat really. It's mostly Chris we talk to. He's such a lovely man, always got a smile and up for a chat is Chris. Always got the time of day. She's quieter, Leah, always has been. Bit shy I think. Reserved. Chris always deals with everything, bills and things, never queries when I tell him how much he owes us, never once in all the years we've been keeping an eye on the place. Pays up just like that. Never a moan, always grateful for what we do. And a nice Christmas box every year, never misses.'

'Right, and how long have you been cleaning for them?'

Irenee frowned thoughtfully. 'Oh a long while now.' She paused as if totting up the years. 'I've cleaned Riverside Cottage since Chris first bought the place, when he was married to his first wife. He bought it with the money his mum left him, he told me. He put a card up in the post office. "Cleaner/caretaker wanted".'

Baker glanced up. 'Right, so, Chris Hills was married before?'

'Oh yes.' She took a breath. 'Linda her name was. Tall girl, blonde, with a bit of a horsey face, but nice looking, and always very pleasant. Well turned out. Liked her clothes. So, I suppose it must have been in the 1980s when I started, my youngest had just started school so it worked out really well. Money came in handy back then when the kiddies were small, and Chris has always paid me a bit of retainer to keep an eye on the place while he's away, and Barry, my husband, he pays him to mow the grass up there and do any odd jobs that need doing. All helps.'

'So Leah is his second wife?' said Baker, turning the conversation back toward Chris Hills.

Irenee nodded. 'That's what I just said, didn't I? Linda and then Leah.' She smiled, quite obviously delighted that she had found a gap in Baker's knowledge. 'Oh yes, Linda and the children, lovely little things they were, Russell, Geraldine and the baby, Lorna. Always beautifully turned out, all of them. Always polite, lovely manners. Used to make me wonder what on earth possessed them to buy the bungalow. So out of the way up there and Linda never struck me as the country type, but I know that Chris loved it and I suppose it was nice for the kiddies, though Linda always used to fret about the river.

'I'd go up there and babysit sometimes if they wanted a night out while they were here. And then Chris would run me home. I used to say to him it couldn't be any fun for him if he couldn't have a drink, and that Barry would come and fetch me, but Chris never seemed to mind. Said it was no trouble. Such a shame when they split up.

'Chris was always saying that he wanted them to move here, move the whole family, lock, stock and barrel. Even used to get me to send him the local paper and things, but she was never keen, I could see that.'

'Linda?'

Irenee nodded. 'That's right; she was a proper town girl was Linda, but when they first came here he was looking to change jobs he told Barry, and had all these plans to have the whole place renovated for her. He put the range in and wanted to have a new kitchen fitted and double-glazing all the way round, new bathroom, another bedroom built on, the works. I mean let's be honest, it could do with a proper makeover even back then.'

Baker said nothing, which was all the encouragement Irenee needed.

'Barry got a digger in and helped him cut that terraced bit out the front and sides ready for the extension. Back then they put flowerbeds at the front and Chris started a vegetable plot, proper picture it looked out the front there when it was finished. Fenced too to keep the children away from the river. Him and Barry spent god knows how long on that garden trying to make a silk purse out of a sow's ear for her and the kids, but Linda wasn't having a bar of it.'

Irenee took a sip of tea. 'I could have told him he was wasting his time from the get go. There was no way she was ever going to move out there. I said that to him once, said he'd be better looking for somewhere closer to town. Like I said Linda preferred the town. She told me she used to worry about them being so far away from everywhere in case anything ever happened. I don't even think she liked them spending all their holidays here. She wanted to go abroad, Majorca and the Costa del Sol, get a bit of sun, sea and sand she said. To be perfectly honest, although it was sad, I wasn't that surprised when they split up, they wanted different things, the two of them, see.'

'And do you know where Linda went after they separated?' asked Baker, making a note to trace her.

'She moved up north first, Manchester I think. With some other man. Took the children. I tell you, Chris was beside himself. It's the only time I've ever seen him upset.'

'Upset?' Baker prompted.

'Well he had every reason, didn't know whether to cry or punch something. Barry had a word with him; they used to talk a lot those two when they were working up there. And then she went off to Spain, got a job running a bar and hotel.' Irenee paused, and pulled a disapproving face, all opinions and judgements. 'I could see that would suit her a lot better but I did wonder what sort of life the kiddies would have out there, but she seemed to think they'd love it. Beaches, the sea – a whole life at the seaside she said.'

'Can I ask how you knew?' Baker asked.

'Knew?' said Irenee.

'About Linda and the children going to Spain. Did she stay in touch? Maybe contact you after she left Chris Hills? Phone you?'

Chapter Seven

Irenee paused and looked heavenwards as if trying to remember. 'You know, I'm not sure how I found out where she was. I suppose Chris might have told me, but I think it might have been someone in the shop. You know how people are.'

Baker nodded, he knew exactly how people were.

'And did you see her again after they'd split up?'

'No, although I did get a card that first Christmas when she went but after that, nothing. That's right, I remember now,' Irenee said. 'She told me that she and the children were doing all right and that she had applied for this job and was looking forward to a fresh start in the sunshine. She sounded happy.'

'Did you take that to mean the job in Spain?'

Irenee nodded. 'I suppose so. She always did say she liked the sun.'

'And she didn't write or contact you again after that?'

'No, but by then I think Chris had met Leah and we weren't really ever that close me and Linda, not really. Polite though.'

'So what can you tell me about Leah?' asked Baker.

Irenee smiled. 'She's lovely, a lot younger than Chris obviously; not that I'm judging, each to their own, that's what I always say. And she is a lovely girl. When they first came down to the cottage for a weekend Barry had been up there to light the range for when they arrived and he said to me that she looked barely legal, just a kid. We've seen her grow up really. I can't believe she's missing, Chris was besotted with her, you know that, don't you? Totally and utterly. He must be in a terrible state at the moment. Leah was his whole world.'

'Was?' said Baker gently.

'I mean *is*,' said Irenee, reddening furiously. 'Slip of the tongue. Sorry. I suppose you read so much these days in the papers, and see it on the telly, don't you? You always assume the worst. What do you think happened to her? I mean do you think–' she stopped herself saying whatever was in her mind, and instead let the silence open up between them.

Baker shook his head. 'Nothing we've found so far suggests that Leah has come to harm.' *Yet*, said a voice in his head, which sounded a lot like Mel Daley. And what was it exactly that they had found, beyond the coat and Chris Hills' statement? Nothing of any consequence to back his story up or disprove it.

'Well that's good,' said Irenee, breaking into his thoughts. 'Let's hope it stays that way.'

Baker wished he shared the old lady's optimism.

'Did you know that Chris was planning to retire here?' he asked.

Irenee laughed. 'Yes, although he asked me to keep it to myself. It was meant to be this big secret, Chris said, but I can't think anyone who knew him would be that surprised. He told me he wanted it to be a surprise for Leah. As if she hadn't guessed,' Irenee laughed. 'He's always wanted to live here full time ever since he first bought the place, and he's always planned to retire here.' She paused to take another sip of tea.

'He was lucky to hang on to it really, given him getting divorced from Linda and all that. I remember that he'd been worried when him and Linda split up that he would have to sell up and give her half of everything and support the children

129

as well, you know how it is, but apparently they worked something out between themselves, he said.' She paused, some thought passing across her face like a dark cloud.

'What is it?' prompted Baker.

'Well I know that he said that what they worked out was quite amicable, given how messy it had all got, but I do think Chris was worried about Linda, what she might say or do if she found him up at the cottage with Leah. He told me to ring him if I ever saw Linda in the village. Or up at Riverside.'

'She could drive?'

'Linda? Oh yes. They'd got an old Volvo estate, you know one of the big square ones, and she was always backwards and forwards with the kiddies all in the back.'

'And did you ring him?'

'What?'

'Did you see her in the village after they split up?'

'No, I don't think I ever did, but then again I can't really remember the last time Linda was here with Chris to be honest, which had to have been when I saw her, but then again it was years and years ago now. Time goes by so fast, doesn't it?'

'And so once the divorce was settled they didn't ever come back here on holiday? Linda and the children?'

Irenee shook her head. 'I don't think so. The cottage had always been his not hers and like I said she was more of a town person. She'd never liked the cottage, I can't imagine any reason why she would come back. So, no, I had just that one card, that Christmas. I remember the postmark was Manchester. Truth is I didn't recognise the handwriting and wondered who it was from when it arrived.'

'But you'd had cards from Linda before? And notes to say thank you?' prompted Baker.

She narrowed her eyes. 'You know you're right. Maybe Chris wrote them, I had always assumed it was her.'

'I don't suppose you kept it?' said Baker.

'The card?' Irenee asked incredulously. 'Hardly. It must have been getting on for…' She paused pulling a face as she did the calculation. '…I don't know, maybe twenty-six or twenty-seven years ago maybe more. So, no, that's long gone. I sometimes keep them if they've got an address in, you know till I've had chance to copy it into my address book but other than that they're out as soon as the decorations come down.'

Baker smiled. 'And do your remember if there was an address on the card from Linda?'

Irenee hesitated. 'I don't think so, I can't remember now, but I'm more or less certain that there wasn't.'

Baker made a note. 'So, you would have made the beds up presumably, when the family came to stay?'

'Like I said it was a long time ago now, but yes, just like now when Chris and Leah are coming; Chris would ring me, usually a few days beforehand and we'd go up there with fresh bed linen. Air the place, light the range. Get the fuel in, logs, coal—'

'So are you saying that those are the children's beds up at the cottage?' said Baker.

Irenee reddened slightly. 'Yes. It was Leah's idea.'

Baker stared at her.

'That and keeping all their toys. Chris took it really hard when him and Linda split up, and then to begin with Linda messed him about with the kids, not letting him see them, denying him access, playing games, then they could see him, then they couldn't. It was really awful for him, you could see that. He doted on those children. Anyway, all credit to her, Leah said that if the beds stayed up then the children could come and stay whenever they wanted. It would show them that they were always welcome. And then when Chris and Leah didn't have any of their own–' Irenee let the sentence fall away. 'Well, it must have been all the harder for her, seeing their beds there, all set up in that room, but the beds and the toys stayed, just in case. There used to be a cot in the corner for Lorna, but in the end they took that down, said Lorna would have grown out of it by the time she came back – if she ever did. I think it's still in the garage.'

'And as far as you know Chris's children have never made contact or been back since?'

Irenee shook her head. 'Not to my knowledge, but then again they'd be all grown up now, wouldn't they? I might not recognise them even if I saw them. Any of them could have been up there and had a look round without anyone knowing – it's not like it's overlooked or anything. I like to think they have been back. Lovely kiddies they were. So quiet, so well behaved, a credit to the two of them really.'

Baker nodded. 'And Chris hasn't ever mentioned them? Or seeing them?'

Irenee shook her head. 'No, no he hasn't but then again he perhaps wouldn't if Leah was about, would he? And let's be honest some men never see their children. I was watching–' she stopped, seeing something in Baker's expression.

'Do you know why Leah didn't have any children?'

'No, Leah's never said anything, not a word. First of all I thought it might be that Chris didn't want any more, not after all the palaver he had with Linda. I mean who could blame him? But then one day when he dropped in with my money I said something in passing about a family, them hoping to have a baby, and Chris said Leah couldn't have any. But he said he didn't mind that much because he had his three, but that he felt sorry for her missing out, you know on having one of her own. He's such a lovely man. And he stayed with her,' Irenee said, 'I mean that says something about how much Chris loves her, doesn't it? Not every man would.'

'And did you go up this week to get the house ready for their arrival yesterday?' asked Baker.

Irenee shook her head. 'No, there was no need Chris said. He'd popped down for a couple of days last week and called in to see me on the way through, said he'd make the bed up and get the fuel in, tidy up and that sort of thing, said that I wasn't to worry. I think he was a bit concerned Barry might go up and see the chimney smoking and think it was squatters or something.'

Baker made a note, wondering why Chris Hills hadn't mentioned his earlier visit to the cottage. 'Can you remember when exactly last week that was?'

Irenee pulled a face. 'Wednesday or Thursday, I think, although I'm not one hundred percent certain. I've always thought it was lovely up there, especially in the summer, if they just did it up. On its own – bit too isolated for me, but if they like that kind of thing. Anyway he was telling me all about his plans. He's finally going to get it sorted out, at long last – he told

133

me he's planning new windows, new kitchen, replacing the old conservatory, getting the garden round, decorating all the way throughout. Him and Leah finally moving over here once he's finished up at his job. Retiring.' She beamed. 'I was so pleased for them. He's been waiting so long. I gave him some names of people who might give him a price for the work. He looked really pleased with himself. Home at last. I said to him that he wouldn't want me once they were living here full time but he said that I wasn't to be daft of course they'd need me. He's so lovely. I can't imagine how he's feeling right now, it must be awful for him. You will find her, won't you?'

DI Baker left his card and asked Irenee to call him if she thought of anything that might be helpful, anything at all, and then he and Sergeant Williams left, after the latter had thanked her profusely for the tea and the scones.

'So,' said Williams as they got back outside into the bright cold morning. 'What do you reckon then?'

'That I need to get back to the station.'

Williams nodded. 'Interesting about the first wife.'

Baker agreed. 'Yes, I'll get a trace on her and see what she can tell us about Chris Hills. Fill in the gaps.'

Williams picked at something in his teeth. 'You think he's good for it? The husband?'

Baker hesitated; most murders were committed by someone known to the victim, but they had no body, no evidence of foul play and nothing obvious or evidence based that suggested Chris Hills had killed his wife, and Baker knew from experience that it was all too easy to let instincts and hunches accidentally lead an enquiry in the wrong direction.

He resisted the temptation to say anything that might be mis-interpreted or take Williams off in the wrong direction. 'We've got nothing,' he said. 'Not on him, not on anyone. Open book at the moment.'

'I've seen the photos, she's a lovely looking little thing – hard to believe she's in her forties – anyway anything else you need, all you got to do is ring me. I'll try and help in any way I can.'

'Appreciated,' said Baker, shaking his hand. As he turned to go back to his car, his phone rang. It was Daley.

'How's it going?' he asked.

*

'We found Leah's phone,' I said. I was standing on the landing of 34 Fieldview Road, looking out of the window down onto the road below. A PC was standing in the gateway. There was tape across the gap in the hedge that the neighbour had used and a SOCO team van was parked up in the drive.

'Good.'

'I tried to ring you earlier but it kept going to voicemail.'

Baker snorted. 'I'm in Wales what do you expect? The signal's piss poor – and then there's the scenery. Way too rural.'

'We also found Leah's handbag, along with her hair brush, make-up, credit cards, debit cards and around thirty pounds in cash, new notes, sequential. It was all wrapped up in a polythene bag in the bottom of the wheelie bin.'

I heard Baker's intake of breath. 'Okay. When's the next collection?' he asked.

'It was supposed to be first thing on Monday morning according to the neighbours.'

'Presumably by then the battery would be long dead and it would be untraceable?'

'That's right. It had got about twenty percent power left when we found it. It was turned to silent, and all calls directed to voicemail. It would probably have been dead by this afternoon.'

'It doesn't mean to say that Chris Hills was the one who put it there,' said Baker, although he sounded as sceptical as I felt. 'And you have to ask why he didn't just turn it off. You said a SOCO team's there?'

'They've just arrived on site.'

'Even with fingerprints we've got nothing that isn't circumstantial. Anyone see anything?'

'No, not even the nosy neighbour, but the last thing Chris Hills did was remind him to put the bins out.'

'It's not evidence though, Daley.'

'It's pretty iffy though, Guv.'

Baker snorted. 'You don't say. Anyway, good find. I'll get Rees to pull Hills back in.'

'We found something else, actually several things that might be of interest.' I carried the phone to the doorway across the landing as if there was some way Baker could see what I could see.

'In the spare bedroom there's a single bed, a chest of drawers and not much else. The bed's recently been moved from the centre of the room and there are marks on the bed frame that would suggest restraints, backed up by the fact we found handcuffs, a blindfold, and various sex toys in the chest of drawers. The handcuffs appear to have blood on them.'

Far away in Wales I heard the slight catch in Baker's breath. 'How much blood?'

'Droplets on the mattress, some on the cuffs and bed frame, nothing else visible at the moment.' I didn't like to say *not enough*, but I knew we were both thinking it.

Unless Chris Hills had been very careful there was far too little blood to suggest that he had murdered Leah in the spare room. Unless he had cleaned down well and nothing was visible or he had used a tarp, with the SOCO team on site we'd soon find out. It was impossible to hide it all from modern forensic techniques.

The room smelt of air freshener.

'Get SOCO to take the place apart,' said Baker in a low soft voice.

'The DS they've assigned me is already onto it.'

'I want to know whose blood it is. You've got something to test against?'

'A comb and the tissues from her handbag.'

'Right. Can we get those fast tracked?'

I made a note.

'Uniform are still searching downstairs and the garden, and there is a shedload of paperwork in Hills' office that's going to take more than a couple of bobbies and me and Carlton to go through.'

'Okay, let's see what the rest of the search pitches up with and then we'll see what else we need to allocate in terms of manpower.' He paused.

'How was Wales, Sir?'

'Interesting – firstly, Chris Hills was here last week according to his cleaner.'

'He didn't mention it before.'

'Probably slipped his mind,' said Baker grimly. 'And Chris Hills was married before and has three children. The whole family were apparently planning on moving to Wales, or at least Chris Hills was planning that's what they were going to do, his first wife wasn't all that keen.'

I looked out of the window on the side of the landing that looked down into the garden. One of the constables was busy trying to open the shed door. 'Sounds familiar. So what happened?'

'His first wife didn't want to go and it ended in a messy divorce, apparently.'

'Nothing strange about that.'

'No, you're right. You've got Hills' sister's contact details? Can you see what you can find out about his first wife? Her name was Linda, I'll email over what details I've got – along with the children's names. Try and get a forwarding address if you can. Add it to the list.' Baker paused again, and I waited.

'You should see the cottage,' he said. 'I wouldn't want to live there; middle of bloody nowhere, damp, bleak –' He stopped. 'I'm heading back to the station. Let me know what you turn up on Hills' ex-wife. I'll get Rees onto tracking her down this end.'

'Right-oh, Sir, I'm going to leave DS Carlton here with the SOCOs and go and see where Leah works and then I'm going to talk to the firm Chris Hills works for in Cambridge.'

'Don't call them,' said Baker briskly. 'I want you to go and see them. The more you can find out about Mr Hills the better, and you'll be able to pick up more if you can see the place, see the people face to face. I want to know more about him, Daley. Keep me in the loop.'

'Right you are,' I said as Mike Carlton came out of the bathroom.

'Your boss?'

I nodded as I ended the call. 'Yeah, some interesting information but no Leah.'

I brought him up to speed with the new information and my plans for the rest of the day. He assigned me a local DC to come with me to both gigs and then paused, slipping his hand into the back pockets of his jeans.

'I was just wondering what your plans are for tonight? Assuming you're not going to be driving straight back to Wales after you're finished, that is?'

I grinned. 'Oh my god, don't tell me, you're the station stud?'

Carlton reddened furiously and then laughed. 'Not these days.'

I smiled. 'Sorry.'

'No, you're all right, I'm flattered – and back in the day – ' he grinned. 'Actually I was just wondering if you'd like to come round to our place for supper tonight. I know what hotels can be like if you're on your own. Me and my wife just moved into a new place. We're expecting our first baby in a couple of months and I know she'd love a bit of female company.'

I lifted an eyebrow. 'Really? Even if it is another copper?'

Chapter Seven

Mike laughed. 'Oh god yes, Carol and I met at a community policing shindig a few years back. She is a youth liaison officer. She misses it, you know, the company, the banter, the challenge of it. Well at least she says she does, but I'm wondering if that is just her way of making me feel better about all the time she spends on the sofa.'

I smiled. 'It's a really kind offer, Mike, but I'm not sure what time I'll be finished. And I really need to write all this up, fire it over to our incident room, so I'm thinking that by the time I've got that done and talked to my boss, my plans mostly revolve around a hot bath, a mug of tea and bed.'

Mike grinned. 'Fair enough, but if you change your mind you have my number. We're planning to eat about seven. Just text or ring, you'd be very welcome. Save us both from conversations about baby names and heartburn.'

'Thank you.'

'Scuse me,' called one of officers from the bottom of the stairs. 'We've got the shed open.'

Chapter Eight

The Studio

I stood on the threshold of the shed in Chris and Leah Hills'
garden, not sure where to look first. I knew that the officers
had searched the building the previous evening but nobody
had reported what was in the shed other than the fact that
there was no sign of Leah.

Inside the anonymous black timber building the walls
were hung with paintings and drawings in various stages of
completion, from the roughest of pencil sketches through to
framed finished artwork. In some places the pictures were two
or three deep, held up with combinations of wire, tape, nails
and drawing pins. Alongside the art, tucked into the tiniest
spaces were postcards and pictures cut from magazines, and
the walls, where you could catch a glimpse of them, were
painted with the same flat magnolia as the rest of the house;
the whole space was a great, vibrant raging collage of colour
and life, talent and passion.

Chapter Eight

There were landscapes and seascapes, still life, flowers and studies of faces, harbours and boats, children, animals, exquisite fluid abstracts, brightly coloured studies that were worthy of being hung in a gallery.

There was a work bench running the whole length of the wall opposite the door, which — totally at odds with the rest of the house's almost clinical tidiness — was littered with tubes of paint, rags, and the chaos of creativity, while along the back were jars of well-used brushes, pencils and pens. An empty easel stood in the centre of the room, turned at an angle, presumably to catch the best of the light. Wedged under the bench was a bookcase, the shelves bowed under the weight of sketch books, reference books of places and animals and architecture, and the books of other artists, the pages well thumbed, the spines broken from years of use and study.

It was totally mesmerising. I stood on the paint- spattered floor, my gaze working along the pictures, trying to take in what I was seeing.

'His?' asked Carlton, picking up a charcoal sketch of a nude woman that was taped down to a drawing board on the desk. I glanced down at the image. The woman was framed by a window, turning towards the artist, the light and shade picking out the delicate musculature of her back and shoulders. While not flattering in any traditional sense, the artist had caught the vitality of the woman, her energy and her joy. The overall look of the thing was haunting, mesmerising.

I shook my head and pointed towards the initials tucked away in the shading around the woman's hips. 'LH,' I said, before turning to take another look at the paintings. 'I think that all these might be Leah Hills' work. Can we get them photographed?'

Mike, his attention still on the walls, nodded. 'Certainly can. We're going to need extra manpower on this.'

I nodded.

I looked at a landscape hanging above the centre of the desk, the sea was so blue, painted so beautifully that you could almost hear it rolling in over the white beach.

'Where are you, Leah?' I murmured under my breath.

Chapter Nine

Looking back

As soon as he had finished the call with Daley, Baker rang the station and was put through to Sergeant Rees. 'I need you to send someone back to the service station and see what CCTV they've got from last week. Apparently Chris Hills was in Wales on Wednesday or Thursday last week as well, see what you can pull.'

'Any idea what day he travelled, boss?' asked Rees. Baker could hear the scratch of a pencil on a pad at the far end of the line. Rees was still old school when it came to note taking.

'Not at the moment, if you can pick up anything they've got for the last two weeks, if I come up with anything more specific I'll get back to you.'

'They may not have kept the material that long.'

'I know but it's worth a shot. Mr Hills is a creature of habit, chances are he dropped into Hoden Gap for a coffee en route to the cottage.'

'Right oh,' said Rees. 'I'll see what I can find.'

'And I want you to get someone onto finding Linda Hills. Chris Hills' first wife. Three children.' Baker read off their names and the detail that he had been given by Irenee. 'Daley's chasing it up in Norfolk as well. Last known address was Manchester, I've got nothing more specific at the moment, and then the word is that she moved out to Spain with a new partner – and no, I haven't got his name either. And can you get Hills back in. We need to talk to him.'

Rees grunted. 'I'm on it,' he said, and with that he was gone.

Baker put the car into gear and pulled away from the kerb, thinking about Chris Hills, Leah's phone and personal belongings and what he might have done with his wife. He caught sight of Irenee Jacklin unashamedly watching him from her living- room window as he moved off.

Chapter Ten

The Garden Centre

It was early afternoon by the time I drove into Charlotte's Garden, an upmarket garden centre and nursery on the A10 a couple of miles outside Denham Market. It was set back amongst a stand of mature trees. Beside the neatly clipped, manicured driveway was a vintage-style hoarding advertising good service and great advice from their team of expert gardeners. I slowed my car to a crawl to avoid a Mercedes van that was busy manoeuvring into one of the delivery bays. The driver, a slight blonde woman wearing a company uniform and baseball cap, raised a hand in thanks as she reversed up towards a set of double doors.

I waved back and waited.

The driveway was flanked by rows of carefully tended shrubs and vast beds of spring bulbs. It was the kind of display meant to inspire Joe Public to pick up a trowel even in the depths of a grim grey spring. Ahead of me the van driver, safely parked, hopped out and opened the back doors, giving me another brief wave of thanks, while I swung right, into an enormous gravelled car park.

The car park was at least half full despite the time of the year. I found a spot a few spaces from the main entrance, locked up and headed inside.

Charlotte's Garden shop was laid out around what I guessed must once have been an old barn and maybe a stable block, though now everything had had a going over with Farrow & Ball paint, fancy skylights, bang-on-trend rustic doors and iron work, so it was hard to tell exactly what its origins had been, and where the original buildings ended and the new began. The planters by the doors were full of low evergreen shrubs under-planted with *Tete a Tete* dwarf daffodils, crocus and snowdrops and might as well have had a sign on them saying, 'You can do this. Look, it's easy.'

Inside it was pleasantly warm and the layout of outdoor lanterns, furniture and fire pits, with big buckets of spring bulbs everywhere invited you to explore further; the rustic barn frontage opened up into a huge showroom, set with displays of houseplants, tools, garden furniture, offering everything you might need from garden gloves to gazebos. There was a café at the back, busy and noisy, with a view out over the gardens, and currently wafting the scent of freshly brewed coffee out into the main trading area to trap the unwary. Just the place for a brew and a spot of lunch on a chilly spring day, and certainly explained the cars in the car park.

147

I unbuttoned my jacket and made an effort to forget that I hadn't had anything to eat since the packet of biscuits on the tray in my hotel bedroom. I felt the phone in my bag vibrate to announce an incoming text and fished it out to check the caller ID.

There were a row of Xs – kisses – where the name should be which had seemed funny when I put it in the menu: kisses, X for anonymity. He'd been texting on and off for the last forty-eight hours. I really needed to deal with it but couldn't bring myself to tell him what really needed saying.

I scrolled through the message. It read: 'Where the hell are you? Are you alright? What's going on?'

I took a breath and considered a reply and then deleted the whole thing and made my way towards the customer service point.

Behind the desk a large, elderly man was tidying the shelves. He'd got a can of spray polish and a cloth on the desk alongside him. He was neatly turned out in a long-sleeved black cotton shirt with an embroidered shop logo above the breast pocket, and jeans so crisply pressed you could have shaved with them. It was a nice touch employing pensioners. My dad would have loved a job in a place like this.

'Excuse me,' I said, pulling out my warrant card. 'I'd like to speak to the manager or the owner, Charlotte Finn, if they're available, please? I believe one of my colleagues called you earlier?'

The man glanced round and smiled, extending a hand like a great paw. 'Hello, I'm Charlotte Finn,' he said, his smile widening out a notch. It obviously wasn't the first time he'd used that line.

'Or more correctly my wife is. We trade under her name. Sounds more like a proper gardener, Charlotte's Garden, and she is, just not the sort who wants to run a garden centre.' His handshake was warm and firm, his hand calloused, which suggested that his role extended beyond manning the tills and light dusting.

'Dick, Dick Finn. I run the place. You must be –' He glanced at my ID. 'What do you prefer to be called?'

I smiled. 'Detective Sergeant Daley will be fine.'

'Pleased to meet you, Detective Sergeant. Have you found Leah?'

He waved towards a young woman who was busy tidying shelves on the other side of the shop. 'Let me just get someone over to cover for me on the till and we'll go into my office. More privacy in there.' He paused for a split second. 'So have you found her?' And then shook his head. 'Foolish question really, I suppose, you wouldn't be here if you had.'

'I'm afraid not, Mr Finn. But rest assured we're doing everything we can.'

He nodded.

'I find it very hard to believe that Leah would vanish like this. It doesn't sound like her at all. Not in her nature, I'd have said. She's always been rock steady at work, never late, always polite, tidy, a model employee in every sense.'

I followed Dick Finn to an office at the back of the shop, which had a view out over a huge outdoor sales area packed with trees, and shrubs, tubs, ponds and statues, corralled by long rustic benches laden with pots of hardier plants, and flanked by bays with rows of fencing and paving.

Chapter Ten

Dick Finn waved me into a chair and sat down behind his desk. I took out my notebook. 'If you don't mind I've just got a few questions.'

Finn steepled his fingers. 'How can I help? Whatever I can do.'

'Thank you. How long has Leah been working for you?'

'Nine years eight months.'

I smiled. 'That's very precise, Mr Finn.'

Dick Finn nodded. 'She started with us the day we opened – actually about a month beforehand. She helped us set the shop up and get everything straight and ready for our big opening. It seems like a long time ago now but we've been planning promotions and events for our ten-year anniversary, so I know practically to the hour when Leah started here. She worked in town, in Denham, before that, at the florists there. She's a good worker, excellent reputation, people ask for her. Never any trouble; we're proud to have her here.'

I made a note. 'And what is Leah like as a person rather than as an employee?'

Finn smiled thoughtfully. 'That is somewhat trickier. She's lovely. Good at what she does. Talented, very creative, hardworking. The kind of person who could have done anything if she had set her mind to it. I've always thought that she should have done more with herself. I often said to her she should go to college, do something with herself. I mean we like having her here but she could really *be* something if she put her mind to it.'

I thought fleetingly about the paintings and drawings in the studio.

'In what way?' I asked.

'Leah's clever, capable, really competent. Good at planning. If we have a problem here in the shop she is always the first person I turn to, but you get the feeling that she's never really stretched herself, stayed safe, stayed close to home. It's always struck me as a bit of a waste – not that we'd want to lose her.'

Dick Finn paused. 'A couple of years ago I had a health scare and decided I ought to slow down. Heart. I took this place on after I retired from the RAF. It was a little, old-fashioned nursery then. It was supposed to be a bit of a hobby for myself and the wife. She's always loved gardening, so we landscaped the back, decided that we could expand. To cut a long story short, it grew well beyond anything we had anticipated and really took off, which wasn't something we'd anticipated. I think we just caught the wave at the right time if you know what I mean.

'Anyway, it was getting to be too much, so I asked Leah if she would consider taking over the day-to-day running of the business as my manager. I could see that she was tempted, and she said she'd think about it, said that she'd like to talk it over with Chris before making a decision, said she'd need a day or two to think it over. Which I obviously respected. I really thought she'd take it. It would have been ideal for her, and for us too, to have someone running the business who we both knew and trusted. But in the end Leah said no; she said she wasn't sure about taking on the longer hours and the responsibility and that she was flattered that I'd asked her, but –'

'But?'

Chapter Ten

'But she had to say no.' Dick Finn pulled a face. 'Even now I'm not altogether sure what the real problem was. She was basically doing the job anyway. I suggested we discuss her concerns to see if there was anything we could do to sort it out, find a compromise. I was prepared to be flexible and she had earned it. It was as if she wanted to take it but didn't, if you get my drift. Anyway Leah said that although she was pleased to be asked there wasn't any point us talking it over, she'd thought it through and didn't want to do it, and in the end you have to respect that.'

'So what happened?'

He smiled. 'I got better, delegated a bit more, stopped doing so many hours, made sure I took time off. As I said in lots of ways Leah was doing the job anyway, picking up the slack. I just wanted to make it official and pay her for the extra responsibility.'

'Thank you,' I said, wondering what it was that had made her turn the job down, and added an additional note to the ones I'd already taken, and moved on.

'So what exactly does Mrs Hills do here?'

Finn laughed. 'What *doesn't* she do would be an easier question. Floristry for the most part, bouquets, wreaths, table centres, button holes, a wide range of floral displays for corporate clients. She's got a real eye for display so she manages a lot of the shop floor design and layout, some of the purchasing, and she deals with almost all of the deliveries. Leah is the kind of person who doesn't mind what she does, and she is good at making sure things run smoothly, good at planning, forward thinking.'

I nodded, jotting down the bare bones as he spoke.

'And what about people she works with? Is there anyone she is especially close to on the staff?'

Finn paused again as if considering his reply, and for the first time since I had introduced myself he seemed to be reaching for an answer.

Finally he said, 'It takes a while for Leah to be at ease with people. Please don't misinterpret that; Leah isn't standoffish. She is always easy to talk to and friendly enough, but she's also quite guarded, closed off. She holds herself back from people, as if she isn't happy or comfortable about getting too close. You have to work to earn her trust – does that make sense?'

I nodded, but said nothing, encouraging him to continue.

'Most of us will swap stories, what we did at the weekend, where we've been, what we've bought, where we're going on holiday – you know, everyday things, but Leah never does that. It took me a while to realise she is the one who is always asking the questions. Even though she has been with us so long, and I trust her implicitly, I don't really know that much about who she is. Does that make sense?'

It was the second time he'd said it, underlining how little he knew about a woman he evidently trusted with his business.

'So do you think Leah Hills was hiding something?' I asked.

Dick Finn shook his head. 'No, not hiding exactly, and certainly not in a bad way, I think Charlotte, my wife, and I have come to the conclusion that Leah prefers to keep her private life to herself.'

I nodded. 'So is there anyone here at work that she is particularly friendly with?'

Finn shifted in the chair. 'Leah talks to everybody and if you asked them they would probably all say that they like her, but I don't think anyone would be able to tell you very much about her.'

'So, no one?' I pressed. 'No special friend or colleague?'

Dick Finn shook his head. 'No, not really. She was very close to Elise, Elise Strawson. They started here together the same week. We took Elise on to run the gardening side of the business for us. Elise was lovely, the most amazing plants woman, gardener, and very talented designer.'

'Okay, so do you have an address for her?' I asked, poised to make a note.

Finn shook his head. 'I'm afraid not. Elise died about eighteen months ago now. Cancer. We all miss her, especially Leah.'

'I'm sorry,' I said, remembering details from Chris Hills' interview, just not being able to put a name to the woman who appeared to have been Leah Hills' only friend. I decided there might be another way to find out who it was that Leah had mixed with since Elise's death.

I glanced towards the window. 'Mrs Hills doesn't drive, does she?'

'No,' said Finn. 'I believe that she had a few lessons but didn't carry on with it – made her nervous.'

'So how did she manage to get to work? You're not on a bus route presumably?'

'No, unfortunately not. To begin with, when we first opened our hours were 8.30 till 17.30. Her husband, Chris, would drop her off and pick her up, every day. I'm presuming he was working locally then because that went on for some time. Then later, when we started opening for longer hours we've always tried to rota round people's needs, and Chris usually picks her up on his way home from Cambridge. But occasionally if Leah is on a short day she'll cycle home, or more often than not one of the others will give her a lift back into town. Different people in answer to your next question, usually those on the same shift pattern. Although I've known her work a few hours extra just so that Chris could pick her up instead. He worries.'

'Do you know why?'

Finn pulled a face, so I pushed a little. 'Why Chris might worry about Leah going home on her own or with someone else?'

Finn looked perplexed. 'No, now you come to mention it, does sound a bit odd, but that's what Leah says, *Chris worries*.'

'Okay, so does anyone give her a lift regularly, besides Chris?'

Finn shook his head. 'No, sometimes if she's been stuck I've run her home myself if no one is going that way.'

'Do you know Chris Hills well?'

'Not well, but socially certainly. Chris is a different kettle of fish altogether,' Finn said. 'He's always smiling, chatty, a lot more relaxed than Leah; always asking me how things were going with business, how Charlotte is. You know, more sociable, more at ease with people. He used to come with Leah to the Christmas parties when we first opened. I remember him laughing about her driving saying he didn't know how she would ever manage on her own, didn't know her left from her right. Chris is quite a bit older than Leah, and he's a bit—' Dick Finn stopped as if trying to find the right words. 'Actually you're right about the worrying – I think Chris sees his role as her guardian as much as her husband, looking after Leah, taking care of her, although personally I never found her like that, vulnerable or needy, but who knows what goes on behind closed doors. As far as I'm concerned Leah is likeable and competent. He told me once that they couldn't have children – or at least she couldn't, so I wondered if he was just being protective.'

'Overprotective would you say?' I asked.

Finn shook his head emphatically. 'No, I just imagine he sees things in her – maybe vulnerabilities – that no one else does.'

'Thank you, Mr Finn. Did Leah ever mention Chris's first wife?'

Finn shook his head. 'No, never, I didn't realise he had been married before.'

I noted his response and then said, 'Would it be possible to take a look at where Leah works?'

'Surely. We have a workshop in the stable block; we do demonstrations, classes, as well as straight floristry.'

'Does Leah teach?'

'No, one of the girls who works with her does the teaching, Although Leah does some of the demonstrations.'

'And what about a locker?'

'Yes, they've got a staff room out there, too. I'll show you.'

'Would it be possible to look in her locker?'

He nodded. 'Yes of course. Anything you need if it helps to find her. I'm not sure if we've got the spare keys here but if not I'll pop home and get them for you.'

The phone in my bag was vibrating and buzzing, I glanced down to read the caller display. It was Baker. I smiled across at Dick Finn. 'If you'll excuse me I have to take this.'

He nodded and got to his feet. 'Certainly, I'll go and find you that key,' he said. 'Won't be a moment.'

*

'Where are you?' asked Baker. It sounded as if he was driving.

'I'm at the garden centre talking to Leah's boss. I'm just about to go through her locker.'

'Anything?'

'Not really, same as before – kept herself to herself, Chris was more sociable and looked after her. The only real friend I've been able to track down so far was the one he told us about, Elise Strawson, who died about eighteen months ago.'

I heard Baker sigh at the other end of the phone. 'We're bringing Chris Hills back in to see if we can get anything else out of him. You're going to Cambridge?'

'That's where I was planning to go after this.'

'We need something else to find out where Leah is.'

'When I left SOCO were all over their house. The more I see the more I can't help feeling we're looking for a body.'

'I know,' said Baker, tone flat. 'We need him to talk and to get that we need something, some leverage.'

'I'm doing what I can, Guv.'

'Okay well let me know if SOCO turn anything up.'

For a second or two neither of us spoke, then Baker said, 'And how are the locals treating you?'

Chapter Ten

I laughed. 'So far so good, I'm liaising with another DS, Mike Carlton; I left him back at the house.'

'Good, keep me in the loop. And bear in mind I'd like you back as soon as you're done.'

'It's not like I'm on holiday, Guv,' I said, sotto voce, as I watched Dick Finn heading my way with a key. 'How's it going there?'

'They're still debating further up the food chain whether Chris Hills should do a TV appeal. Given the circumstances I've suggested they hold off. We're getting a lot of calls in already from the radio broadcast and the press release. I'm just hoping we find Leah before we get pushed into giving Chris Hills centre stage. At the moment if I was a betting man I'd have him coming in as the hot favourite.'

The truth being of course that we had no one else – unless it was a random snatch by a complete stranger we had no obvious candidates except for Chris Hills, and the phone, the handbag, the blood in the spare room were sending us in his direction.

'You think he's good for it?' I asked.

There was a long moment's silence that told me everything I needed to know.

'We've got nothing conclusive on him yet and I don't want to be the one jumping to conclusions,' said Baker quietly. 'Let me have anything you find. I'm just going in to update the Superintendent.'

I hung up and smiled at Dick Finn. It was essential not to jump to conclusions, to follow the evidence, but the truth was that so far it was all pointing Chris Hills' way, but we still needed to unpick what was going on.

Chapter Eleven

Chris Hills' Office

The drive to Cambridge took far longer than I had anticipated, mainly because I seemed to have managed to hit every last school run across East Anglia. Searching Leah's work room and locker hadn't turned up anything very interesting; a spare uniform, a fleece, a pair of waterproof trousers and jacket, all tagged with the garden centre's logo, along with wellingtons and gloves, a box of tampons, tissues, roll-on deodorant, hair brush and a packet of hair ties, certainly nothing that gave anything obvious away.

In the pocket of the fleece was a receipt for two slices of cake from the Garden Centre café, with a code Finn explained meant she had staff discount, along with a packet of mints and two crumpled tissues. Nothing at all that looked promising. I arranged with Finn to keep the locker secured until Mike Carlton could arrange for the contents to be bagged, tagged and taken into evidence, and then rang

Cambridgeshire Police to tell them about my visit to see Forth & Row, as it was across the county border.

And Finn had been right about the rest of the staff. The consensus was that Leah was lovely, kind, warm and kept herself to herself but nothing anyone said shed any light on why she might have disappeared. I arranged to have an officer go back and take statements from all of them.

Sod's law being what it was I had to wait for the same delivery driver to back out as I was leaving, before I could get onto the A10 and head over to Forth & Row's offices.

*

Cambridge Research Park was a new development a few miles out from the city centre, closer to Waterbeach than Cambridge, despite the address on the signage. The buildings, off a purpose-built roundabout, were all turquoise glass, chrome, bleached wooden panels, and pleasing ergonomic shapes. They said cutting edge, they said expensive. The companies in the offices on the site map were big names in Biotech, pharmaceuticals and technology, which I only know because I Googled them while trying to find the office for Forth & Row.

Finally I tracked them down, sub-letting two floors of office space in one of the main hubs, which was in a cul de sac off the main thoroughfare. The building was huge and according to the blurb on the website was designed to *facilitate synergies between disparate disciplines* and featured luxury break out areas, a gym, sauna and pool and top-class sports facilities, which made it sound more like a hotel than an office. It was set amongst carefully manicured lawns and arty flower beds heavily mulched with woodchips, while their atrium was full of very healthy looking trees in huge concrete tubs that wouldn't have stood a chance outside in the fenland wind.

I parked up, went inside and introduced myself to the woman on reception, then waited while she tracked down Chris Hills' boss and someone from HR.

A few minutes later a smart, sharply dressed man came over to greet me. He was somewhere in his mid-thirties, around five feet nine and dressed in a beautifully tailored dark grey suit, crisp white shirt and red tie, all of which whispered *finance department.*

'Detective Sergeant Daley,' he said, extending a hand. 'Gareth Jameson. I'm Head of Finance here on site.' Mr Jameson was tanned, tautly muscled with a strong handshake and a public school accent. It was hard not to notice the way the smile lines cut into his tan or that the skin around his eyes was a shade or two paler than the rest of his face. Skiing or snowboarding was my best guess. He had the triangular shape of a fitness bunny.

I glanced round the atrium. 'I read the spec on the internet for this place, I was expecting it to be all coffee machines and sofas,' I said.

He smiled, although I noticed it didn't go all the way to his eyes. 'God bless Google. We don't do much in the way of synergy in finance, although the R&D guys upstairs did get a pinball machine for Christmas, apparently it's art, done by someone who was short-listed for the Turner prize, and they're not allowed to use it. Just admire it from afar. Now, how can we help?' he asked. 'I'm a little short on time today.'

'Thanks for seeing me at short notice, Mr Jameson. I'd just like to ask you a few questions about Chris Hills if I may?'

'Sure, although I'm not sure what I can tell you, but let's go up to my office, shall we? I think Angie from HR will be joining us?'

I tipped my head, implying a question.

'Company policy when discussing any employees,' he said, guiding me towards the lift. 'They're all clued up on what we can discuss and what we can't. Would you like a tea or coffee, water?'

'No thanks. The HR policy, is that just for Chris Hills or across the board?'

'No, not at all. Same for everyone,' he said briskly, avoiding my gaze, which made me think that he was lying.

The lift travelled noiselessly up to the first floor. I took a long look around the elegant understated office spaces wondering how much the rental set Forth & Row back. This much minimalism usually cost a mint. The place put my office to shame. Everywhere was quiet and tasteful, a combination of soft blonde wood, acres of charcoal grey carpets, and great swathes of spotless glass.

'So not a sniff of widescreen TVs, jelly beans and table tennis?' I said.

Gareth Jameson pursed his lips. 'Like I said we're finance. This way –'

He opened an office door and stood aside as I stepped in. The room had a view out over an inner courtyard with benches and a sculpture with a water feature. I also noticed that Mr Jameson had a secretary working in an outer office but had chosen to come down to meet me himself.

In Jameson's inner office was a desk and chair with their back to the view, and in one corner an informal arrangement of black leather armchairs and a sofa set around a low glass coffee table. This was where Gareth Jameson sat and indicated that I should join him.

'Are you sure you wouldn't like tea or coffee?' he asked, glancing towards the outer office.

'No, I'm fine thank you. I was wondering what you can tell me about Chris Hills? Or would you prefer to wait for your colleague from HR?'

'May I ask what this is in connection with?' asked Jameson. He sounded cagey. 'I mean,' he looked left and right as if there was some chance we might be overheard. 'Is this something I should be aware of?' He laughed nervously. 'Did I miss a meeting?'

'We're investigating the disappearance of Mr Hills' wife, Leah,' I said, taking out my notebook.

Jameson stared at me and for the briefest of moments I saw shock and then a look of relief on his face and wondered what it was exactly that Gareth Jameson was hiding.

'You seem surprised,' I said, as Gareth Jameson made a show of regaining his composure.

'Sorry, I suppose I am if I'm honest. I had no idea Chris Hills was married.' He paused, as if gathering his thoughts. 'We've spoken quite a bit over the time he's been working with us but I had no idea. He always struck me as the kind of

chap who might well still be living at home with his mother.'
Jameson laughed again. I didn't.

'What makes you say that, Mr Jameson?' I asked.

'Sorry. I didn't mean to be flippant. It just never occurred
to me that he was married. Chris has always seemed quite
staid, conventional, kept his distance, but then he is several
years older than most of the staff here, so he tended not to
join in with the things that were going on – the banter, the af-
ter-work activities, the social side of things, not that he wasn't
invited of course.'

'What sort of things?' I asked, glad that I had caught him
off guard. If we waited for HR the chances were he would be
less candid.

'Carting, we've got a staff team, there's squash, volleyball.
Cricket in the summer. And a few of us go skiing when we
can. The company owns a chalet in Verbier. We're quite a
sports-orientated workforce. Trips to see the rugby, the cricket,
that sort of thing. Helps with team building. I think Chris
came down to Lords with us once on a corporate junket, you
know the kind of thing, but he's not a regular participant.'

I nodded. 'And did that cause any problems, any friction?
Mr Hills not joining in?'

'No, not really, although I suppose the danger is that it
causes a bit of distance, really the opposite of what we're
trying to achieve here. I'm not sure how much you know but
Chris came to us after a merger about four years ago. He
came from a more…' Jameson hesitated again, as if he was
searching for the right words. 'A firm with a more traditional
trading portfolio and outlook.'

'You're saying that Chris Hills didn't fit in here?'

I had expected Gareth Jameson to deny it and maybe hang back till the woman from HR showed up, but instead he took another swift look over his shoulder. 'I'm assuming this is in confidence?' he said.

'I can't promise that, Mr Jameson, if it proves pertinent to our inquiries.'

Gareth Jameson bit his lip. 'No, I suppose not; I should wait for HR to put in an appearance really,' he said, glancing back towards the door. And then he sighed and began to speak as if it was a relief to get it off his chest.

'Realistically Chris ought to have taken redundancy when Forth and Row bought his old company out, but the board wanted a few of the old guard to come across and give us a steer.' Gareth snorted. 'As if we'd never done a takeover before. Anyway, since he's been here he's been overlooked a couple of times when it came to promotion. Don't get me wrong that wasn't about his age, but it was about his outlook. His attitude. Chris is old school with no real aptitude or desire to embrace change. He's certainly not what you'd call a team player. I know he didn't like it when he didn't get a more senior role. He came in a foot soldier and left a foot soldier.'

I looked up from my notes. 'What do you mean *left* a foot soldier?'

'Didn't Chris tell you? We're making him redundant. He's currently on three months garden leave while we sort the whole package out. I mean he'll leave with a very nice nest egg. When he came to us his years of service and pension were guaranteed so he won't lose out. Golden handshake, handsome final salary pension at sixty – very nice little retirement package under the circumstances.'

'And why garden leave?'

'He's working in a sensitive part of our operation, and while I'm not casting any aspersions we would prefer him away from the coal face, so to speak, now that he's definitely going.'

I glanced at my notes. 'So are you saying that you're concerned Chris is the kind of person likely to cause trouble?' I asked.

'No, not directly. He was a quiet man in many ways but he has a way of creating discord if things didn't go his way. And we had a couple of incidents that we couldn't get to the bottom of.' Gareth Jameson reddened. 'I thought that's why you were here.'

'Incidents?' I pressed gently, not wanting to spook him into silence.

'Nothing to write home about, a couple of inappropriate images downloaded onto his laptop and someone logging into some dubious websites. I mean it's all adult stuff, nothing illegal as such, but against company policy. And then there were some accounting irregularities –' He stopped and looked towards the office door. 'I shouldn't be telling you this. You didn't hear this from me. Okay?'

'He was on the take?' I said, raising an eyebrow.

Jameson's colour deepened. 'No, not really, I mean the monies turned up.'

'But you thought it was Chris Hills?'

Gareth nodded. 'We couldn't prove it. A decision was made to keep the whole situation in house; these sort of things can easily shake shareholder confidence, which was why I was surprised to see you. We have an ongoing investigation, but the porn was on his laptop, there was no ambiguity there. It's a sackable offence, though it was probably just another weight on the scale.'

'And what about the money?' I said. 'What have you turned up?'

He bit his lip as if weighing up whether or not he ought to say anything.

'Far harder to prove; we know someone was moving small amounts of money around without authorisation, as I said we couldn't prove it was Chris, but we had our suspicions.'

'Is his laptop still here?'

'Probably but before you ask it will have been sanitised by now, and even if it hadn't we wouldn't allow you access without a warrant. Not, I hasten to add, because of the porn, but because of the sensitive data and information relating to our company that would have been on it.'

I nodded. 'Can you remember what sort of websites Chris was alleged to have visited?'

Gareth shook his head. 'Not really, I didn't see it personally, it was reported to me.'

'By whom?'

'IT support when they were doing an upgrade.'

'So are you saying that reporting him for it wasn't likely to be personal?'

Gareth nodded. 'He swore blind it had got nothing to do with him, that someone else had to have done it.'

'Is that possible?'

'Yes, but highly unlikely. Either he really pissed someone off and they planted it or the truth is more likely he did do it. Although I hasten to add I have no proof. He's not alone in falling foul of the porn rule, it's just that—'

'Not everyone who gets reported for it gets dismissed?' I looked up and met his eye. 'His face doesn't fit in, does it?'

Gareth Jameson said nothing.

'You didn't like him?'

Gareth Jameson opened his mouth to say something and then thought better of it. 'Let's say he wouldn't be the first person I would pick for my team, no,' he said. 'And I think if we're going to pursue this it might be better if we did it with a company lawyer present.'

There was a tap on the office door, and a large blonde woman in a floral skirt, sweater and scarf came in. 'Hi Angie Bloom,' she said, extending a hand dripping with rings. 'I'm so sorry to keep you waiting. Thanks for hanging on. Now, how can we help you?'

An hour later I was back in my car and checking the phone, having heard the official company line from Angie Bloom about how they had decided to let Chris go because they were reshaping and streamlining their workforce in line with some great management shake-up from above, all this without a single mention of porn, missing money or how Chris Hills didn't quite fit the Forth and Rows personnel profile.

When I brought up the suggestion that images had been found on Chris Hills laptop without mentioning or even glancing in Gareth Jameson's direction, the warm and oh so

Chris Hills' Office

helpful Angie Bloom said that Chris Hills was aware that it was against company policy and that he had been issued with a written warning for a petty infringement regarding privacy but not porn. The suggestion of any financial irregularities brought a blank expression and another offer of tea. I left my card with both of them.

Back in the car there was a message from DS Mike Carlton on my phone asking me to ring him back.

He answered on the third ring. 'Hi, how's it going?'

'Not so bad.'

'So what have you got?' I asked.

'No patience some people.' He laughed. 'Well we've got all sorts of bodily fluids in the spare room, some blood droplets, along with plenty of signs of sexual activity. And when we were going through the upstairs again I noticed something odd. I'm not sure if it means anything but there are keys in locks on the bedroom doors.'

'Meaning what, exactly?'

'The key in the main bedroom door is on the outside, and in the spare room it's on the inside.'

Although I couldn't see him I nodded, trying to process what that meant. 'That is weird,' I said.

'That's what I thought. How about you? How's it going with the geeks?'

'Hills was made redundant rather than retiring. There is also a suggestion that he was involved in some sort of financial irregularities, but no details of what or how. He was also reprimanded and received a written warning for downloading porn onto the company hardware.'

Chapter Eleven

'I'll resist the temptation to go for the cheap joke,' said Carlton. I could hear the amusement in his voice and decided to ignore it.

'Good plan. The thing is it's another lie. Chris Hills told us he was taking early retirement.' I paused. 'How much blood did they find?'

'Not much, a few droplets on the carpet, and the dresser, more like a cut dripping than anything else.' We both knew what anything else implied – a murder, a violent assault. 'There's no sign of a clean-up.'

'And on the cuffs.'

'Yeah, oh and by the way the SOCO guy said they're fake – the cuffs? You don't need a key. Just press and click and they're off.'

'But there's blood on them.'

'Maybe whoever was wearing them didn't know they were quick release,' said Carlton. 'Or maybe they didn't want to take them off. SOCO are busy taking the carpet up. Oh and there's something else. I had someone go back and take a look at reports and files that still haven't been digitised. We finally found something on Chris Hills –'

*

As soon as I had hung up I called Baker to let him know what I had found out and tell him about the state of play at Fieldview Road. And what Mike Carlton had turned up on Chris Hills.

Chapter Twelve

Talking to Chris Hills

'You do not have to say anything. But it may harm your defence if you do not mention when questioned something which you later rely on in court. Anything you do say may be given in evidence.' Baker glanced at Chris Hills. 'Do you understand that you're under caution and what it means?'

Chris Hills nodded.

'Yes, I understand what you said, although I'm not altogether sure why you think it's necessary. My wife is missing–'

'I'm obliged to point out that at this stage you're not under arrest, Chris. You're not obliged to remain here and answer the questions, and that if you wish you may obtain legal representation. We have a duty solicitor available if you don't have your own.'

Chris Hills shook his head. 'I don't need a solicitor. I'd just like you to tell me what the hell is going on. I've already told you that what I want is to get Leah back safe and sound.'

Chapter Twelve

'That's exactly what we want, too. If you change your mind and feel you want a solicitor then let me know.'

The interview room at Hereford had been recently refurbished and there was still a slight odour of new paint and fixative lingering in the air. The grey utilitarian lino was – at the moment – stain and scuff free. The interview was being videoed, together with a separate audio recording. A tiny red light glowed in the corner of the room to let everyone know that the interview was being recorded.

As he settled himself at the table the light caught Baker's gaze and triggered a thought that he couldn't quite catch hold of, something that he had seen recently, something that wasn't quite right.

'What exactly is this about?' Hills' voice broke into Baker's train of thought. 'I don't understand what's going on. Why did you bring me in?' He paused. 'Have you found Leah?'

Baker shook his head. 'No, Chris we haven't.'

'Where the hell is she? It's impossible just waiting around for news. Is there any reason why I can't go to our cottage? I mean it makes more sense rather than staying here. I keep thinking that Leah might turn up there. I keep thinking that maybe she has had some kind of a breakdown.'

'I understand your frustration but it's not possible for you to stay there at the moment.'

'And what about the TV appeal? That woman from the media office said she would talk to me. The media woman, you know who I mean?'

Baker nodded. 'We've already aired an appeal on the news last night and this morning. The consensus at the moment is that it's probably better if we handle it.'

Chris stared at him. 'What do you mean *better*?'

Baker, poker faced, opened the notes on the table. 'There are a few things we need to go over. To get straight.'

'Again?'

'A few things we need to clear up. You understand that you're being questioned under caution?'

Chris Hills nodded. 'I understand that, I just don't understand why. I haven't done anything.'

Baker glanced down at his notes.

Hills was opposite him on the far side of the table in the interview room. He looked tired and drawn but unruffled; he was dressed casually in a pale blue sweater over a shirt, and jeans with a crisp crease. He looked annoyed rather than overly concerned at being brought in from the hotel they had found for him. He was sitting a little way back from the table with his shoulders back and legs crossed at the ankle. Confident, composed, slightly annoyed.

'Let's start with the cottage in Wales, shall we?' said Baker. 'Is there any particular reason why your wife doesn't have a key?'

Chris hesitated, apparently wrong footed. Baker wondered what it was he had expected to be asked; obviously not this.

'Not really. I've always been the one to look after things. You know, the practicalities, bills, insurance–' He paused as if gauging Baker's reaction. 'I've already told you this. Leah is quite a bit younger than me. I'd already got the house and the cottage when we first got together, and it seemed natural for me to carry on sorting things out. We've never really felt the need to change the arrangement.'

Chapter Twelve

'So, she didn't have a key for the holiday cottage you share? Does she have one for your house in Denham Market?'

'Yes, of course she does.' Chris ran his hands back through his hair. 'I'm not sure why this is relevant, and I suppose it sounds a bit odd not having a key to the cottage when you say it like that, but Leah doesn't drive, we've always gone to Wales together, so there's never been any real need for her to have one, not really. I thought I'd already explained that to you?'

Baker nodded. There was no way he could imagine his wife trusting him to run things.

'And does she know about the spare set in the guttering?'

Chris appeared to consider the idea for a moment and then shook his head. 'I'm not sure, but no, not that I know of. I can't say I've ever told her about it, or come to that not told her about it. It was meant for emergencies, we have Irenee who comes in and keeps the place tidy, cleans up, airs it, when she knows we're coming. She's got a key.'

'We've already spoken to Mrs Jacklin. When we spoke yesterday you didn't mention that you had been at the cottage last week.'

'Didn't I?' Chris frowned. 'Sorry, I didn't think it was that important. I was in the area on business and I thought I'd stay at the cottage rather than shell out for a hotel, and it would give me chance to get it ready, air the place, that sort of thing, for when we came down this weekend.'

'So you'd already got this trip planned?'

Chris nodded, 'Yes.'

'And you were in the area on business last week?'

'That's right.'

'Would you care to tell me what sort of business?'

Chris stared at him. 'I don't see how that fits in to anything. I want to talk to you about the TV appeal. Can you tell me why I wasn't involved? I mean I'd be more than happy to do it, anything to get Leah back safely. I can't help wondering where she is. Where she was last night. It's eating me up.' He paused, hands working over each other where they sat in his lap. 'We're hardly ever apart, I can't imagine–' he stopped himself from saying whatever was on the tip of his tongue.

For a moment there was silence and then Baker said, 'I appreciate that this is difficult for you. But I need you to tell me where you were going on business?'

'Swansea.'

'And the name of the company you were visiting?'

'Is that strictly necessary?'

'Yes, yes it is. Where did you go?' Baker's pen hovered above the note pad.

Hills opened his mouth to reply and then thought better of it. 'Actually I was going to talk to a builder. To get a quote. For work on the cottage.'

'Okay. May we have his name?'

'I haven't got it with me but I could find it for you.'

'Did Leah know about your visit?'

'No, no I told her it was work related.'

'Do you often lie to your wife?' said Baker in his low, even voice.

The question took Hills by surprise and his face flushed crimson. 'What the hell is that supposed to mean? No, of course not.'

Chapter Twelve

'But you told her you were at work.'

'It's not like that. I've got holiday entitlement owing to me so I thought I'd get quotes for the work on the cottage. I didn't want to tell Leah. Like I said, I wanted it to be a surprise for her.'

'And you thought it would be easier to go and see these people rather than ring them?'

'Yes, it meant I could be at the cottage, show people around if they wanted a site visit. It seemed like a sensible idea.'

'And you say that you'd got some leave owing?'

'Yes, that's right. I don't think I've ever taken my full holiday entitlement. I'd got weeks owing all over the place.'

Baker nodded, taking another brief look at the notes on the table. 'And you told me when we spoke yesterday that you're taking early retirement?'

Chris nodded. 'That's right. Not for a while, but yes.'

Baker lifted his gaze. 'One of my officers went to see your manager at Forth and Row this afternoon – a Mr Jameson, is it? He said that you had been made redundant and are currently on garden leave awaiting your financial settlement being finalised.'

Chris Hills' face dropped. 'You've been to see them?'

Baker nodded. 'Now would you like to tell me again what you were doing in Wales and what you told Leah?'

'Look,' Chris Hills said hastily, his earlier confidence evaporating. 'I can explain everything. There's been some confusion.'

'You see there are lots of things that you've told us, Chris, where there appears to be some confusion. You didn't tell us you had been in Wales last week, you told us you were planning to retire – and you said your wife was wearing a camel coat when she got out of the car. Did you tell your wife that they had found pornography on your computer at work? Or that you had had a written warning? Or that there was some suggestion of financial irregularities? I'm not sure what that means – did they think you were on the take, Chris?'

A muscle in Chris Hills' jaw tightened. 'That wasn't me. It had nothing to do with me, any of it. I certainly wasn't going to upset Leah with something that wasn't true.

'Someone set me up with the porn thing – gay porn. Those little shits in the office thought it was a huge joke and the money was a misunderstanding, an accounting error, which has been rectified.' His voice was as tight as a piano wire. 'They've been looking for a reason to get rid of me since I arrived there. It's like a boys' club, no sense of respect, nothing. And Jameson? Head of Finance? I mean that's a complete and utter joke.'

'And what about Leah's coat? Can you explain how that got into the boot of your car?'

'No, I can't, because the last time I saw her she was wearing it,' Chris Hills took a long breath, steadying his voice. 'And I told Leah I was taking early retirement because I didn't want her to worry about how we would manage. She's a worrier. She always has been, the last thing I wanted was to make her anxious. I've negotiated a good redundancy package. We can easily get by on that and I can always pick up a bit of private work if I ever needed to top it up.'

'So how have you managed to keep your garden leave a secret from your wife, Chris?'

Chapter Twelve

Hills took a deep breath. 'I've been going to work every day the same as always.' He took another noticeable breath. 'I told Leah the trip to Wales was for business but actually I just fancied a few days away. Time to think. Time to plan.'

'So there is no builder in Swansea?'

'No.' Chris shook his head and looked down at his hands. 'I'm sorry. I didn't realise I'd be in this situation.'

''What do you mean?'

'I've been keeping the redundancy to myself. The lie just came out without thinking. I was going to go and see a few people, see about the renovations, get some quotes, but in the end I just stayed at the cottage – walked down by the river. It's a peaceful place and I wanted to think about what I was going to do next. I mean my whole life is about to change.'

Baker's eyes didn't leave Chris Hills. 'Is there anything else that you've been lying about that you'd like to tell me about, Chris?'

'No, no. You have to understand that I was just trying to protect Leah, that's all.'

'Can you tell me about your first wife?'

Chris looked startled. 'What?' He looked up, eyes bright.

'Linda. You didn't mention that you had been married before. Or that you have a family. Three children.'

'I didn't think that it was relevant. We were divorced before I met Leah, and it's years ago now,' he said, wrong footed and sounding defensive.

'Have you any idea where your first wife is now?'

Chris Hills waved the question away. 'Not a clue. Why would I have? Last time we spoke she was off to Spain, I think.

She was planning to help run a hotel and bar.' His tone was matter of fact.

'And taking your children with her? That must have been difficult for you?'

The muscle in Chris Hills' jaw was working overtime. 'Yes it was difficult at the time, but in the end you have to be philosophical about these things. Look, Linda and I were too young to get married and when it went wrong, it all went wrong really fast, despite the children or maybe because of them. It was a lot for us to cope with, having a family put both of us under a lot of strain. When we split up she got in with this man who'd bought some sort of hotel over in Spain. And then she upped sticks and went out there with him.'

'And she took the children?'

Chris Hills nodded.

'And you didn't object?'

'I didn't see that I had much choice,' he said, voice tight with emotion. 'She'd made up her mind. At the time it was messy, we both said a lot of things – I'm not proud of what happened between us but these things do happen. I was working all the hours that god sends and Linda was lonely and bored, stuck in the house with three small children and ended up sleeping with our next door neighbour. Then she went off with some bloke up north somewhere. By that stage I was glad to see the back of her.'

'And what about the children?' Baker pressed.

Chris sighed. 'That was the worst part. To begin with Linda used to bring them round, drop them off so I could see them, spend time with them, have them for the weekend, holidays, but then all of a sudden all that stopped.'

Chapter Twelve

'Before they went to live in Spain?'

Hills nodded. 'Yes, before they went to Spain.' He leaned back in his chair, fiddling with his cuff, as if there was something he was reluctant to share and then he said, 'Looking at it now I even wonder if they were mine, biologically. I couldn't trust her. I never could if I'm honest. Linda was always the life and soul but a terrible flirt. In some ways, if you want the honest truth, it was a relief really when she moved away.'

'And have you heard from her or the children since she left for Spain?'

Chris Hills looked Baker square in the eye as if trying to prove a point. 'No, I haven't seen them or heard from them since she told me she was going to Spain.'

'Doesn't that worry you?'

'Yes, of course it did, but it got less as the years went on. She was—' he paused. 'I assumed that she poisoned them against me. It would be just like her. And after all they had a new daddy.' He spat out the word *daddy* as if it had an unpleasant taste.

Baker made a note. 'Did she ask you for money, maintenance for the children?'

Chris Hills shook his head. 'No, I think her new boyfriend was well off. Loaded was how she put it, I seem to remember. I'm assuming Linda thought that she was better off cutting all ties. At least that was what it felt like.'

'And she didn't ask for any kind of financial settlement?'

'No.'

Baker made another note.

'Can you remember her new partner's name?'

Hills' expression hardened. 'No, I can't. I didn't want to know then and I don't want to know now.'

'And what about the hotel where they were going to live, your ex-wife and your children?'

'No, I've got no idea, and I don't see how this is relevant at all. You're supposed to be looking for Leah.'

'So you were going to let your ex-wife and your children go off with a man you didn't know, whose name you didn't know, and had no idea where they were going?'

Hills looked up from under greying eyebrows. 'That's right and in my opinion whatever she got she deserved.'

Baker met his gaze wondering exactly what Hills meant by that. 'What did she get?'

Hills shrugged. 'I've got no idea. As I said we never spoke once the divorce was final and she told me she was off to Spain.'

'And did she tell you to your face or by phone.'

Chris hesitated, his brows knitted. 'I can't remember,' he said.

Baker waited.

'It must have been by phone because she was living with him by then.'

'But you can't be certain?' said Baker.

Chris shook his head. 'No, I can't be certain. It's a long time ago now. Is this relevant in any way? How can Leah disappearing have anything to do with my ex-wife. Or my children?'

'You tell me,' said Baker in the same low, even voice he had used throughout the interview.

'What the hell is that supposed to mean,' snapped Hills.

Baker turned the page on his notes. 'In September 1989 officers were called to a flat in King's Lynn by your then-wife Linda Hills, as the result of a 999 call. Mrs Hills told the attending officers that you refused to leave the premises and had threatened her and her children with violence. She told the officers she was afraid of what you might do, and that you "threatened to burn the place down with her and the children in it".' Baker read the final words from the police report.

Chris Hills' colour drained. 'For god's sake. Are you serious? That was years ago. Years. I was never charged. The policeman cautioned me because he said he had to be seen to be doing something, wanted to make a show of how they were dealing with domestic violence he said. I was just angry and upset. It was one moment of madness. One moment. It was as much her fault as mine, not the other way round. She invited me in, led me on, said she wanted to make things right between us.'

'By which she meant?'

'Linda only knew one way to make things right,' Hills said grimly. 'She was a slut. I just didn't recognise it until it was too late.'

'She offered you sex?'

Hills looked away. 'She said she was sorry, said she had made a terrible mistake. As I said they let me off with a caution. It was stupid. Something and nothing.'

Baker looked down at the pages that had been scanned and emailed over to him from King's Lynn. 'According to the officers' report, your wife said that she was afraid of you and had been advised by her solicitor to consider taking out a

restraining order. It says here that she said you were a manipulative bully and had threatened her and the children on more
than one occasion.'

'That's rubbish, total and utter rubbish,' protested Hills.

'Have you ever been violent towards Leah?'

'No, of course not. Look, Linda's solicitor told her if she
wanted to get rehoused quickly and there was any suspicion
of violence or abuse that she would go straight to the top of
the housing list. Linda told them I was violent so she would
get a sodding council house, that's all. That's the kind of
woman she was.'

'So you're telling me that this was some kind of put-up job?'

'I don't know now – but I wouldn't put it past her. Seriously,
she was a piece of work. I was supposed to be having the
children for the weekend but when I got there she said they
were staying over with friends. Friends? What friends? Lorna
was only two. Linda said she wanted to make things right between us. She – she was all over me like a rash from the minute
she opened the door, and it was obvious that she had been
drinking before I got there. Anyway I told her it was too late,
that I wouldn't touch her with a bargepole. Said I didn't know
where she'd been – and at that point she started to scream at
me. She came for me–'

'So you hit her?'

'No, no it wasn't like that.'

'But you threatened her?' said Baker, his voice still as even
as before.

'No, of course not.' Hills stopped and sighed. 'Maybe I did.
I can't remember now. I was a lot younger then, a lot more hot

headed, angrier, but those days are long gone. We were both upset, both shouting. When the police arrived she burst into tears, telling them what a bastard I was. She was upset that I'd turned her down. I was angry. They took her side. Looking back I can see why. In their situation I'd probably have done the same thing.'

Baker nodded, giving the appearance perhaps of being satisfied with Hills' explanation. He didn't tell Hills that they were trying to trace Linda and the children. It seemed too much of a coincidence that two wives had vanished.

'And what about Linda's family? How did they react?'

'She was an only child, her dad died when she was little and her mum died a few months after we got married. Cancer. It was touch and go whether she was going to be there for the ceremony.'

Baker nodded; another vulnerable woman on her own with no one but Chris Hills to turn to for support. 'And was she also younger than you?'

A flash of fury passed over Chris Hills' features. 'What are you implying?'

'That you have a taste for vulnerable young women.'

Hills snorted. 'Linda wasn't vulnerable, she was anything but and no she wasn't *much* younger. She was eighteen when we met and I was twenty two. And don't for one minute think that she didn't know what she was doing. She set her sights on me right from the start. Good job, prospects. She knew exactly what she was doing.'

'And what was that, Chris?'

'Got herself pregnant – we'd been going out less than six months, she swore blind it was mine, though back then there was no easy way to tell. And of course I did the decent thing and married her.'

Baker nodded. 'And you were married how long?'

Hills pulled a face. 'I'm not sure now. Six or seven years, eight I think, till the divorce came through.'

Baker glanced back through his notes. 'And you married Leah in 1990. You mentioned it's your twenty-fifth wedding anniversary this year.'

'Where is this going?' asked Hills looking bemused.

'Well the maths suggest Linda wasn't the only one dating other people.'

Chris Hills glared at Baker. 'Yes, yes all right I was still married when I first met Leah but I was in the middle of getting a divorce, a messy, furious, angry, bloody divorce. And she was the only good thing to come out of it.'

'Did Linda know about her?'

'What? Look, what has this got to do with finding my wife, Inspector?'

'Is that a yes or a no?'

Chris Hills held his hands up in despair. 'Yes, yes I think she knew.'

'So were you trying to patch things up with Linda, while having your cake and eating it?'

'No, no there was no way back with Linda, I've got no idea what she had been up to, inviting me round, but she didn't want me back and by that time I didn't want her either.'

'Because you had met Leah?'

'In part, yes, but that wasn't the only reason.'

'And you say Linda knew about her?'

Chris nodded. 'I think she did, I can't be certain.'

'Is there any chance that they stayed in touch?'

Chris stared at him. 'What the hell are you getting at?'

'Maybe they stayed in touch. Maybe your first wife helped Leah to disappear – after all Linda's done a pretty good job of vanishing, hasn't she?'

'She hasn't vanished; she is in Spain as far as I know. What I do know for certain is that there is no way Leah would have anything to do with her – Leah saw what Linda did to me.'

'Okay, so let's go back to Leah's coat.' He flicked through the file in front of him.

Chris held his hands up in a gesture of defence. 'For god's sake what good is this doing? I've already told you I have no idea how the coat ended up in the boot of the car. I saw Leah put it on. I saw her get out of the car in it.'

'You'd been driving a long time.'

'You think I imagined her putting it on? I didn't. I saw it with my own eyes.'

'And what about her bag, you mentioned her handbag?'

'She had her coat and her bag.'

Baker took one of the photographs from an email that Mel Daley had had the Norfolk Crime Squad send him and slid it across the table. Chris Hills stared down at it. 'Is this the bag?'

Hills nodded. 'Yes, that's Leah's bag,' he murmured. 'That little silver thing on the side, the lucky charm, a friend bought it for her one Christmas.'

Baker looked at the picture. The silver charm was in the shape of an acorn. 'You're certain?'

Chris nodded. 'Yes. Where did you find it?'

Baker ignored him. 'Which friend? I thought you said Leah hadn't got any friends.'

Chris shook his head. 'I did. She died. Elise Strawson. I told you about her. They used to work together at the garden centre.' He looked up, eyes full of tears. 'Where did you find her bag? Please tell me.'

'This morning one of my officers found it while searching your house in Denham Market. We found your wife's mobile phone and handbag, along with her credit and debit cards inside, in a carrier bag in the outdoor wheelie bin. Can you explain that?'

Chris looked stunned. 'No, no I can't. What the hell is going on here?'

'Did you put them there, Chris?'

'No, of course not.'

'Hoping we wouldn't find them? Hoping the bins would be collected before we got around to looking?'

'No, no of course not. We packed the car Wednesday evening, and left first thing Thursday morning. Leah put her coat on the back seat with her bag and we drove to the service station on the way to Wales. Leah got out of the car with her coat on and had her handbag with her.' Chris Hills mimed the bag. 'It's a small bag, maybe six or eight inches square on a long strap and goes across your body like an old fashioned satchel.'

'This bag?'

Chris Hills looked again at the picture and shook his head in despair. 'Yes, that bag.'

'And who packed the car?'

Chapter Twelve

'I did. On Wednesday evening so we could leave first thing on Thursday morning.'

'And did anyone else go to the car after you'd packed it?'

'I don't think so.' And then he paused. 'Leah took out a box of groceries. There was no room in the boot so she said she was going to put them on the back seat.'

'And did you see her do that?'

Hills shook his head. 'No, no I didn't, but I did see her in the coat and bag.'

'So you're saying you can't explain how her bag and her phone were in the bin? Or how her coat got into the boot?'

'No, I don't know.'

'Okay, well let's come back to that, Chris. I want to talk to you about the spare room at your house at Denham. My officer found evidence of sexual activity, restraints, blood–' Baker paused gauging Hills' reaction. 'Can you explain that or is that something else you don't know about?'

There was an unsettling and subtle shift in Hills' body language as if, despite the nature of the question, he was back on safe ground.

'No, I know about it,' he said.

'Would you care to enlighten me then,' said Baker.

'It's not what you think, and not something I usually make public but yes, I can explain. Leah and I are both consenting adults and we have always enjoyed role play. We've always had a very healthy sex life.'

'We're looking for your wife, Chris, there is blood, tissue–'

'How explicit do you need me to be, Detective Inspector?'

There was something in his manner, a little glint of amusement almost hubris that caught like a splinter, and made Baker's flesh crawl, but nonetheless he kept a poker face. 'I want you to explain the blood on the handcuffs, the splashes on the wall and carpet.'

And now Chris Hills smiled. It was as unsettling as it was unexpected. 'Have you done a DNA test on them yet?'

Baker said nothing.

'Because if you had then you would be aware that the blood belongs to me.' With his gaze not leaving Baker's, Chris Hills rolled up one of the sleeves of his sweater. His forearm above the wrist was marked with a mesh of fine silver scars, one or two of which were still raw and in the process of healing.

Baker waited.

'I'm attracted to hematolagnia; I always have been.' He paused, and presumably seeing no comprehension in Baker's eyes, continued. 'I'm aroused by the sight of blood. 'He rolled his sleeve down. 'My own, I hasten to add, not the blood of others. And the exquisite touch of the blade.' He shivered. 'I know it's not to everyone's taste so it's not something I care to make public knowledge.'

'And does Leah share your interest?' said Baker calmly, masking his sense of revulsion.

'Not really, or at least not with the same degree of enthusiasm, but over the years we've both learned to accommodate each others' little idiosyncrasies.' He grinned. 'So that's where your blood comes from, Detective. Now have you got any other questions or can I go back to the hotel?'

Chapter Thirteen

Chris's Sister

While DI Baker was talking to Chris Hills, I was making my last call of the day accompanied by a PC that Mike Carlton has assigned me. It was getting dark when Helen Norman opened her front door as far as the security chain would allow and peered out beyond the glare of the security light.

'Hello? Can I help you?' She sounded cultured with the slightest hint of a Norfolk accent.

' Hello, Mrs Norman?' I said.

'That's right. What do you want?'

'I wonder if we could have a word with you?' I produced my warrant card. 'We're investigating the disappearance of your sister-in-law, Mrs Leah Hills?'

Helen Norman stood for a second or two and then slipped the security chain off the door. 'You better come in,' she said, waving us inside.

Gratefully I stepped in out of the cold wind, followed by the uniformed PC.

'I do know about it. This thing with Leah. Someone rang me,' Helen said grimly, directing us into the sitting room. She picked up the remote control from her armchair and muted the TV.

'She is friends with someone who works at the garden centre, and wanted to know if I knew about Leah going missing. She said she drove past their house this morning and saw the police car outside.' Helen pulled a face. 'Actually I suspect she wanted to know *what* I knew rather than *if* I knew. Do you want some tea? I've just made myself one.'

I shook my head. 'That's very kind, but no thank you.'

The sitting room was spotless, not a thing out of place. It reminded me of Chris and Leah Hills' house on Fieldview Road. Helen Norman waved us to sit down and then took a prime spot in the armchair by the hearth.

'Is there anyone else here,' I asked, glancing round. 'Your husband?'

'No, he's down the club, darts match tonight. Not really my cup of tea; I prefer to stay in and watch my programmes. I record them.' She nodded towards the TV. 'Save them up for when he's out. So, is there any news yet about Leah?'

I shook my head. 'I'm afraid not. But we've got everyone looking.' From my bag I heard the little metallic scuttering sound that my phone made when it was on silent and a call came in. Casually I glanced down; there were six Xs on the caller display. Leaning forward I switched the phone off in one smooth movement before looking up at Helen. 'Anything you can tell us might help. Anything at all.'

Helen took a sip of tea. 'I'm not altogether sure what I can tell you really.' She sniffed. 'We're not close, me and Leah, or Chris come to that. It's been years since I've spoken to either of them.'

'Would you like to tell me why that is?'

Helen took a deep breath as if considering her options and then said. 'Do you think that Chris killed her?'

I felt a little kick in the pit of my stomach. It was maybe not a strange thing to think but it was a strange thing to ask, particularly of a police officer.

'We don't know what's happened to Leah at the moment.'

Except that her phone, her bag and her credit cards were tucked up in the bottom of the wheelie bin, which Chris Hills had wanted to ensure was collected and disposed of, said a little voice in my head. Who willingly leaves home without those things?

'What makes you think that Chris might be involved in Leah's disappearance?' I said.

Helen shrugged. 'I don't know, but if you want the truth nothing would surprise me when it comes to Chris. I've been thinking about it since that woman rang to ask me about Leah. He comes across all sweetness and light, chatty-chatty but that isn't what he's like once you get to know him, you know, underneath. People sometimes say, "Oh I saw your brother in town; he's such a nice man".' Helen looked up at me. 'But trust me he isn't.'

I said nothing. It was an old trick, people aren't comfortable with silence, the temptation is always to fill the empty air. I tipped my head to one side, another indication that I was listening – and waited.

Chris's Sister

Finally Helen Norman said, 'The thing about Chris is that he is cruel, he was cruel when he was little, cruel as a teenager. He used to find ways to get everyone else into trouble but never himself. He'd set something up and then when you took the bait seemed to enjoy watching you fall head first into trouble. I learned in the end. The hard way.

'You know he was married before? To Linda, she was a lovely girl, but he treated her badly, madly jealous, wanted to know who she'd talked to, where she was, what she'd been doing, every waking minute. It would have driven me mad.

'Once Linda had had the children he wasn't so bad because she was home all the time but then when the youngest one, Lorna, was about eighteen months old Linda wanted to go back to work a few hours a week, for the company and a bit of money, so I said I'd have them for her. Their oldest, Russell, was about six I think, Geraldine was five, they were both at school – anyway Linda got a job in King's Lynn, part-time receptionist.

'She'd been a receptionist when they first got together. That was how they met, Chris and Linda, at Walker and Jones, the accountants in town when she worked there on the front desk. Anyway Linda got this job at the hotel – she was so pleased about it. Well the way Chris carried on you'd think she'd gone on the game. He called her everything, and me even worse for helping her out. It was mad, he used to check the phone bill, the mileage on the car, turn up at her job during the day to try and catch her out. All she wanted was a bit of money of her own, and a bit of independence.

'I think it was the final straw, she told him she couldn't stand it and said she was leaving him. She'd found a flat. And

Chapter Thirteen

then all hell broke loose. I can't tell you how awful he was, threatened to burn the place down with her and the kids in it, followed her to work, nearly got her the sack by making this great scene in reception. They called the police in the end and got him taken away. Then later she met someone. He was lovely. Ray he was called —'

I nodded. It sounded as if Helen had been waiting to tell someone.

'Do you have a surname for Ray?' I asked.

She nodded. 'Burridge. Ray Burridge. He used to be the head chef at the hotel where she worked. 'The Orb and Sceptre in King's Lynn. It's just off the market square.'

I made a note but Helen hadn't finished.

'They moved in together but Chris wouldn't stop. He was round here begging me to talk to her. He swung between begging her to come back and being so horrible to her, you wouldn't believe. He kept saying he'd change if only she would have him back, but me and her both knew he couldn't change. A leopard doesn't change his spots just like that, but I think she was tempted a couple of times, you know, for the sake of the children. She used to ring me in one hell of a state.

'In the end Ray said he thought it would be better if they moved away, had a fresh start for her and the children, so they went to Manchester. She'd ring once in a while to let me know how she was and then she told me that they were moving to Spain.'

'How did Chris take that?'

'It was horrible; he was icy cold, totally different to how he had been, and it was worse somehow, he frightened the life out of me. He said he never wanted me to mention her again, said as far as he was concerned she had made her bed and she could lie on it.'

'So he didn't see the children?'

'I don't know, but I don't think so.'

'Did he stay in contact with Linda?'

'I really don't know. He just said he didn't want to talk about her, and when he said that, well I said he could be cruel. I just never said anything about her or the kids.'

'Do you know where she went in Spain?'

Helen shook her head. 'Ray had got the chance of running a hotel or a bar, buying it I think – I'm not sure which now, but I know Linda was really excited. Apparently it had a lovely flat and was right near the beach. She said that we could come out and stay with them once they'd got settled in.'

'And did you?'

Helen shook her head. 'No, once they'd gone we never heard another word, but I used to think, who could blame her?'

'So you didn't hear anything from Linda after she went to Spain?'

'No, but then again in those days there was no internet like there is today, no *Skype* – you couldn't just ring up from abroad without it costing you an arm and a leg, and she'd moved on. I could understand that. Probably wanted to forget all about Denham Market and Chris Hills.'

'Not a Christmas card or anything?'

Helen shook her head. 'No, I was a bit hurt if I'm honest but I can't blame her wanting to get away.'

Chapter Thirteen

'And what about Leah?' I asked. 'What can you tell me about her?'

Helen shook her head and looked heavenwards, her eyes bright with tears. 'I always said she was far too young for him. I think Chris thought if he went out with someone who was young and impressionable that he could make them into the sort of wife that he wanted. The first time I went round there I couldn't believe it. Chris was still married to Linda then, and as far as I knew trying to get her to come back, and there was Leah cooking dinner in Linda's kitchen. She was like a little girl playing house.

'He used to buy her dresses, shoes, took her to have her hair cut.' Helen looked at me, the distress obvious on her face. 'It was like she was a doll for him to play with.'

I nodded, encouraging her to go on.

'I didn't know what to do,' she said. 'Who could I tell? She wasn't under age or anything, but it didn't feel right. I said to Linda it wasn't right.'

'You told Linda?'

Helen nodded. 'I didn't know who else to tell.'

'And how was she when you told her?'

'I don't know really, hurt, angry–'

'So, just to be clear, Chris started going out with Leah when Linda was still in the country?'

'Oh yes, she was still living in King's Lynn I think, although I think she and Ray were an item by then.'

'So do you know what Linda felt about Leah?'

'Angry, I think – and she said we ought to say something, tell someone, but like I said, who? We both knew what he was like, and Leah was so young. I wondered if one of us ought to talk to her. But then again if we said anything would she understand? Would she believe us?'

'Did you say anything to Chris about your concerns?'

'No, there's no way I could talk to Chris about it.'

'And did you talk to Leah?'

Helen shook her head. 'No, I didn't know what to say and Linda had moved. I wish I had now.' Her voice faltered and faded.

'So what happened then,' I prompted.

Helen looked up. 'Chris's divorce came through, and they got married and when I saw how happy they looked I thought that maybe I'd got it wrong, maybe it was all right. They seemed all right together, really happy. Leah always struck me as a bit fragile, and I think that suited Chris. And then one day I met her in town doing some shopping. She said she had been to look at a litter of puppies but hadn't realised that Chris was allergic to cats and dogs so he had said they couldn't have one. It was news to me but I never said anything, and then she said, that maybe it was a good thing because she was hoping to have a baby.

'They'd been trying for a while apparently, and she said she had had all sorts of tests and things and they couldn't find anything wrong, but she was young so the doctors were hopeful that it would just happen in time. Told her not to worry.'

Helen glanced at me, her expression fixed, her lips pressed into a tight unhappy line. 'I opened my mouth without thinking really, because I knew that Chris had had a vasectomy when he was with Linda. She said he didn't want any more children. So I asked Leah if he had had it reversed. Well, it was obvious from her face that she had no idea that he'd been sterilised.

Chapter Thirteen

How could he not have told her? How could he have let her go through all those tests? Knowing it wasn't her who couldn't have kids – cruel, he is, totally heartless.

'He came round a few days later for something or other and I asked him about it. And he flew at me, called me everything. I've never seen anything like it, never seen anyone so angry. He told me it was none of my business and that it was my fault Linda had left him and there was no way I was going to destroy what he had with Leah. My husband came home and told him to leave, and thank God he did, or I don't know what would have happened. He told Chris he should leave and that he wasn't to speak to me like that. Chris stood on the doorstep, face like thunder, fists clenched down by his side like he could barely hold himself back. I remember it like it was yesterday. Chris said not to bother myself about him speaking like that, that he wouldn't ever speak to me again as long as he drew breath, and he's been as good as his word. We've not spoken from that day to this.'

'And what about Leah?' I said. 'Denham's a small town; presumably you've seen her again?'

'Yes, a few times in the street, but never to speak to. One time I saw her on the market and she practically ran away from me. I've got no idea what Chris told her but whatever it was, it worked. 'Helen paused and looked across at me. 'I often wondered what would happen when Leah grew up and started to push back, maybe want a bit more independence. I saw Chris's face that day in the kitchen when he was angry with me. I can't see that he would ever let Leah leave him like Linda did.'

*

When I got back into the car I called DI Baker to update him and then called Mike Carlton for a progress report on the house on Fieldview Road.

'I tried to call you, we've got a body.'

I felt the icy track of fingers down my spine. 'Where?'

'Just out of town in the Relief Channel by the railway station. We've got an officer on site, coroner and forensic pathologist are on their way. Couple of people heading home from work called it in, saw it as they were walking over the bridge, thought it was a mannequin.'

'Do we think it's Leah?'

Mike cleared his throat. 'Female. Right height, the body's been in the water a while and there's a lot of damage. There's a possibility it was caught up in the debris when they were opening the sluices further upstream. So at the moment we've got no way of telling.'

I felt sick. 'Where are you?'

'On my way to the scene. I was about to go off duty.'

'And me. I'll be there as soon as I can. We've got a description of what she was wearing according to her husband.'

'The man who drove her to Wales, you mean,' said Carlton.

I took the point.

I called Baker back and told him I'd let him know the identity of the body as soon as we had it. If it was Leah and she had never left Norfolk then everything Chris Hills had told us was a lie.

Chapter Thirteen

*

Two men in a punt had managed to haul the body up onto a floating jetty that ran parallel to the bank in the relief channel that served the Great Ouse. Further down, the river divided at Denver Slice, on one side feeding into the Tidal Ouse beyond the lock gates and sluices, while on one side it went into the relief channel. In the fens water management was a matter of life and death for the land and the people on it. Visitors driving along the miles of river and dyke banks were shocked when they realised that, in lots of instances, the water held back by them was far higher than the road alongside it.

By the time I got to the river, technicians had already erected a white tent over the body. An unmarked ambulance and other official vehicles were pulled up on the grassy area above the dock. Mike Carlton got out of his car as soon as he clocked me driving in. A couple of uniforms had got the area taped off.

Out of the car the night air was bitter, rain blowing in horizontally across the open site. I pulled my collar up around my ears and went to join Mike. He moved past the niceties at a rate of knots. 'Usually when it's this cold the rate of decomposition is slowed, but unfortunately our body had some kind of altercation with a propeller or maybe the lock further upstream. Even without the bloating there's a lot of damage. Not a hope in hell of getting anything from facial – do you want to look?'

Realistically, no, but I didn't see I had much choice.

The lights in the tent were daylight bright so that the whole structure glowed white hot in the darkness. I could make out the shadow of figures working inside.

The smell of decomposition is very distinctive, once you've smelt it you never forget it. It hangs in the air like fog, clinging to you, so heavy and so dense that it lingers not just in your nose but your mouth, too, so that after you leave the scene you feel as if you can taste it, and – even if you can take an emotional step back – there is something deeply unsettling about seeing another human, a mirror of yourself, reduced to biology, to blood, bone and tissue.

In the confined space the lights brought everything into sharp relief, the lights and body heat from those alive inside brought the smell up from the poor broken thing on the grass.

The hair, what was left of it, was the right colour. There was no face to speak of, and the clothes were muddy and ripped or gone altogether, but there was one totally unscathed hand and it was that that held my attention. The fingers were long, the nails perfectly painted in a delicate shade of pink, without a single chip, as if she had been getting ready for a night out. I made a note to check if Leah wore nail polish.

The doctor looked up from his task. He had the brightest blue eyes, visible above his mask and the clear splash visor. 'There's very little I can tell you at the moment. The extent of the trauma from immersion in the water and what looks like propeller damage is masking any other injuries. All I can tell you is that she is female, probably 40s.'

'Is that all?' asked Carlton.

The two had obviously met before. 'You know the way this works, Mike,' said the pathologist. 'I take her back to the lab–'

'And we wait,' said Mike grimly. 'We've potentially got a murder victim here, Beau. We need anything you can let us have.'

Beau? What sort of name was that?

Mike hesitated as if he had read my thoughts from my expression, and then said, 'Doctor Beau Shepherd, this is Detective Sergeant Daley, all the way from Herefordshire.'

The man nodded an acknowledgement. 'A long drive to come and hang about on a river bank with DS Carlton.'

I nodded. 'Anything else you can tell us about the victim?'

'Five four or five tall, slight build.'

All of this was adding up to the body being Leah's.

'Oh and there was this caught up in the clothing, I saw it as we were turning her over.'

He handed me an evidence bag. Inside was a loop of red string, tied with a knot.

Mike peered at it. 'Your girl a Buddhist?'

'I don't know, why?'

'It's a symbol some people wear, like a protective thing or a blessing.'

Dr Shepherd nodded.' We also can't definitely link it to the body, it was tangled in the clothing, doesn't mean it belongs to our girl here.'

'When will we know if this is Leah?'

'We've collected DNA for comparison,' prompted Mike.

'As soon as I know you'll know,' said Beau Shepherd. 'Now if you'll excuse me, folks, the sooner you are out of here the sooner I can get her back to the lab.'

As we slipped back outside Dr Shepherd was bagging her one good hand to retain any evidence trapped under those per-fectly painted nails. Outside the wind whipped my breath away.

Mike looked at me. 'What do you think?'

'I don't know. I need to check on whether or not Leah wore nail polish. We didn't see any signs of polish or remover in the house, did we?'

Mike hesitated. 'Isn't that the sort of thing she might take with her?'

'You mean like her handbag, credit cards and phone?'

Mike and I walked back to the cars.

'Beau's good,' he said. 'When you ring the station get them to ask if Leah was a Buddhist.'

'You don't think it's her, do you?' I said.

He shrugged. 'I'm no wiser than you are. I'm heading back now. You sure I can't interest you in supper?'

I smiled. 'I'm afraid not, Mike. I'm going back to the hotel to write this up, but thanks anyway.'

'You think Chris Hills is good for it?'

I sighed and glanced back at the shadowy figures inside the tent. 'I'd be lying if I said no, but it's not evidence, is it? If that is her I can't see how he hasn't got a hand in this. He lied through his eye teeth about taking her to Wales. And it all fits. Jealous, manipulative – and a liar, but we haven't got anything to link it to him. '

'Yet,' said Mike as two men in coveralls carried a stretcher into the tent.

Chapter Fourteen

The Girl Next Door

Back in my hotel room I finally eased off my shoes, lay down on the bed, connected my laptop to the wi-fi and began to update the files, type up my notes and complete reports on the day's events, all the while mulling over what we knew, although every thought led me back to the woman on the river bank. I pored over the images we had of Leah; there was nothing where she was wearing nail polish. I wondered about going back to the house to see if we could find any of the para-phernalia that it required – polish, emery boards, remover – I couldn't remember seeing any of those things, but perhaps she had had it done professionally, but that didn't stack up with the image I was creating of her.

It had been a long day and I was tired, hungry and brewing up a killer headache.

Around ten I phoned out for a takeaway having found a place that would deliver. All the time I ate and all the time I was typing, I kept one eye on my mobile phone wondering if it would ring again, wondering if Beau Shepherd would do the autopsy straight away, and if he did whether Mike Carlton would ring me.

It occurred to me halfway through a container of chow mein that it might still be on silent, so I flicked through to settings, which made me think about the call I'd had while I was at Helen Norman's. It wasn't like Mr XXXXXX to call me, usually he sent just the briefest text, which I guessed he would delete the moment it was sent and would leave a far less obvious trail. Maybe it was something important. Maybe there had been some kind of an emergency. I took a long look at the phone. Who was I kidding? I knew exactly why he had rung and what he had in mind.

Just after eleven when I had finished off the last of the prawn crackers and picked the tasty bits out of the special fried rice, the phone rang again, the row of Xs coming up in the caller display.

I thought about the things I had found out about Chris Hills, about the girl on the river bank with her delicately painted nails and about a man who told lies, and manipulated and bullied women. I picked up the handset and pressed the button to take the call.

'Where are you?' he asked, before I could speak. He sounded breathless, speaking quietly and quickly, as if there was some chance he might be overheard.

'I've been thinking about you all day,' he said. 'I was thinking that we could get together, although it's a bit late now. Where have you been? Can I come round?' I could hear the urgency in his voice and the need. 'I could pick up some wine, maybe grab a takeaway. What do you fancy?'

I didn't tell him that I was in Norfolk or about the day I'd had or about the girl on the river bank. I didn't tell and he didn't ask because I knew when it came right down to it, he didn't care.

'We've got to stop this, Jimmy,' I said, my tone firm, all business.

'Oh come on, Mel,' he purred. 'Don't tell me you've already eaten?' He laughed. 'What's the matter. Don't you want to see me? You know you want to. Come on, just half an hour.'

'We can't keep doing this.'

'You said that last time and the time before. You know you just can't resist me. Can you? ' His laugh was throaty and seductive and made something in my chest tighten. 'I can be there in ten minutes.'

'No, you can't. I'm away on a case.'

'Even better, you won't have to explain anything to that nosey neighbour of yours. Where are you?'

'Norfolk.'

Jimmy snorted. 'Oh for fuck's sake, Mel, why didn't you tell me you were going off somewhere.'

'Why would I?'

'Because –' he began.

'Because I'm at work. It's what I do and it's none of your business?'

'Did you do this deliberately? *Hands up I'll take the job*? You knew that I was trying to get away so I could see you. You could have let me know you were going to be a no show.'

I felt a flare of outrage. '*A no show*? For fuck's sake it's not like we were on a date, Jimmy. At no time ever did I say I'd see you tonight.'

He didn't reply. I plunged on into the angry silence.

'So you're saying it's my fault that you can't nip round to my place and get your rocks off?' I said incredulously. 'Jimmy, if you're trying to make me feel guilty, you're barking up the wrong tree. I didn't want you to get away. I don't want to see you. I don't want you coming round. We're done, finished, over. Okay?'

'You said that last time.'

I looked heavenwards, the trouble was that Jimmy was right. I *had* said the same thing, almost word for word before and had regretted it ever since. If anything pissed me off more than his smug attitude it was my lack of self-control. That one mad time, which I thought we would both be ashamed of and never mention again, had turned into lots of times, something almost regular but not quite and a lot, lot hungrier and more potent than I ever imagined possible. But that didn't mean that it was right or that it didn't have to stop.

I could hear him breathing. Hear him waiting to talk to me, to say I was missing him, that I wanted him. And I did, that was the trouble.

My poxy poxy arrogant bastard of a brother-in-law, Jimmy, with his big cheesy grin and those broad muscular shoulders, who was always there when I needed furniture moving, or a tap fixing, always there to help when I was confronted by something I couldn't manage on my own. I shivered, thinking about the way he looked at me, the way he made me feel, the way my insides turned to jelly when I saw him and when he touched me. Oh I know it's wrong.

I'm not proud of this or any of it, quite the reverse. I'm ashamed, and appalled. I'd die if someone did this to me, and I still couldn't help myself. What does that say about me? Nothing good that's for certain. It's why I hadn't answered his calls or his texts for days. It's not him I hated, it was me for being so bloody weak and stupid and selfish.

It had to stop. Kathy, my sister would die if she ever found out what was going on, but not until she had killed both Jimmy and me, slowly, painfully. And who could blame her? Kathy would be devastated, hurt and then furious, beyond furious – and the chances were she would blame me, despite it being Jimmy who had made the first move.

And she would most probably be right. I should have said no. I could easily have said no, made a gentle joke of it. All blindingly obvious in the cold hard light of day but not when he had shown up one night when I was half cut, sad, feeling lost after dumping the man I had thought was my happy ever after, and consoling myself with a bottle of wine and a box set. It was cold and dark and the heating had packed up and I was a wreck.

'I just wanted to see if you were okay,' Jimmy said, as I opened the front door. 'Kathy told me about you and Liam. I'm sorry. I thought you two were solid. I thought you might like someone to talk to?'

He had brought more wine and said he'd take a look at the heating for me. I was in my pyjamas and had cried so much that it looked like I had been punched in the face. He poured another glass of wine, made me some cheese on toast and then went to look at the boiler.

And then when he'd fixed it and I'd had more wine he told me that I was lovely and that Liam had to be mad, and then he put his arms round me and hugged me, tight, up against his chest and he smelt beautiful and I had felt so alone and so miserable and there he was, and he made me feel safe and I loved the feel of his strong arms round me. And then I looked up and he looked down and there was a moment then when we could have smiled and one of us could have stepped away and laughed, and gone and put the kettle on or something, but we didn't.

It sounds so corny now but it had been so easy. And afterwards we both agreed that it had been a terrible mistake and that we wouldn't ever mention it and never, ever do it again, that confessing would only hurt Kathy more, that it was best just to forget the whole thing had ever happened. It had been an accident, an error of judgement. We were both sorry and apologetic. And then the next week Jimmy had been there on the doorstep with a big bunch of flowers to say sorry and I was pleased to see him there and he asked if he could come in, maybe just for a coffee. And he'd stayed.

A little showreel of guilt ran through my head; Kathy at Christmas dinner weeks later, spooning out the vegetables into *Tippee* bowls for the kids, while Jimmy – master of all he surveyed – carved the turkey at the top of the table.

'You should get yourself someone like Jimmy, settle down, shouldn't she, Jimmy?' Kathy had said, while she was cutting the kids' meat into little squares and ladling on the gravy.

Chapter Fourteen

My eyes had met Jimmy's across the crackers and the bowls of sprouts and roast potatoes, and I had seen the grin on his face as he looked up and licked his lips. Even now I could feel colour rising at the thought of it. It had to stop. Jimmy was so cocksure, so very certain of himself, so confident about what we were doing that I couldn't help wonder if he had done it before – and there was another irony, because if I had have ever found out that he was cheating on my little sister it would have been me who would have felt obligated to kill him.

'When are you getting back?' Jimmy purred, breaking into my thoughts.

I looked out of the window into the courtyard of the hotel, for a moment, considering the appeal of just disappearing and never going back.

'Jimmy, please. Don't ring me again. I'm done, okay?'

'You know you don't mean that, kitten. You know you want me.' His voice made me tingle; I should hang up but I couldn't.

'It would break Kath's heart if she ever found out,' I said. 'You know that, don't you?'

'Then let's make sure she doesn't. Come on, when are you back? I could make an early morning call.'

I took a deep breath and hung up. The trouble was, I suspected that, far from dissuading Jimmy, setting myself up as a challenge made me more exciting rather than less.

I had barely had time to put the handset down on the table before it rang again. I snatched it up and was about to reject the call when I saw it was from Mike Carlton.

'Have you found something on the body?' I said.

'No, still nothing, but don't worry, Beau will ring when he's got anything.'

'So what is this? A social call?' It sounded snippier than I'd intended but Mike sailed on.

'I've just been reading through the reports; one of the uniformed officers who was canvassing the area said that Chris Hills has been giving the neighbour's teenage daughter extra maths tuition. The parents are fine about it. Dad told the PC that Hills was a lovely man, really helped their daughter Amy with her grades, he was polite, the same kind of stuff we've heard before. Anyway the PC made a particular note of it, and he said there was something felt off about it and flagged it up when he got back to the station.'

'Okay, so did anyone get a chance to talk to the daughter on her own?'

'No, but I'm just emailing you a photo that one of our guys found on Facebook. I think you should take a look.'

I reached over the remains of supper to wake up my laptop, clicking through to my email and opening up the email attachment. What appeared on my screen was a picture of a young woman sitting in a car. The car door was open, and the girl was turned towards the camera; she was barefoot, dressed in a tight, white tee-shirt and little layered miniskirt, denim and something floral. She was laughing, leggy and slim but quite small framed, and bore more than a passing resemblance to Leah Hills.

'Do you see what I mean?' said Mike Carlton.

'She looks like Leah,' I said.

'Uhuh, well that's Amy Cooper, the neighbour's daughter on a day out at the beach, the album name is, quotes '*with good friends'*. But it looks to me like just one friend. Can you zoom in on the image?'

'With a bit of fiddling about,' I said, concentrating on the screen and the track pad. 'Can you give me a clue?'

'Do it. You need to look at the reflection in the rear window behind the girl. Take it in as close as you can.'

I dragged the .jpeg onto the desktop and opened up an image-handling programme. 'This is going to take me a couple of minutes, do you want to put me out of my misery?'

'It's Chris Hills. He took the photograph. The caption on the image reads, 'Before breaking out the bikini.'

I felt another chill ripple down my spine.

As soon as Mike was off the phone I rang Baker, knowing that he wouldn't mind being disturbed at home.

*

DI Baker was at his desk before eight the following morning, checking what had come in during the evening and overnight. He glanced out of his office window across to the desk in the bullpen where Mel Daley usually worked. It was empty, not really a surprise, but there was some part of him that had hoped that she might be back for the morning briefing, but understood why she wasn't. While he was ruminating Sergeant Rees knocked on the door.

'Everyone's in, Sir.'

Baker nodded, 'Still nothing from Norfolk on the identity of the body?'

Rees shook his head.

From the corridor behind Rees there was another voice. 'Excuse me, I think you need to come and see this, Sir.'

The urgency in the constable's voice was enough to get both men to their feet and hurrying after him.

They followed him through to the media suite where Sheila Hastings was at her desk in the CCTV room, but what was playing on the screen was not footage from the service station or the motorway but instead a picture of Chris Hills on the steps of the Laurels Hotel in the centre of town.

He was talking to a TV film crew. 'I'm extremely concerned about the way the police are handling my wife, Leah's, recent disappearance. Rather than search for her they have treated me as a suspect and as a result I've been marginalised and excluded from the hunt for my wife,' he was saying. 'I am extremely worried about her and I want to say to Leah, wherever you are, my love, my precious darling, please just come home. I love you, my darling. Just, please, come home.' At which point Chris Hills broke down in tears. A photo – the same photo the police were using, flashed up on the screen with contact details for both the police and the TV station news desk.

Baker swung round. 'For fuck's sake, who is supposed to be with him. Where is the liaison officer?' But Rees was already on the phone, trying to answer exactly the same question.

'Is this going out live?' asked Baker.

Sheila shook her head, 'It was on the local news about ten minutes ago; I've just pulled it off their website. Someone on their day off rang it in. The TV station are planning to run it in their news bulletins throughout the day.'

'Jesus. Get someone down there with him will you.'

Chapter Fourteen

*

Amy Cooper was thin as a whippet with shoulder-length brown hair, streaked through with blonde highlights, tendrils of which were escaping from a scrunchie and framing her face. Although she was probably no more than five feet two, she had long, rangy limbs and elfin features, neatly arranged in a symmetrical, triangular face. In person she looked less like the photo they had of Leah Hills but there was still something about her, a ghost of a resemblance that kept surfacing and resurfacing as I spoke to her.

With her parents' permission we had arranged to interview Amy in the local police station with an appointed responsible adult present. It had taken some doing. Her father was defensive and slightly perturbed and wanted to be there with her, but I knew from experience that Amy was far less likely to tell them anything about Chris Hills if either of her parents were present.

Amy was in year 11, had turned sixteen in October, and when I met her was dressed in black leggings, paired with converse trainers, under a miniskirt and long sloppy sweater that had sleeves so long that they hung down over her fingertips. Although we were in a purpose-built interview suite with an informal seating area, it didn't take a genius to realise that Amy was nervous about the prospect of being questioned by the police.

I left her parents in the waiting room and showed her and the designated adult – a social worker called Lynn – into the interview suite. 'Thank you for coming in, Amy, I'm sorry to intrude into your weekend. It's really appreciated. We'll try not to keep you too long. Have you got anything good planned?' I said, keeping the tone light and conversational.

Amy shrugged. 'Not really.' She had a high, slightly nasal voice. 'I don't really know how I can help,' she said, looking up at me. Her voice suggested a bright, nervous per-sonality, bright but not necessarily confident. 'I've already told the policeman who came round everything I know.'

I nodded. 'I understand but sometimes it's just the smallest thing – you know stuff that you don't think is important. Can I get you anything? Tea, coffee, water? I'm not sure they run to anything much beyond that here.'

She smiled nervously. 'I'm fine, thank you.' The girl's nails were bitten down to the quick and I noticed that she had a flower doodled in biro on the inside of her wrist, which re-minded me of the red string bracelet found with the clothing of our unidentified female from the night before.

'Maybe some water?' Amy said after a second or two.

I glanced at Lynn who shook her head to a drink of water, and then nodded to the female PC who went off to get some. I explained that we were going to record the interview rather than take notes and that we could stop at any time, that this wasn't about anything she had done but was about finding Leah. Amy nodded.

We talked for a while. The water arrived. Amy wasn't stupid, and I guessed she knew that I was trying to put her at ease. We talked about school and music and what there was to do in Denham – I told her I'd grown up there – and what Amy planned to do when she left school, and then gently, very gently, guided her back to the conversation I really wanted to have.

'I'd like to talk to you about your neighbours, Chris and Leah Hills,' I said, glancing down at the notes I'd got balanced on my knees.

Amy nodded. 'Yeah, I know. Mum said Leah had disappeared. I mean that is so weird. How can someone just disappear? So awful. She seems really nice.'

It seemed as if no one had joined the dots and associated the body found by the river with Leah yet, or maybe Amy hadn't watched the local news. I'd seen the report on the TV: woman's body found in the River Ouse near Denham Market, and was just glad that they hadn't had the cameras there when Mike and I had been looking at the body.

'Do you know Leah well?'

'No, not really. I mean I've seen her about, in the street and that. And I think she was at a barbeque we had when we moved in.'

'How long have you lived there?'

Amy tipped her head on one side as if she had never considered it. 'Maybe four or five years. I'm not sure. We moved when I was in year six.'

'So you were eleven?'

Amy nodded. 'I s'pose so. We moved that summer so I could start at the new school in year seven when everyone else was moving up to High School.'

'Okay. And have you known Chris and Leah all that time?'

Amy shook her head, but then paused and said, 'Yes I suppose so, but not really known them. Just that they were about, you know?'

I nodded.

'And have you ever spoken to Leah?'

'Leah? Yeah, a few times, we had a street party and she did the banners and I helped. She seemed really nice, but a bit quiet. Shy. My mum thought she was stuck up.' Amy flushed red. 'Not that she didn't like her or anything. She just didn't say very much. Leah.'

'And what about Chris?'

Something in Amy Cooper's demeanour subtly shifted. She would certainly never make a poker player. 'What about him?' she said, her tone defensive. 'He teaches me maths and stuff.'

'Yes, your mum and dad told one of our officers that Chris is tutoring you in – 'I made a show of looking at the notes on my lap. 'Is it just maths?'

Amy nodded. 'That's right. Maths.'

'Never my strong suit,' I said with a smile. 'Do you like maths?'

Amy looked up at me from under her eyelashes. 'I'm not really very good at it, but I need a B or above to get into uni.'

'What are you hoping to do?'

'I want to be a vet,' said Amy, more comfortable back on neutral territory. 'Small animals, not cows or sheep or anything like that. I've always wanted to work with animals. Since I was little.'

'Sounds good, do you know where you're going?'

'I'd like to get into Nottingham.' Amy paused. There was something there that was uncomfortable, too. 'But it might be better to try for something closer, you know, so I could live at home.'

'A lot of studying?' I said.

Chapter Fourteen

Amy nodded. 'Yeah, but I don't mind that and I'm on target for my grades.'

'Even in maths?'

Amy nodded.

'That's great, so the tutoring from Chris has really helped? Your mum and dad said you'd been struggling a bit.'

'Yeah, I was.' The prickle was there again, a tiny ripple that made me sure that there was something else going on.

'So,' I said, tone deliberately light. 'Strict is he – Chris? – always making you turn your homework in on time?'

For a second Amy's eyes widened and then she said in a low, even voice. 'No, not at all he's really nice. He makes maths fun. I've improved a lot since he's been helping me out.'

I nodded. 'That's brilliant. How did he start teaching you, do you know? I mean did he offer or have a card in a shop window or something? Maybe your dad found him through the school?'

Amy pulled a face. 'I don't know; you'll have to ask my dad.'

'Okay, so how often do you and Chris get together for extra tuition?'

'Once or twice a week, depends on what we're doing.'

'That's quite a lot.'

'I know but I was really getting behind, and it's only an hour at a time, and Dad thinks it's worth it if it can get me the grades. And then Chris sets me some homework to do between times, just exercises really to make sure I've got it.'

'Sounds like you're really dedicated.'

Amy blushed. 'I really want to be a vet.'

I nodded. 'That's brilliant – good to have a plan. And your dad pays Chris for your tuition?'

Amy nodded and pulled a face. 'Yeah. I think it's quite expensive. He's always telling me how much I'm costing him.'

'Your dad?'

'Yeah, but like I said my grades have really improved.'

'And where do you have your maths lessons with Chris?'

'At my house. In the kitchen.'

'Okay. And do you always have them there?' I moved her out, step by step, slowly edging towards the questions I wanted to ask.

Amy hesitated for a second. 'Mostly.'

'But not always?'

'No.'

We were almost out on the thinner ice now. Amy looked unsettled and uneasy. *Gently, slowly*, I reminded myself, keeping the tone even and warm, my posture open and relaxed as if I hadn't spotted the subtle tell in Amy's body language.

'So, where else did you go; the library?'

Amy shook her head. I smiled but stayed quiet, leaving her the space, not crowding her answer out with another question or another suggestion.

'Sometimes we used to go to his house,' said Amy after a few seconds more silence.

I nodded. 'Okay, I can see that, it's convenient, and it's only a couple of doors up the road. Makes sense.'

When she realised that I wasn't going to jump on her for telling her the truth or for being stupid, Amy continued, 'Yeah. We only went there once or twice though, just when my mum was out.'

I nodded again but said nothing.

'He'd forgotten his laptop,' said Amy in answer to an unasked question. Her discomfort was obvious. It was a lame excuse. They lived four doors away, how long would it have taken for him to go home and get it? Rather than pointing out the obvious I smiled.

'And was Leah there when you went round?'

Amy shook her head. 'No, she was at work. But like I said it was only a couple of times.'

'Okay,' I said, making a mental note. 'That's great. And so did you ever meet Chris anywhere else? You know maybe grab a coffee or something?'

Amy shook her head. 'No.'

'Are you sure? Just maybe once or twice?'

She stared at me from under the tendrils of hair, trying to front it out, while her fingers worked nervously in her lap, picking at a stray sliver of skin on her thumb.

'You see I don't mind if you did but I'd rather you told us the truth. This isn't about you, Amy, it isn't about trying to trick you or get you into any kind of trouble, it's about us trying to find out what's happened to Leah.'

I waited. She carried on staring, although her gaze was no longer focused on me but on a spot just above my shoulder. She chewed her lip.

'Maybe not coffee, maybe out for a drive? You said Chris was nice – I can see that you might want to meet up with him,' I suggested, and as I did I took the printout of the photo Mike Carlton had emailed me and handed it to Amy.

She flushed scarlet. 'Where did you get that? That's private. You said you wouldn't trick me. You're trying to trick me, aren't you? What else have you got in that file?' she said.

The social worker flashed me an icy look.

'What else do you think there might be?' I asked, tone still measured.

'I don't know,' Amy snapped back. 'But that's private.'

'It was on Facebook. And your profile is set to public.'

Amy reddened.

'So can you tell me where the photo was taken?' I asked, pointing to the image on the coffee table between us.

'I don't know where it was.' She was prickly now, defensive.

'But you were with Chris, weren't you?'

She held out for a moment or two longer.

'Amy we know you were, his reflection is in the window on the car.'

'It's none of your business.'

'I think it is, Amy. Leah's missing and we are trying to find out what's going on. Chris is really upset.' I paused. 'He's worried that something might have happened to her.' Momentarily I see perfectly painted finger nails. I blink to clear my mind. 'You two sound like you're really good friends?'

'We are,' she said after a second or two.

'Then please, we're only trying to help him. Tell me about the photo.' I pushed it towards her.

I could see the cogs turning, could see her weighing things up and then finally Amy looked down, avoiding my gaze. 'Chris said we both deserved a day off for all the hard work we'd been doing and did I want to go for a ride out somewhere? We ended up at the seaside. We went to this really posh place to eat and then we walked along the beach. That was it. No big deal.'

'So when was this?' I said.

Amy looked at the photo, considering her reply. 'In the summer. After exams. May or maybe June.'

'Last year?'

Amy nodded. 'Yeah.'

'And did your mum and dad know where you were going?'

Amy started to pick at a stray thread on the hem of her sweater. 'God, no. No, they don't care where I am as long as I'm in by ten, getting good grades and not answering back.'

I waited again, giving her time, trying to resist the temptation to push her along; I needed Amy to tell me what had happened, along with the how and the why. She looked down at the photo.

'Dad was off playing golf with his mates and Mum was on a Spa weekend with her girlfriends.' Amy emphasised *girl* so that it sounded like an insult. 'She's always out somewhere. Dad was supposed to be at home working and looking after me, but then one of his friends rang up wanting to know if he'd come down to the club –' she paused again. 'He asked me if I'd mind if he went out for a little while.'

'And what? You said you would be okay on your own?'

'Yeah, I mean it's not like I'm a kid or anything. They are just so protective, it's crazy. So I told Dad that I would be okay, that I'd just go round and see a friend, so he needn't worry.'

'But you didn't say which friend?'

Amy looked away. 'No, but he doesn't know who my friends are anyway. I was going to go round to see Lacey but I texted her and she wasn't in.'

'Lacey is your friend?'

'My best friend.'

'So did you text any of your other friends?'

Amy shook her head.

'So you texted Chris?'

She nodded. 'Yeah, he said I could always ring him or text him. Anytime.'

'So you could talk to him?'

She nodded again. 'My mum and dad are always busy.'

'And what did you talk to him about?'

This time she shrugged. 'Just stuff, you know –'

'Maths?'

She laughed.' No, about stuff.'

'What sort of stuff?'

'I dunno, friends, what I'd been doing, what he'd been doing, you know, just stuff.'

'So did Leah come with you? To the seaside?'

Amy wriggled uncomfortably on her seat. 'No.'

'So was she out too maybe?'

'I don't know. I didn't go round the house, Chris picked me up from the playing field at the bottom of the road. He said it was easier –' she left the words hanging.

I waited; easier than what, I wondered.

'So have you still got the messages on your phone?'

Amy glanced up at me. However much I wanted to find out about Chris Hills I didn't want to frighten Amy Cooper

223

into clamming up, so my expression remained resolutely in neutral. Seconds ticked by. Amy bit her lip.

'Chris gave me a mobile phone. Just for me and him. He said it was all right to use it to ring him if I ever needed anything. You know, like with homework or to talk or anything.'

I said nothing.

'And so I just texted him and said that Mum and Dad were out–' Amy's discomfort was palpable. 'And Chris said did I want to go somewhere, like for a ride or something. Like a celebration for getting through all the exam stuff and for all the work I'd done.'

'And you said yes?'

Amy glared at me. 'Yes, I said yes, but nothing happened if that's what you're trying to say. I was bored and Chris is always so nice to me. Not like my mum and dad, he treats me like a person, not like I'm stupid or in the way. We went to this really nice place to eat, on a harbour, you could see the boats from where we were sitting, and then we had champagne.' She paused as if daring me to say something. 'Chris said I deserved it. Although I'm not sure why people go on about it. I thought it would be sweeter. Anyway he understands, he listens to me, he doesn't treat me like a kid, he said –' Amy, up on the crest of a wave, grabbed a breath and stopped herself.

'What did he say, Amy?' I said gently.

Amy shook her head. 'You wouldn't understand.'

'That's possible, but you can tell me anyway.'

Amy said nothing.

'Have you still got the mobile Chris gave you?'

Amy nodded.

'May I see it?'

She hesitated for a second. 'Chris said I wasn't to let anyone see it, that people might get the wrong idea. You know what people can be like.'

I nodded. 'Yes, but I'm not people, Amy, I'm a police officer and we're trying to find Chris's wife. He is really worried about her. We think there is a chance that Leah might be in danger. You want to help him find her, don't you?'

'I'm not a child,' snapped Amy. 'Don't patronise me. Of course I want to help but Chris wouldn't hurt anyone.' And then she picked up her rucksack from the floor and began to unfasten the straps. 'I don't see how my phone can help.'

And then unexpectedly she said. 'He loves me, you know.'

The breath stopped in my throat. Amy's attention was apparently fixed on the bag, her eyes still down. 'He told me that I'm really special – and I know what you're thinking but it's not just bullshit. He said that if he wasn't married that we could be together. Me and Chris. I mean I'm really sad for him that Leah's vanished but it was over you know. He told me. He was only staying with her till he could find the right moment to explain about us. I've tried ringing him. Just to talk to him, to say how sorry I am, to help him, but he's not answering.' Amy looked up, her gaze meeting mine. Her eyes were bright, her expression determined. 'You know that he's only with Leah because she can't cope without him, don't you? He said so.'

I held out my hand. Amy dropped the phone into it.

*

Chapter Fourteen

'Hills told her to delete the texts and the pictures but she didn't – couldn't bring herself to get rid of them. The texts are still on her phone and she downloaded the images onto her laptop.'

I was sitting at Mike Carlton's desk in Denham Market's police station talking on the phone to Baker back at the station. 'We've picked the laptop up from her house and we've got Amy making a statement. Her parents are beside themselves. They were paying this guy to teach her maths. She was fifteen when he offered to help her. We've got the local guys going through the laptop we found at his house.'

'And –'

'And from what we've turned up so far, Chris Hills was extremely circumspect about what he kept on his laptop, the techies are pretty confident that if there's anything on there, they'll find it. He's clever, but Amy not so much – he started having sex with her the day she turned sixteen,' I said grimly, looking down at the printout of the texts that had come from Amy's phone. It never got any easier.

'He promised her that one day they would be together. One day they'd get married. We've got him on grooming and making indecent images of a child under the age of eighteen.'

Baker sighed. 'I'm sending a team to the Laurels to pick him up now.'

'It doesn't get us any closer to finding Leah.'

'No, but at least we can charge the bastard with something.

'Anything on the body yet?'

'No, Mike is chasing it up at the moment but they know the situation.'

'So are you on your way back?'

'I soon will be,' I said, glancing round the office. 'Just saying my goodbyes. One other thing, Amy Cooper said that Chris Hills was planning to take her away for the weekend. Said that they were trying to work out a cover story between them.'

'Don't tell me.'

'He told her he had got a cottage in Wales right by a river. Have forensics been over it yet, Sir?'

'No,' said Baker. 'But they will be.'

Chapter Fifteen

Talking to Ray Burridge

'I'll need to question Chris Hills about Amy Cooper,' said Mike Carlton as he walked me out to my car. I dropped my holdall into the boot and closed the lid.

I nodded. 'We'll be expecting you,' I said as I climbed in. 'I can't offer you a home-cooked supper but we've got a cracking kebab van on the market square. You'll let me know if anything else comes up? And you'll ring me when they've got a definite ID on the body from the river?'

He nodded. 'Beau says he should have something definitive by the end of the day.'

I extended a hand. 'Thank you.'

'Least I could do. 'He grinned and slapped the roof of my car. 'Safe journey. Let me know you make it back safe and sound.'

I laughed. 'You sound like my dad.'

Before heading home I drove up to Fieldview Road and walked down between the hedges and down the steps onto the playing field where once upon a time, a lifetime ago, I had kissed Charlie Falconer under the lee of the graveyard wall, and fumbled around in the way that teenagers do. Or at least that's what they do if left to their own devices, I thought grimly.

Running parallel to the playing field was the roadway where Chris Hills had driven round to pick up Amy Cooper. The knowledge that we'd got him because of his involvement with Amy Cooper was no comfort at all. Far from it. People like Chris Hills go unnoticed, under the radar all the time, but that didn't help me to find Leah. I needed Doctor Shepherd to call.

The consensus was that Chris had arranged for Leah's disappearance to make way for a newer model, but knowing it and proving it were worlds apart. Norfolk Police had scaled up their involvement and allocation of resources but we still had the thick end of bugger all on Hills.

My one hope was that, confronted with the information we had on Amy, Baker would get him to confess. I hoped so – wherever she was we needed to find Leah and bring her home.

The wind was still cold, still edged with rain. The playing field had barely changed since I had last been there; there were still the same swings and a climbing frame, a slide and a sandpit, surrounded by closely cropped grass and a few stunted trees. Odd that it was the same when so many other things had changed.

I watched two women walking across the grass, one with half an eye on a child running ahead, the other ambling, eyes down, deep in her own thoughts. The woman was wearing a camel coat. For a moment I froze and stared, watching her, willing her to look up. When the woman did and glanced in my direction it was obvious she bore no resemblance to Leah Hills. I shook my head to clear it; of course she didn't. Why would she? Leah Hills could be anywhere. But where? The question nagged at me like bad toothache. Three days in and we were no nearer to knowing what happened.

CCTV cameras around the sluices and the roads coming out of Denham couldn't place Chris Hills's car on a road that took him anywhere near the Great Ouse, although given the miles of riverbank – all of it unmonitored – that was small consolation. We needed more.

I stuffed my hands in my pockets and headed back towards the car thinking about Leah, thinking about Amy and wondering what else Chris Hills was hiding. The phone pinged in my handbag. I glanced down at the row of Xs in the caller display and pressed the red key to cut it off.

As I got back to the car it rang again. I was about to reject the call when I saw it was from Mike. 'You driving?' he said.

'No, I'm fine, just visiting old haunts before I head home. Did you hear from Beau?'

'It's not Leah. We've just had a missing persons report in. Sounds like that's our woman, although we'll be waiting for DNA confirmation. Tina Howarth, 42, lived on a narrow boat – friends saw her last after a party four nights ago. They said they'd all been drinking pretty hard, one of them called round to take her out to lunch today and found the boat deserted. The friend who reported her said they'd have a girlie day out the day she disappeared, they all had their nails done – oh and Tina was a Buddhist and wore one of those red string things.'

'Sounds like we've got a name.'

'They're down at the boat collecting DNA for comparison, but apparently the bank and the jetty are slippery as hell. You can easily see how someone might slip in. Beau found no signs of foul play but did find signs of blunt-force trauma to the skull – chances are she slipped and fell in.'

'Thanks, Mike, can you let me know when it's official.'

'Certainly can.'

He didn't ask me if I had hoped it was Leah, didn't ask if I was disappointed, because who wants to know that someone you are searching for ends up like that. But if she wasn't in the Ouse, where was she? I rang Baker to let him know that our body was unlikely to be that of Leah Hills.

By the time I finally drove into the police station car park it was evening. The yellow lights around the perimeter gave everything a strange jaundiced tint. Baker's Audi was still in his spot, away from the lights, tucked in close to the wall so that you had to know where to look to check if he was in or out.

When I got inside I found him in his office at his desk, head down, notebook alongside him as he ploughed through a pile of files. He glanced up as I knocked on the door and nodded a hello. 'So there you are. I thought we'd lost you. I was just about to send out a search party. How was Norfolk?'

'Flat,' I said, slipping off my jacket. 'And cold. Do you need a hand?'

'I thought you'd be going straight home.'

I nodded. 'Me too, but I wanted to see if anything else had shown up.'

Chapter Fifteen

Baker indicated the screen on his desk. 'We've got this from a traffic camera, came in about an hour ago.'

I looked at the image. It was not exactly crisp but it was possible to see Chris Hills driving, with Leah Hills in the passenger seat, her eyes closed, head tilted on one side. The footage wasn't clear, the weather poor but it was definitely them. Leah Hills looked as if she was asleep. It was the first real proof we had that she actually had been in the car en-route to Wales.

'At least it proves that she was in the car with him.'

Baker nodded. 'So she definitely left Norfolk.'

'Where was this taken?'

'From a footbridge on the A38 junction of the M50.'

'So not so far from here.'

'They picked the Mercedes up in other places en route – Rees has already put it up into the timeline, but this is the only one where we've got any kind of decent shot into the interior.'

'Still plenty of places he could have hidden a body.'

'We've widened the search parameters. Bad weather is keeping the heli grounded but the forecast looks better for tomorrow.'

I looked up at Baker across the table. This far in we both knew the chances were we were looking for a body.

'How did it go with Hills?'

Baker pushed his chair back from his desk. 'Like a charm,' he said grimly. 'Apparently Amy Cooper is a needy fantasist and has had a crush on him for some time, and he can't understand what this has to do with finding Leah. Chris had been at the point of telling her father that he couldn't tutor Amy any more because he felt her behaviour was inappropriate. And he had never had this problem with any of the other people he's tutoring.'

I stared at him. 'There are others?'

'Seems so, although I think he regretted letting that slip. Mr Hills declined to give me a list.'

'Maybe Amy Cooper will be able to help. I'll make sure Mike Carlton knows.'

'And then when I showed Hills the images from Amy's laptop he clammed up and said that he wanted a solicitor.'

'Surprise, surprise.' I took half a dozen files from the pile he had already been through.

'But the good news is we've tracked down Ray Burridge.'

I looked up. 'Where?'

'Spain, he's retired out there. We've organised a Skype call in…' Baker glanced at the office clock '…about ten minutes, do you want to sit in?'

I nodded.

*

Once upon a time Ray Burridge must have been a very handsome man, but long years under the Spanish sun had turned his skin the colour and texture of old leather. He had close-cropped, wavy, white-grey hair and eyes like dark, glittering buttons in his copper coloured skin.

'The man who contacted me earlier said this was about Linda?' said Ray, once the niceties were out of the way. 'I'm not really sure how I can help you.' He stubbed out a cigarette in an unseen ashtray. 'It's been years since we've been in contact.'

Behind him I could see a string of lights, bright against the dark sky, swinging gently on the breeze and a distant glimpse of sea under a silvery moon. The view from Ray Burridge's balcony in his apartment in Denia looked a lot more inviting than grey, wet and windy Hereford.

'We were told that you were planning to run a bar or a hotel together in Ibiza?'

'That's right, we were. Back in the dark ages.' He laughed. 'God knows how many years ago that was now. Lot of water has flowed under the bridge since then, and not just water.' He screwed up his eyes as if trying to remember. 'It was a little family bar – Fernando's, with a couple of holiday rental apartments attached if we wanted them. Nice place. Linda had done some bar work and worked in the hotel where we met. I'd worked in hospitality all my life. Anyway, we found this bar for sale while we were on holiday. Seemed like a dream come true really, fresh start for both of us, bit of paradise and a decent living all rolled into one.'

'And you bought it?'

'After a bit of negotiation, yes, the original plan was that me and Linda would run it and me, her and the kids would live in one of the flats upstairs. It was a family place, little bar in the corner, few tables, did coffees and lunches as well as open in the evenings and we had the option to buy the apartments next door to rent out to tourists. I stayed there about three years, built the business up and then sold it on, bought somewhere bigger, bit more commercial and then got myself another place.' He grinned. 'Start of my business empire that was.'

'We were told you had gone out there with Linda?' said Baker.

Ray nodded. 'Yeah, that's right, that had been the plan but in the end she decided she couldn't leave the UK.' He stopped and lit another cigarette. 'She said she wanted to try and sort things out with Chris.' He sniffed. 'Like that was ever going to work; the man was a total and utter bastard. Anyway, I ended up with four bars and a hotel before I packed it all in. Eventually got married to a local girl, Agata.' He nodded towards someone unseen outside the range of the camera.

'We retired out here after selling up, got out just in time too, missed the crash by a gnat's.' There was a glass of beer alongside him on the table and from somewhere close by came the sounds of a television. He took a long pull on his cigarette. 'Didn't do too badly in the end.'

'Can we talk about Linda?' asked Baker.

Ray nodded. 'Sure, although it was a time ago now.' He adjusted his chair, leaning forward so that his face was closer to the screen. 'Is she in some kind of trouble?'

'No. We were hoping you would be able to help us find her. We're looking into the disappearance of Leah Hills.'

Ray's brow furrowed. 'What? Did they have another kid?'

Baker shook his head. 'No, Leah is Chris Hills' second wife.'

Some kind of comprehension dawned on Ray's face. 'So they did finally split up in the end then? I'm not surprised, the man was an arsehole –' He stopped. 'In that case I'm really not sure I can be of much help. I mean Linda and I split up before I moved out here. She wanted to give it one more chance, one more go round with her old man. I thought she was nuts to even think about trying, but there you go, each to their own. You'd be better talking to her.'

'That's the problem. We've not been able to locate her.' Baker glanced across at me. 'We thought you might be able to help. When did you last see her, Mr Burridge?'

Ray Burridge frowned. 'I'm not sure. I came out here in…' he paused. 'Hang on.' And with that he vanished from the screen only to appear a few minutes later with a box of photos, which he started to flick through. 'I think it was the late 80s, early 90s, I'm not sure exactly. There might be some dates on these photos. I took them when me and Linda came out here first time with the kids.' He thumbed distractedly through the box, shaking his head as he flipped them over. 'I can't see any dates.'

'Would it be possible for us to have copies of those?' asked Baker.

'Yeah, sure, I can scan them in and email them to you if you like.'

'Can you tell us what happened between the two of you?' said Baker. 'Anything you can remember could be useful.'

Burridge nodded. 'Like I said it was a long time ago now. She was something else.' He smiled. 'Lovely. Her and the kids. She'd not long left Chris when we first met. She was working in a hotel and I was doing some agency work there. I'd not long been made redundant, my dad had died and left me some money and I was working out what I wanted to do with the rest of my life. Anyway we chatted and eventually I asked her out. Friends at first, mainly because she was worried about upsetting Chris. We got on really well. Chris was giving her a lot of grief and I'd got a contract coming up in Manchester so I said why didn't she and the kids come up there with me.' He frowned. 'It was just platonic then – although it changed.' Ray pulled a face. 'I'm not sure about the order of all this now, like I said it was a long time ago. She came up and stayed with me. I remember that there seemed to be a lot of to-ing and fro-ing, and then we all went out to Spain for a holiday and found the bar and we started making plans to move over there and make it permanent. Linda was really up for it, then Chris starts all this *I want you back, I can change, please for the sake of the kids*, stuff.

'I could see moving to Spain was a big step for Linda.' Ray paused. 'I didn't want to lose her but owning my own place was one of those big dreams I'd always had, you know? So we talked about it and talked about it, and I could see she wasn't ready to go, so I said when she was ready I'd be there. I thought she would come out and bring the kids – I would have laid money on it.'

Ray looked up. 'I rang her a few times after I moved out here, but no one ever answered.'

'And do you know if Linda went back to Chris Hills?' I asked.

He shook his head. 'I don't know. I know she said that he wanted them to have one last go at it, on a trial basis, have a holiday, no strings, just to see if they could sort it out.'

'Do you know where they were going to go on holiday?' Baker asked.

I glanced across at him; I'd have staked a month's wages on the answer.

Ray laughed. 'Yeah. I do. I've never forgotten. She said he was taking her and the kids to Wales. I mean for god's sake. I thought she was joking at first when she said it. You'd think if he was trying to win her back he could do better than that. Linda was a woman who loved the sun, the sea and a bit of nightlife.' He shook his head. 'It was February, who goes to Wales in February, for fuck's sake?'

We wrapped up the conversation with a promise from Ray to send over the photos and let us have the addresses of the flat and the hotel where he and Linda had lived in Manchester, and let us know if anything else came to mind.

Baker glanced across at me.

'We need to take the cottage in Wales apart.'

As we spoke the light on the top of the computer flicked from green to red to let us know the video feed had been cut.

Baker stared at it and then at me, more exactly through me.

'What is it, Sir, are you all right?' I asked.

Baker nodded. 'When I was in the cottage in Wales the place was freezing, I mean bitterly cold inside, the fridge and washing machine had their doors open and the immersion heater was off, but in the cupboard under the stairs the electricity meter was running – there was a red flashing light. I noticed it at the time and it didn't really register.'

I looked at him, watching his mind ticking over.

'What the fuck had Chris Hills got on?' he said. 'There's something on that site using electricity.'

He picked up the phone and began to dial. 'We need to get someone over to the cottage. I missed something. I just hope it's not too bloody late.'

*

It was hard to drag myself away but I was dead tired and realistically there was nothing more I could do. I knew Baker would keep me in the loop if anything changed, so I headed home in darkness, bone tired and hungry.

The temptation was to pick up a curry on the way back to the flat and try to forget about the plans to diet; there was some chicken in the fridge that needed eating up, and probably the makings of a salad – like that would hit the spot. The Curry House was on the way home. The car almost seemed to steer itself into the empty parking space outside. As I got out of the car the mobile rang. I pulled it out of my pocket to check the caller display. It read. 'Kathy'.

I hesitated. Up until a few months ago a call from my sister would be something to look forward to, time to chat and have a catch up, but that was before Jimmy.

I took a deep breath. 'Hi, Kathy, how're you doing?' I said, making the effort to sound cheery and praying that Kathy wouldn't pick up that I was faking it.

'Where are you?' she asked.

'Why, what's the matter?' I said, picking up the tension in her voice.

She sniffed. 'It's Jimmy,' she said. 'I can't find him. He hasn't come home. He's not answering his phone. I'm supposed to be going to late night ladies' swimming tonight. I go every Sunday. He knows that. He said he would be back and he's not.'

I waited, composing myself, trying to remember if I had told him I was coming home. 'Maybe he's working late?'

Chapter Fifteen

'It's Sunday, nearly nine o'clock, Mel.'

'Maybe he had an emergency call out. When did you see him last?'

'About four. He said he was going to pick up some gravel from Andy.'

'Well maybe they got talking, had a beer, you know what boys are like. Have you rung Andy?'

'Of course I did. He was the first person I called. He's not seen him and he didn't know anything about the gravel. And if he was going to be late or something came up why hasn't he rung me?'

'Maybe he lost his phone, maybe the battery is dead. Maybe he left it in his van – c'mon there are a dozen reasons why he's not picking up. Just don't panic. I'm sure he's okay. Do you want me to come round?'

'No.'

'I could mind the kids for you till Jimmy gets back if you like.'

I closed my eyes, what the hell was I saying? The last thing I wanted was to be alone in the house when he came home.

'No, I don't want to go now,' said Kathy. 'I just want Jimmy to come home.'

'I'm sure he'll be home soon.'

'Easy for you to say,' said Kathy. 'And why did he lie to me about the gravel?' Her voice cracked. 'The thing is we had a bit of a row. I mean not anything that major but there's something not right, Mel. I can feel it. It's like he's always somewhere else at the moment. I just said–' her voice finally broke into ragged sobs. 'Oh god, Mel, I think he's seeing someone else.'

I felt something dark and cold tighten in my gut. 'What makes you think that?' I said, as evenly as I could. And what the hell was the right answer?

'I don't know. Just a hunch. He's been pricing a lot of jobs up, after work, so he's been coming home getting himself all spruced up and then going back out again. Anyway, Andy came round to bring some gear over and I heard him and Andy talking about not having a lot of work on. So I said to Jimmy, just casually, haven't any of those jobs firmed up? Mel, I tell you, he gave me such a look, and Andy laughed and said, "What jobs, you moonlighting again, are you?" And then Jimmy made a joke about it, but I know something wasn't right. They both looked like I'd caught them out. So after Andy went I asked Jimmy about it and he flew at me, Mel. He was really angry, said I shouldn't have said anything in front of his boss. So I said, "Are you moonlighting then?" And he wouldn't answer.'

I took a breath. 'Maybe he is moonlighting,' I said. 'Maybe he didn't want Andy to find out.'

'Well there's no more money coming in if that's the case. And also when he was on his own when we first got together, you know, self-employed, and he was out looking at a job he used to take a notebook, write everything down, take the measurements, sketches, contact details all that sort of stuff.'

I waited.

'The thing is he hasn't got one for all this new work.'

'He could be using his phone,' I said.

'To do drawings? I don't think so.' She sounded tired, sad, and disillusioned.

Chapter Fifteen

'So what do you want me to do, Kath, come round there and arrest him for not having a notebook?'

Kathy sighed. 'I don't know, Mel. I was thinking that maybe you could have a word with him. Try and find out what's going on. He likes you.'

I closed my eyes and looked heavenwards. 'Okay,' I said. 'Leave it with me. I'll see what I can do.'

'Thank you,' she said.

I couldn't bear the sound of the gratitude in her voice. I glanced at the Curry House and, no longer hungry, pulled back out into the evening traffic. In the space of a phone call my appetite had vanished.

I pulled out my phone to ring Jimmy, more or less certain that even if he wasn't answering Kath's calls he would most probably answer mine, and then thought better of it. It would be better if I called when I got home, so I had a chance to consider what it was I was going to say.

As I pulled into my road I passed Jimmy's van parked up in a side road and swore under my breath. I hadn't told him I was coming back tonight, had I? I tried to remember what I'd said to him last time we'd spoken when I was in the hotel. I pulled into the parking space feeling a flutter of fury. What made him think I wanted to see him?

For a moment I imagined him waiting outside my door, sitting on the top step, drinking a beer. It wouldn't be the first time. Or maybe he'd let himself in with the spare key I kept taped on the ceiling of my mailbox – I wouldn't put that past him either. I could see him now upstairs, feet up on the sofa flicking through the channels. The last thing I needed was him thinking of my place as a bolthole when he fell out with Kathy. This needed sorting out once and for all.

I tapped in the door code, preparing a speech for Jimmy in my head as I made my way inside and climbed the stairs. As I reached the first landing I heard a voice, a familiar voice, and hung back. From where I was standing I could see my neighbour Fiona's front door and there was Jimmy standing on the threshold, Fiona was there in a robe, tied up but barely. He leaned in to kiss her.

'I'll call you,' he said.

'Be sure you do,' she purred.

I stepped back into the shadows under the stairwell. Jimmy, so full of himself, jogged down the stairs, whistling just under his breath, not once looking in my direction. As I stepped out from the shadows he was out of the front doors and vanishing back into the street.

A second or two later my phone rang. It was Jimmy.

'Hi,' he said. 'Where are you?'

'Why?'

'I've just seen your car.'

'Really,' I said, climbing the stairs and fishing my key out of my pocket. 'How come?'

'I was on my way home and just swung by to see if you were about.'

I laughed.

'What's so funny?' he said, sounding perplexed.

'I was about, Jimmy. I was about at just the right time.'

'What is that supposed to mean?'

'I saw you just now, you bastard. With Fiona on the fucking landing.'

Chapter Fifteen

There was a silence, and then it was Jimmy who laughed. 'What's upsetting you more, Ms Goody Two Shoes, that I'm cheating on your sister or that I'm cheating on you?'

If he had been within range I would have punched him out and then punched the smug self-serving bastard some more; as it was I took a long, slow breath.

'Kathy is far too good for you, you slimy fucker. You disgust me.'

'That wasn't what you said before,' purred Jimmy and with that he hung up before I had time to tell him that she had rung me.

I rested my head against the door frame, feeling my heart banging like a drum in my chest. Inside on the doormat was a postcard of a lean, tiger-striped tabby. I took one look at it and ripped it into tiny pieces before dropping it into the bin.

I stripped my clothes off where I stood, headed for the bathroom, showered till the water in the tank ran cold, and then fell into bed, slipping unexpectedly into a deep, dreamless sleep.

*

It was still dark when the phone rang, for a few seconds I had no idea where I was, and then wondered if the call was from Jimmy, or worse still from Kathy. I'd put nothing past Jimmy. Disorientated, I rolled over and picked up the phone from the bedside table; it was Baker.

'We're going to Wales,' he said. 'I'll pick you up in half an hour.'

I sat bolt upright in bed, instantly awake. 'Have you found Leah?'

'Not yet,' said Baker. 'But they've got a team there, they're taking the place apart.'

Chapter Sixteen

Searching Riverside Cottage

Mist hung across the valley like smoke, obscuring the view of the trees and hills opposite Riverside Cottage and closing it in, cutting it off, making it feel even more isolated than it already was. The forensic team had been working all night.

Baker and I were parked up on the grass, far enough away from the house to ensure we didn't get in the way. Bill Williams, the local sergeant, was there, too, along with a constable in a patrol car, the police pathologist and an unmarked ambulance. A white tent had been erected across the entrance to the garage.

Another police car was parked across the entrance to the lane that led down to the cottage from the main road, cutting it off from Joe Public should he want to drive the mile or so down the lane to see what they were up to. And I guessed that he would.

The story of Leah's disappearance had broken in nationals that morning, after Chris Hills' emotional unscheduled TV appeal, and the subsequent arrest in connection with Amy Cooper had caught the media's attention. The story and Leah's disappearance had made the headlines in most of this morning's papers. A lot of them had the story on the front page and used the shot of Leah from the Garden Centre alongside one of Chris Hills, a still taken from his TV appeal, his face fixed in a snarl, his finger jabbing angrily towards the cameras.

Someone had dug up a wedding photo from somewhere. It was an unflattering photo, which highlighted the age difference between them so much that I had found it hard to look at without wondering why someone close to Leah hadn't stepped in or said something. Chris looked more like her father than her husband. He was smiling, leering almost, while she looked whey-faced and lost despite her smile. Chris Hills had his arm round her in a clumsy, proprietorial embrace. Looking at the grainy print that we'd been sent I couldn't help think about Amy Cooper and the other girls that he had tutored.

'Child abuse monster's wife vanishes' read the headline in one of the tabloids, which was almost inevitable given the offences Chris Hills had already been charged with. But they didn't know the half of it, not yet. I just hoped that the search for Leah wouldn't get lost in the maelstrom.

Officers who had responded to the call from Baker the night before had gone back to the cottage on the river. The light was still flashing on the electricity meter in the hall cupboard and with a bit of savvy and a search round the outside of the house they had come across a cable that came out of the back wall of the kitchen and vanished under the hardcore and granite chippings between the bungalow and the garage.

Chapter Sixteen

A search of the outside had shown no signs of any electrical appliance that might be burning juice and so they had broken into the garage. A first pass had shown up nothing and then one of the constables had found a door concealed in the tongue and groove wall at the rear of the garage, the opening barely visible amongst the upright lines of the painted wood and hanging tools. It was locked, the handle and keyhole concealed by a sieve.

Conscious that Leah was still missing and at risk, they had found a pry bar and jimmied open the door. What confronted them was a kill room, lined floor to ceiling with polythene, a row of hooks set into the roof joists, and against the back wall a commercial chest freezer, wired into the mains, and padlocked shut.

At that point they had retreated and called in the cavalry. The local SOCO team had been working all night.

*

Bill Williams, the local sergeant, got out of his car and headed over to our vehicle, which was parked up a hundred yards or so away from Riverside Cottage. Baker stretched and made as if to get out. 'C'mon, Daley let me introduce you to the natives,' he said.

The warmth of the car hadn't prepared me for the dank, wet chill of a Wales morning, although this time I had come prepared and brought gloves and a hat. I glanced out of the windows as figures in white, all-in-one suits moved backwards and forwards in the arc lights set up in the house and garage.

'Inviting, isn't it?' said Baker, buttoning up his jacket.

Bill Williams looked grave, and from the hint of stubble on his broad, open face hadn't been home all night.

'Can we go inside?' Baker asked.

Williams nodded.

Flat, rubberised metal plates like stepping stones had been set down by the forensic team so that everyone came in and out by the same route, which lessened the risk of any forensic evidence being compromised. Floodlights had been set up to illuminate what seemed like every corner of the site.

The stepping plates led across the yard, in through the double doors, and down the length of the garage, guiding us towards a narrow, open door. The glow from the doorway, framed by painted wood panelling and racks of tools, was an intense, unforgiving white.

I followed Baker inside, stepping in his footsteps. As we got closer I noticed that some of the hooks on the partition wall were empty, their outline on the painted wood suggesting most were bladed tools, which SOCO had presumably already bagged and tagged and taken away for analysis.

Baker and I both stopped at the doorway. Inside, the SOCO team's white lights standing on metal tripods and revealing a room around eight feet deep by twelve feet wide lit the concealed space. The floor was covered with thick polythene sheeting that had been meticulously taped down around the edges, similar material hung from the ceiling in overlapping curtains fixed on rings onto long metal poles. Behind the polythene, the walls were painted white. In the ceiling, across one of the joists were a row of hooks. The whole place reeked of bleach, so pungent that it made my eyes sting. In the centre of the room, protected by the polythene, was a large grating, covered with a fine mesh screen, presumably leading into a drain, while against the far wall was a large chest freezer, now open.

One of the senior SOCO team, Ena Lowering, looked up at us. She was covered from head to foot in a white, protective tyvek suit and was gloved and masked.

'This was what was draining the power,' she said, nodding towards the freezer. 'Turned right up to fast freeze; it'll chunk through the power. Specially running it on empty.'

'It's empty?'

Ena nodded.

'So have you got *anything*?' asked Baker.

Lowering stretched and eased her back. 'So far nothing.'

Neither of us said a word. I didn't want to find Leah in the freezer, I didn't want her to be dead, but every fibre of my body told me she was.

Baker glanced round the room. 'Did you cover the floor?'

'Do I look like I've got time to redecorate?' asked Lowering, grimly. 'No, the whole thing was like it when we got here. Floor, walls, all covered.' She stepped back a little and pointed to the wall behind the freezer. 'There was a stainless steel worktop and trestles stored behind here. We're going over it now for any trace but it's mostly bleach and more bleach.'

Baker sniffed. 'Tidy worker?' he said.

'Forensically aware is the phrase you're looking for. But whatever is here, don't worry, we'll find it. And you'll have more when I know more.'

'Thanks,' said Baker.

'Once I've finished with the freezer and the rest of the room, we'll cut through to the drain cover. Hopefully we can find something there. He might be good but we're better.'

Baker nodded. 'Anything else?'

Lowering pulled a face. 'I'm going to complain to whoever designed the chest freezer. My back is killing me.'

We went back outside; there was nothing Baker or I could do in the garage other than get in the way. I think we both knew that the answers were there, we just had to find them.

'Come on,' said Baker. 'Let's take another look around.'

'Get the lie of the land?' I suggested.

Baker snorted.

The place was as bleak and damp and uninviting as Baker's earlier report. A second SOCO team were at work in the house so all we could do was wait.

While Baker discussed the current strategy with Sergeant Williams and patched a call in to Rees and the search teams, I took a look around the garden. The mist hung in ribbons above the river, the banks on both sides were heavy with frost and water droplets that caught what little light there was. Trees, underplanted with snowdrops, the only flowers to brave the weather, framed the far side of the house. The snowdrops were clumped under each tree, creating little pools of light, nodding in the breeze.

I pulled out my phone and scrolled down to Kath's number. I hadn't called her since seeing Jimmy the night before, mainly because I was afraid that, being so angry I might say something I would live to regret. Calmer now, I needed to know that she was all right and – after Baker's early morning call – this was the first chance I'd had to ring her.

Kathy answered after the third ring. 'Yes?' she snapped.

'I just called to see if you were all right.'

'Right,' she said. 'Like you would fucking care.' And hung up.

I called straight back but the line was engaged and her mobile went straight to voicemail. Jimmy's phone too. Not good.

*

The day went slowly. The local force brought up a caravan to use as an incident room, and the team from the forensic unit worked the garage, the woodshed and the bungalow inch by painstaking inch, photographing, bagging and tagging as they went. It was slow work and after hours of searching there was nothing obvious to show for their efforts other than a growing pile of evidence bags.

I wondered if we wouldn't be serving Leah better by going back to the station and carrying on the search through the CCTV and phone calls, but it was Baker's shout and he liked to be close to the action, and today the action was at Chris Hills' holiday cottage.

The hours dragged, and try as I might to concentrate, my mind kept being pulled back to Jimmy and Kath. I wondered what the hell he had said or done.

As the day cleared, a helicopter passed low overhead, almost undoubtedly manned by a news crew looking for an exclusive.

I took another look around, watching SOCOs move around the place like ghosts, wondering if I ought to suggest to Baker that we go back to the office.

As I stood in the sunshine, thinking about Jimmy and Kath rather than Leah Hills, something caught my eye. In the sun by the woodshed was a plastic flowerpot full of snowdrops, with the plant label still stuck into the compost. I had to have walked past it before but it was the first time I'd really noticed it. It was one of the few things that SOCO hadn't carried off yet, and it looked incongruous and out of place tucked away out of the wind in the lee of the woodshed.

The first flowers of spring, so much at odds with the events of the day. They are one of my favourites and for a second or two I wondered who had put them there before realising that it had to have been Chris Hills. But why leave them there, out in the open? Why not plant them along with the others?

I looked up, partly to try and work out where else he could have left them and partly to try and work out his mindset. I bent down to take a look but didn't touch them and then walked round the bungalow one more time to check if I was right, trying to get my thoughts in order before hurrying back towards the temporary incident room that the local force had brought on site.

'Excuse me, Sir,' I said, as I opened the door.

Baker looked up from a computer screen set up on a desk that he was sharing with Bill Williams. 'What is it, Daley?'

'The snowdrops.'

Baker stared at me. 'What about them?'

'There's a pot of them standing by the woodshed. They can't have been there that long or they would have dried out. Hills had to have brought it with him the last time he was here. I've just looked at the label. They came from Charlotte's Garden, where Leah worked. He must have brought them here from Norfolk. He said that this was the first trip they had made together this year.'

Baker pulled a face. 'I'm not seeing the connection, Daley.'

'Why bring snowdrops with you when they've got them in the garden already? Chris Hills could have easily split a clump. And why leave them there when he could have easily put them in the garden with the others? There are four clumps in the front garden planted under the conifers. You can see them from the pathway. You can see them from the front of the house. They're the only flowers in the whole garden.'

Baker stared at me. 'Who brings anyone to Wales in February?'

He was quoting Ray Burridge. I nodded.

Baker was on his feet. 'We need to get ground penetrating radar in–'

Bill Williams stood up. 'Wouldn't it be easier just to dig? We've got the manpower available and with this terrace the ground here can't be more than three or four feet deep. GPR might not be able to pick anything up with all this bedrock.'

Baker nodded. 'Okay, I need to talk to Ena.'

We went back out into the cold, damp, wet Wales morning. The snowdrops under the contorted conifers fluttered on the edge of the spring breeze. I pulled my coat tight around me and made my way across to the trees, as I did my phone rang. It was Jimmy. I rejected the call and followed Baker across the garden.

Searching Riverside Cottage

*

The team brought in a tent to cover the first grave, which contained the bones of a tall, slightly built woman, who the police pathologist placed in her mid to late twenties. The teams worked all night to excavate the other three areas – in the second grave were the scant remains of a child between six and eight, in the third was one aged around four and in the last, the tiny, heartbreakingly fragile, paper-thin bones of a toddler.

The finds quietened the site to a hush, people spoke in whispers and the sense of tragedy and loss seemed to hang in the air with the mist that cloaked the valley.

There was no evidence, no solid proof but neither Baker nor I had any doubts that we had found Linda Hills and her children.

Finally, Baker and I made our way back to the car.

As I unlocked it I turned to DI Baker. 'Do you think those snowdrops were meant for Leah?'

Baker pulled a face. 'If so, where is she? If he buried her with the others then we'd have found her. Maybe he killed her elsewhere and intended to pick her body up and bring her here later, but if that's the case why report her missing in the first place? Why attract our attention? Why not just bring her here? It makes no sense.'

When we got back to the station I looked at my phone. There were sixteen messages, all of them, bar one, from Kathy.

*

Less than a week after reporting his wife missing, Chris Hills confessed to and was charged with the murder of Linda Hills and his children at Riverview Cottage sometime in late February 1990. But despite continued questioning he refused to tell us what he had done with Leah. Teams of officers and volunteers searched verges and barns, derelict houses and dykes within miles of the motorway, Hoden Gap and the cottage in Wales and found nothing, not a trace.

We all had our own ideas about what he had done with her, including a theory that he had hidden her somewhere, perhaps still alive and was withholding the information until he was sure she was dead. I didn't want to contemplate what that would be like.

Almost every police officer has cases that haunt them; the man we couldn't convict because we couldn't find the evidence, the child not found, the murderer not put away or caught. And I had a hunch even as I was heading back to the office that day after we found Linda and the children's bodies that Leah Hills was going to be mine.

As days and then weeks passed we carried on looking for Leah as we built the case against Chris for the murder of his first wife and children. We carried on looking during the long months while Hills was held on remand, and even after Kath caught Jimmy in bed with my nextdoor neighbour when she came round to confront me about flirting with her Jimmy – his story.

We carried on, on the day that Jimmy, contrite and desperate for absolution told Kath that my nextdoor neighbour wasn't the only one, and even on the day when I applied for a transfer to join the Norfolk Police force to get away from Jimmy and Kathy, on the day when he started to believe that confession was good for the soul. I knew it was only a matter of time before he told her about me. But even then I never gave up on Leah.

By then it seemed like the trail had grown cold. The manpower had been slowly reduced and cut back to a bare minimum, despite the fact that the case was constantly reviewed and any new information logged. But we couldn't close the file on Leah; until she was found or was declared dead, she remained a missing person.

Which was why, eight or nine months after Leah vanished, I was sitting at my desk sifting through the boxes of files and reports that related to the Leah Hills case, going through the computer record, taking one last look, a swan song that I had volunteered for before packing up and leaving for Denham Market. Busy work really, as Baker couldn't assign me to a current case as we didn't know exactly when the transfer would be completed.

In the months since Leah had vanished I had been through the case file time and again until I could practically recite it word for word, so in the review process I made a point of constantly broadening my search. The truth of it, the science of it is that Leah Hills had to be somewhere.

Going through traffic reports for the day she disappeared I found stills of Chris Hills' car on the motorway as he made his way through road works with an average speed limit section on the M6. I remembered it, driving to and from the service station in the pouring rain the day she had vanished.

At the end of the file someone had downloaded a list of fines issued for speeding on that section of road on the day of Leah's disappearance, along with registration numbers and corresponding names.

Looking back I have no idea what it was that made me read through them but as I did, my gaze idling down over the list, one name caught my attention and knocked the breath out of my chest.

In the early hours of Thursday morning a white Mercedes van registered to Elise Strawson had been caught in an average speed trap on a stretch of road works on the M6.

Elise Strawson, the name was like a splinter that caught in my flesh. What were the chances of someone called Elise Strawson, Leah Hills' only friend, being on the M6 on the day Leah vanished? Elise Strawson who had died eighteen months before Leah had disappeared? It was too much of a coincidence.

I pulled the details from the database and within minutes had traced Elise Strawson back to an address in Denham Market, and pulled up the records from the DVLA. The vehicle, a white Mercedes van, had been bought and registered two months prior to Leah's disappearance, bought by and registered to a dead woman. I couldn't believe that someone hadn't picked it up before.

For a moment I sat very, very still staring at the information on the screen, then went back over the detail to reassure myself that I hadn't imagined it. The penalty fine was still outstanding, marked unpaid, as Elise Strawson no longer lived at the registered address and the DVLA had been unable to trace her.

With a registration number, a vehicle and a name I began a new search for Leah Hills. At 04.45 am on the morning of Leah's disappearance Elise Strawson's anonymous white panel van had been caught on camera less than a mile from Hoden Gap Services and at just before eight it had been caught on camera on the M4 heading towards Swansea.

With a name and address there was a chance we could chase the financials. Someone had to have bought the van with real money, someone taxed and insured it, someone was driving it.

I picked up the phone and called Sheila Hastings, the woman who had worked the original CCTV footage.

'I've got something I need you to look at,' I said, my gaze fixed on a still image of a white van on the M4. 'It's from the Leah Hills' case.'

It was mid afternoon when Sheila Hastings rang back. 'Can you come down?' she said. 'I've got something I think you might like to take a look at.'

Chapter Seventeen

The Woman in the Camel Coat

'So,' I said, sliding into a chair alongside Sheila Hastings. 'What have you got?'

'Well, not your white van for a start. I've checked from when it was within a few miles of Hoden Gap to when it shows up on the way to Swansea. It wasn't picked up by the plate recognition cameras at the service station and you know as well as I do if it didn't come in to the service area then we didn't track the vehicle or the driver.'

As part of the operation to trace Leah and to eliminate possible abduction we had contacted every driver who had passed through Hoden Gap Services on the day she had vanished.

I frowned. 'Bugger. So what have you called me down for?'

Sheila smiled, and clicked onto the security camera footage from the entrance foyer of the service station. 'I want to show you something. Something has always bugged me about the Leah Hills case. I've been through this footage dozens of times trying to find other angles.'

I glanced at the screen. 'Is that Chris Hills?'

Sheila nodded. 'That's him coming in to get his coffee.'

'Still no sign of Leah?'

'Well –' Sheila pulled a face. 'I kept thinking about Chris Hills. In his statement he said he saw her go into the service area. He was absolutely certain.'

I nodded. 'It wouldn't be the only thing he's lied about.'

Sheila nodded. 'That is true. But that look on his face when he caught up with the woman who he thought was Leah, nothing about that struck me as fake or staged. Well, that's the thing. After you rang I pulled the stills photos of Chris Hills' car in the car park. I was trying to check on what he could see and what he couldn't. It's been a while since I've been through this stuff, so I suppose I've come to it with fresh eyes. Here – tell me what you see.'

She clicked on an image that had been taken outside during the morning of Leah's disappearance, before Hills' car had been taken away.

'Chris Hills' car parked outside the doors of the food court?'

She nodded. 'Right, but if you look – either side of the automatic doors there is a manual door, presumably a failsafe if the main doors fail. The picture's not great; I didn't notice before.' Sheila pulled up a film file, now showing footage from inside the service station foyer aimed towards the main entrance doors, which we had both viewed dozens of times.

'So we've got the main automatic doors here, front and centre,' said Sheila, pointing with a pencil. 'And then this is the manual door on our right as we look into the car park here. But the camera doesn't pick up the one on the left at all. I don't know how I missed it. I suppose we assumed Leah would be on the screen if she was there, that she would just be there, be obvious – and I've looked at this footage hundreds of times. Anyway…' Sheila let the film run forward a frame or two. 'Can you see that disturbance in the top left-hand corner?'

I stared at the footage. In the top left of the screen there was an intermittent flutter, barely noticeable unless you were really looking for it.

'From looking at the right-hand side door I'm pretty much certain that that's the top of the left-hand side door when someone opens it fully, so the camera just about registers the door opening, but not who comes through. And if you stayed tight into that wall on the left, you wouldn't be seen. The camera only covers three doors and maybe the first fifteen feet of the foyer, so once you're past them you're inside and home free.'

'You're sure about that?' I stared at her.

Sheila nodded. 'Pretty much, although you might want to get someone to go there and try it out. Someone small, slightly built.'

'Someone like Leah Hills?'

Sheila nodded.

'But who would know that?' I said, watching the film as another flutter registered on the screen.

'The staff possibly,' said Sheila with a grim expression, clicking onto another still photo. 'There is a bank of CCTV

monitors situated slap bang in the entrance hall. I found
photos of them on file and rang the office at Hoden to verify
what they show. I'm assuming that they're meant to give the
punters a sense of security, because they're also fed into the
security office, but I reckon ten minutes with a coffee browsing
the papers and you could work out where the blind spots are.
The only thing you can see in all the footage we've got is the
very tip of an umbrella – which suggests in order to register
you'd need to be over six foot six'

'So Leah Hills could have got in and out without being
seen?'

Sheila Hastings nodded. 'It is possible, if she knew where
the blind spots were, but it would have to have been very deliberate.' Sheila ran the film through a bit further. 'If the left
and right side of the foyer are the same size the blind spot is
about two foot six at the widest place. You would have to walk
sideways to ensure you weren't picked up by the camera.'

'That's possible, she is small. So are we saying that Leah
Hills *was* at Hoden Gap?'

'I can't swear to it.'

'So what *are* you saying?'

'That we can't be certain, but that there is a way Leah
could have gone into the service area and not been seen. So
there is a chance that Chris Hills was telling the truth. But
there's something else I want you to see. Let me show you
this.' Hastings glanced down at a pad on her desk listing a
variety of time stamps, and then flicked through to another
CCTV recording. 'Here we are in the foyer: 05.21. See that
woman there?'

Chapter Seventeen

I shifted focus to pick out the figure Sheila was pointing to. The woman was dressed in a heavily padded black duvet jacket and had a baseball cap pulled down tight on her head that obscured her face.

'We can follow her as she makes no effort to conceal her arrival. Now here we are, this is a couple of minutes later.' Sheila flicked between screens. This time there was the footage from inside the burger bar overlooking the main foyer, although the camera's range didn't extend to giving them a view through the windows.

'What am I looking at, Sheila?' I asked.

'Same woman, see?'

The woman had her back to the camera and was busy buying a coffee, and cakes from a cold cabinet. The server put them in a box for her. The woman had a newspaper tucked under one arm and a rucksack slung over one shoulder. She didn't look at the CCTV.

'Now watch what she does,' said Sheila. 'All the tables have been cleared and wiped down except for that one.' She pointed. 'And yet that's the one she decides to sit at. And notice she makes no effort to clear the table either.'

'Maybe she likes a bit of a mess,' I said, eyes fixed on the screen.

Sheila nodded, working the mouse so the image was as clear as possible. 'Or maybe that's the one with an uninterrupted view of the front doors to the service area and the only table in the place where unless you look up you can't be seen on CCTV. She sits there for well over an hour nursing a coffee and reading the paper, but can you see – it's even more obvious when I fast forward it – how she keeps glancing up at the window as if she is watching and then at 06.49 she gets up, leaves her paper and walks out.'

'Getting a lift? Needing the loo. Bored rigid,' I said, wondering where this was leading.

'Her coffee is still half full and stone cold I'd imagine,' said Sheila. 'And she's left the cakes on the chair. Just take a look at the bag she's carrying.'

I did as I was told. The rucksack was tightly packed, full, and looked heavy, the fabric pulled tight over the seams.

'Do we see where she goes after the burger bar?'

'Looks like towards the women's toilets.'

'And then?'

'Just keep watching.' Sheila fast forwarded through more interior footage of the café. 'If we go back to the café a little while later.' She clicked between screens. 'Here we are. You can see a woman, now in a long coat, going back in to pick the cake box up. I'm certain it's the same woman, same build, same walk, same stance, same rucksack.'

I stared at the image as the woman picked the cake box up; as she turned she held up her hand to thank the man behind the counter, not that he was looking. There was something familiar about her, something that rang a bell, although it was nothing I could put into words.

'Bear with me.' Sheila glanced at another time stamp she had written down on a pad beside her, and found the piece of footage in another file. 'Here we are. Here she is in plain view heading towards the exit.'

Chapter Seventeen

'In the camel coat,' I said, leaning forward, willing the woman to turn round. The woman wasn't walking fast but her sense of purpose was obvious as she headed towards the exit, her head down, the strap of a rucksack clearly visible over her shoulder.

'The thing is as you know we can't find any footage of anyone coming in, in a camel coat. And I've been through hours and hours of footage.'

'Unless they were in the blind spot?'

'Unless they were in the blind spot,' Sheila repeated. 'Here, she is nearly at the doors.'

'Which was when Chris Hills mistook her for Leah,' I said, somewhat unnecessarily. On screen there was an altercation as a man – Chris Hills – swept in from the side and grabbed the woman in the camel coat by the arm. The image clearly showed her swing round with her fist clenched almost as if she intended to punch him.

'If you look she's still got the cake box,' said Sheila.

I nodded. 'And even when he grabs hold of her she keeps her chin down and her face away from the camera. She definitely doesn't want to be seen.'

And then as she shook off Chris Hills, the woman turned a fraction and adjusted her bag. 'There,' said Sheila. 'Look at the bag.'

I narrowed my eyes trying to pick out the details of her bag and her face. From the CCTV it was obvious that it was the same bag, but now far from full. 'Okay, so where does our mystery woman go after she exits the food court.'

'Well that's the thing. You know the service station had a series of break-ins last year and they moved a lot of the cameras to cover the back doors of the food court, which was where the thieves got in.'

'Are you saying all that is linked with Leah's disappearance?'

'No, not at all, they caught the lads who did it, couple of locals who saw themselves as *gangstas*. No, what that means is that there was really good coverage for the back doors and service doors, and great coverage for the HGV bays at the back, and then great big dead zones. After all they've got the numbers and cars coming in and out, doors in and out and round the back; the management probably feel they've got the best coverage they can get with the cameras available.'

'And so you're saying our woman in the camel coat slipped into one of the dead zones. Are we sure that woman,' I stabbed my finger towards the image on the screen, 'is definitely not Leah Hills.'

'Chris Hills said she wasn't his wife.'

I nodded. 'I suppose that's about as good as it gets, but that also means that if she knew where the cameras were then maybe Leah Hills did, too.'

I stared at the screen for a few seconds more, trying to work out what it was about the woman in the camel coat that triggered some kind of memory.

Sheila glanced up at me. 'There's something else,' she said in a low voice. 'I can't be certain about this, it's purely speculation, but I think there is a chance I might have found Leah Hills.'

I stared at her. 'Seriously?'

She nodded. I waited.

She scrolled the footage back, back before Chris Hills was grabbing the woman's arm. Back when he was on the phone trying to call his wife on a phone that had been left hidden in Norfolk, back to an instant where he appeared on the screen, looking desperate, clutching his phone to his ear. The image was so compelling it was hard to look anywhere else in the frame but there, off to his left, about to vanish back into the blind spot was someone dressed in jeans and boots and a heavily padded black duvet jacket that looked too big for her, the same style as the woman in the café had been wearing with the same baseball cap pulled down hard on her head, only this time there was a long ponytail of dark hair protruding from under the backstrap. The woman was looking back, just a fraction, as if attracted by something behind her.

Sheila Hastings zoomed in as far as she could before the image pixelated. I leaned in closer too. It was impossible to be sure but I nodded. 'I think you might be right,' I said in an undertone. 'They swapped coats. I think that's Leah Hills. I think she is alive.'

Chapter Eighteen

Finding Elise Strawson

The brightness of the daylight took me by surprise as I drove off The Swift in Dublin. The crossing on the catamaran had been smooth as silk and taken me less than two hours from Anglesey.

I stopped to fill up with fuel and grab a coffee at the service station not far from the quayside, and as I paid for it looked round at the anonymous faces, the straggle of people coming in and out, most in transit, finding myself unconsciously looking for someone familiar in amongst the crowd.

The moment and the sensation were not lost on me. I had spent months looking for Leah Hills' face in the crowd. I took my coffee from the guy behind the counter, paid for my diesel and then headed west.

The motorway out of the city was broad, busy and looked new, though I had been warned by colleagues that the multiple lanes leading out of the city were a way of lulling travellers into a false sense of security. Turn off the main drag and you were back onto narrow roads, barely more than lanes, all ruts, bumps, no white lines and lord only knows what, coming the other way.

Although at least on the local roads they weren't ripping you off with a toll charge every half mile, I thought grimly, handing over another handful of euros to a smiling Irishman in a bright shiny new toll booth. From the cheeriness of his demeanour I wondered if he was on commission.

I made my way out along the M6, through to Galway, the hills welcome after the flat peat bogs and rolling plains that had flanked the road for mile after mile in the country's centre. I was even pleased, at least for the first few miles as I turned off the motorway, for the change of pace, driving on criminally poor roads, through colourful busy little towns, with strings of empty bungalows on their outskirts, built in the boom and now left high and dry by the financial crash and the recession.

By early afternoon I had made it to Clifden and stopped long enough to stretch my legs, buy a sandwich and visit the loo, but not too long – there was a feeling of eagerness that I hadn't expected because I knew I was so close now, so very close to getting answers to all the questions that had bugged me since Leah vanished. It was another forty minutes' drive before I finally reached the place I was looking for.

Nearly five hours out of Dublin, the cottage was perched on a narrow rocky headland with a view out to Omey Island over a stretch of beach so white and a sea so blue it could have easily been taken for the Caribbean rather than the Atlantic. I slowed down to take the last bend and admired the scenery; who wouldn't want to live there? It reminded me of the watercolour I had seen pinned above the bench in Leah Hills' studio.

The cottage sat at the end of a narrow trackway, a single lane covered in chippings that crackled and spat under the wheels of my car. I parked up on the grass behind a little silver estate car with Galway plates, got out and stretched, trying to ignore the ache in my back and the stiffness in my legs.

The woman who owned the house had been expecting me, and opened the door as soon as I got out of the car. Framed in the doorway she looked tiny and far younger than in the photos I had seen, her hair cut short and spikey and dyed white blonde, although there was no mistaking who she was. Leah Hills watched me walking up the path, her expression guarded and closed.

As I got to the front step. I pulled out my warrant card. 'DS Mel Daley,' I said. 'We spoke on the phone?'

Leah nodded.

'You better come in,' she said, waving me into the darkness of a tiny hallway hung with coats and strewn with boots, shoes and walking gear. 'Come on through, you'll have to excuse the mess. I'm not much of a one for company.'

I followed her inside, eyes adjusting to the gloom.

I wasn't ready for the view when Leah guided me through into the main room of the house, part kitchen, part sitting room, part studio, with a covered easel standing by a table covered with paints, a palette and jars of brushes. A huge triple-glazed window filled the whole of the end wall of the room, giving a view of the Atlantic, framing the sea, and the blue of the sky cut with the odd scudding clouds, as effectively as any oil painting.

The room was warm and comfortable, littered with the detritus of everyday living, and in a basket by the range a huge brown and white mongrel slapped his tail against the tiles in welcome.

'Tea?' asked Leah, indicating the kettle.

I nodded. 'I wouldn't mind. It's been a bit of a haul.'

'I remember. Please, sit down if you want to. Make yourself at home.'

'Thanks, but I think I'll stand for a few minutes, get the kinks out after all the driving.'

Leah nodded and slid the kettle onto the stove.

I watched her intently, impressed by how still she was, how unflustered by my arrival, although I could see the wariness in her eyes.

'You've got a fabulous spot here,' I said, nodding towards the bay and the beach.

Leah smiled for the first time since she had waited for me by the door. 'It's amazing, isn't it? I am so lucky to have found it. It's heaven.'

After a moment or two I pulled out a seat at the table and settled down to let my gaze and attention rest on the view, enjoying the sense of calm, while Leah found mugs and milk. It was a view that you would never tire of, I thought. Neither of us spoke again until the tea was brewed and poured.

I took the mug Leah offered me. 'So how did you find it, Leah? The house, this place?'

'The internet,' she said, casually. 'We looked for months, and it's Elise now, if you don't mind.'

I took a sip of tea. 'Elise Strawson?'

Leah nodded. 'I like it that I have her name. It's like she is still alive, still here with me. Sharing it. It's the only gift I can give her after all the things she did for me; she gave me so much. She let me have a glimpse of what life could be like without him – and then she gave me another life.' Leah paused, her fingers laced around the mug. 'What happens now?'

I looked back out at the ocean. 'We won't tell your husband where you are, if that's what you want, but we do have an obligation to let him know that you're safe and well.'

Leah tipped her face towards me and laughed. 'Oh he will hate that. You have no idea. What concerns me is that if you can find me then there is a chance that he will, too.'

I nodded. 'I can understand that, but rest assured he won't find out from us. And there are other things on his mind at the moment. But I guess you already know that? Do you get the British news over here?'

Leah nodded and sat down on a stool by the kitchen table. 'On the internet.'

'He'll be going to prison for a long time for what he did to Linda and the children.'

Leah nodded. 'I'm glad.'

There was no malice in her voice just a sense of relief. 'So, what *are* you here for?' she said.

'We have to make sure you're all right, and not at risk.'

'Well I am all right and the only risk is from you. Can I ask how you found me?'

Chapter Eighteen

'First of all on the day you disappeared a van was caught in an average speed trap on the motorway; the van was registered to Elise Strawson. I'd interviewed your boss at the garden centre – so when I finally I saw it, the name rang a bell and once we had a name as well as the van, it was like a key.' I paused and took another sip of tea. 'And then I went back to your financial records, back a lot further than we had when we thought you had just vanished, and I followed the money. The money that you'd inherited from Elise, and that you had transferred from your account over to Ireland into an account in the name of Ms Elise Strawson, which was odd given Elise was already dead.'

Leah reddened. 'I'd thought about bringing cash over but I wasn't sure if the Irish bank would be suspicious.' She smiled. 'I know better now. They'd not have noticed, or cared.'

I smiled. 'Like I said, once we had a name it made things a lot easier. We found the van, and the ferry tickets.'

Leah nodded. 'I thought about coming across as a walk-on but there were things I wanted to bring with me. I put it in an auction as soon as I was settled.'

'And then we found a payment made to a surveyor who came out to survey the cottage.'

Leah looked up at me and sighed. 'You make it sound so easy. Are you saying that I'm not safe anywhere?'

'I think you're safe here. I can assure you that we won't tell Chris where you are.'

Leah flinched. 'You know I can't even bear the sound of his name.' She looked out over the sea, her eyes fixed on the middle distance. 'He would never have let me go, you know that, don't you? He told me. He said he couldn't live without me. That he would rather die than see me go. He used to say it would kill him if I ever went.' She paused.

'He would cut himself, deep, deep cuts so the blood would drip out of him, and I'd beg him to stop, I'd promise him anything, and then later I wondered what he might do to *me* if I ever truly wanted to go. By then of course I knew what I'd got myself into, and I couldn't find a way out.'

I stayed still, cradling my tea, waiting for Leah to continue. I wanted to know everything and I knew that she wanted to tell me.

'Elise found the cottage for us, she said it would be perfect. That was when we both thought there was a chance there would be the two of us here together. She'd got it all planned. While she was still well enough to travel she came over and took a look around at half a dozen places, but she said right from the beginning that she knew this was the one.

'While she was over here she sorted out a bank account, all that sort of stuff. I hadn't realised how hard it must have been for her to travel till I did it. God knows how she managed. We'd got it all planned.'

'You were going to come here with Elise?'

'Yes, although it seemed like a dream really, by then we both knew she wouldn't last that long, but we kept talking about it, planning it. I'm sure it was what kept her going. We both knew her cancer was terminal but she said I should do it anyway. I couldn't see how, and then she told me about the money. She hadn't got anyone else to leave it to, she said. I did say she shouldn't leave it to me, but she said the only alternatives were the taxman or a cats' home. My choice, me or some mangy moggy. Typical Elise.

'So we used her address for everything, which made it simple enough, and then when she was gone, I sold the house and set up a post office box in Cambridge in Elise's name, and got all the post redirected there. It's got a proper address and everything, they just held it for me till I could get in to pick it up. I could get there and back on the train while Chris was at work.'

I nodded. 'And now they send it here?' I said.

Leah shook head. 'God no, I closed it. I was worried Chris might be able track me down if I left it open. Tell them some cock and bull story. He was good at that.'

She glanced out the window, her eyes bright with unshed tears. 'I just wish that Elise could have been here, too. I miss her so much. Every day. We made so many plans over the years about how we could make a new start together, just the two of us.'

'How did you manage to get the time to do it? I get the impression that your husband never took his eyes off you?'

'He didn't, but where there's a will; Elise and I had been friends since I started at her dad's flower shop in town as a trainee. Chris worked away a lot of the time then and he was worried about me being in the house on my own, a few times he took me with him to hotels and things, but I think I cramped his style. I'm not sure how it came about really now, who suggested it, but I started to stay with Elise and her dad on the nights he was on the road. Her dad wasn't well, they had carers in – he was on oxygen, barely able to get out of bed.'

'And Chris didn't mind?'

'No, he didn't see Elise as any kind of threat. She could come across as shy, you know – a bit of a mouse if you didn't know her, and she was stuck at home looking after her dad, given up a lot to care for him. But I think I recognised a kindred spirit straight away. And she certainly recognised Chris for what he was.'

'How long were you friends?' I asked.

Leah smiled 'I'm not sure, twenty years, probably more.'

'And then you worked together at the garden centre?'

'Yes, and like I said at the florists in town that her dad used to own.' Leah looked up. 'When he finally died Elise sold up. He'd got four shops and ran a gardening service and at the end she was managing them all, as well as taking care of him at home. She didn't want anything to do with any of them once he was gone. So we both applied to go to Charlotte's Garden.'

'And carried on working together?'

Leah nodded. 'Her dad was a bully, controlling, abusive – but everyone else always thought he was such a loving man, the life and soul. Just like Chris in lots of ways. When he died her dad left her everything – the house, money, his business. She didn't really have to work, she just liked it. Elise told me how he used to beat her mum and how she would hide under her bed, terrified that he would come for her. Of course he did in the end, but she always felt she had let her mother down by not standing up to him. I'm sure that's why she wanted to help me. She wanted us to run away together within weeks of us meeting, but I couldn't do it back then, I just wasn't brave enough. But we talked about it all the time. Planning, imagining what it might be like to be free, but I always knew that Chris would come after us. He would never let me go. So Elise and I just stayed friends. All those years. All those years we could have had together.' A tear rolled down her cheek unhindered.

'Friends?' I said gently.

'Up until Elise I'd only ever been with Chris. I didn't know anything could be so lovely, so gentle.' Her voice cracked. 'She truly loved me. Real love. That's my one huge regret that we hadn't done this sooner. I keep thinking now that there had to have been a way.'

'Elise was diagnosed with ovarian cancer?'

Leah nodded, sniffing back more tears. 'Yes. By the time she was diagnosed it was more or less too late, although that isn't what either of us wanted to believe. And that was when she really started to plan. Proper plans. You should have met her, she was such a powerhouse – and she wouldn't take no for an answer. It was as if by helping me she was helping herself to escape.'

'The passport, learning to drive?'

'All her idea, though I didn't say no. You have to understand we had the time to plan, and both of us knew that we couldn't leave anything to chance. She made me promise that once she was gone that I'd do it – that I'd really go.'

'And so you have a passport and driving license in Elise's name?'

'We looked vaguely similar, about the same age, so while she was still living at her house in Garret Road we filled in an application with her name and my photo. We used her documents, birth certificate, utility bills. Then we had a couple of the customers in the shop sign the pictures on the passport application as a valid likeness. They never take that much notice of what we're called anyway. We had swapped our badges and one of them always mixed us up, so it seemed like an omen.'

'And you learned to drive?'

Leah nodded. 'That was Elise's idea as well. We'd got the time to plan my escape you see. She worked it all out, bank account, the whole works. And then we tried to decide how best to do it, where to go, where we thought no one would look for us. To begin with it was like a game – we'd look at houses on her laptop on Right Move. Somerset, Cornwall, France, Italy – she had been to Ireland a few times when she was a teenager and was convinced I'd love it here–'

'And you do?'

Leah smiled. 'Yes, I do. She came over on her own to look at the house, opened a bank account with my documents. No one noticed that she didn't look much like the photo.

'And how did you get from Hoden Gap to here?'

Leah went very still. 'If I tell you will there be any trouble?'

'Trouble?'

'For whoever helped me?'

I shook my head. 'Did they break the law?'

'I don't think so.'

I smiled. 'Then they're fine. I would just like to know how.'

Leah took a long breath. 'There's a girl who delivers to the garden centre, her name is Katya. She's from the Ukraine.'

I stared at her, the penny finally dropping. The girl I had seen on the CCTV footage, the girl buying cakes had been the same one I had seen delivering to Charlotte's Garden. The girl who had raised her hand in thanks. That's why she had looked so familiar.

'Katya understands all about keeping quiet,' said Leah. 'She would sometimes arrive early at the garden centre and I'd let her in, get her coffee. She'd told me a few stories about her life back home, just in passing and I thought I could trust her. She was used to keeping her head down and her mouth shut. So I offered her five hundred pounds to help me. She drove the van up to Hoden Gap for me and parked in a service road on the back of the industrial estate. I don't think anyone uses it, but I'd seen it before when we'd stopped there, when they were laying the roads out before they built the banks, and then when I checked it out on the map it seemed like a good place to park up and avoid the motorway.

'Katya arrived first, parked up and came in over the bank, went in to get a drink and waited for us to show up.

'When I got there she followed me into the disabled toilet. She'd brought me a change of clothes and we swapped coats. She put on the camel coat I'd bought from a charity shop. Then I went outside and headed for the van. The plan was that she would follow me out, it took her a while because she had bought cakes and left them in the café. She said she nearly died when Chris grabbed hold of her.'

The breath caught in Leah's throat, as if she was reliving the moment.

'And the blind spot?'

Leah stared at me, and then reddened, as if she was surprised that we had found it, and then said, 'I noticed it when I was waiting for Chris once. It was like a bizarre magic trick. I was watching the screens and realised that some of the people coming through the doors were invisible. I think I turned round and walked into someone having been looking at the screens and not realising he was even there. I thought it would be good not to be seen, then maybe the search would begin somewhere else. It didn't matter so much when I came out because by then I'd changed clothes. I was so scared he might spot me, I tried not to think about it. I mean I wouldn't have been able to explain – he'd have known.

'Anyway Katya told me to walk like I belonged, not to rush, to amble out. I waited for her round by the fences and bins. Got out a packet of cigarettes that she had left in the jacket pocket of her coat and lit one, so it would look like I'd gone out for a smoke.'

Leah laughed. 'I've never smoked in my life, so I just lit and held it. I've got no idea how long she was but when she got there she'd already taken the camel coat off, rolled it up under her arm and stuffed it back in her bag. And then she lit a cigarette. "Talk to me," she said. "Like we're on a break." She'd got this slicker thing on underneath the camel coat and took another cap out of the bag, and then we both headed for the far side of the lorries. She said that if there was CCTV it would be on the back so they could see if anyone was breaking into the trailers. So we skirted round the side. When we got to the top end near the big skips we just slipped over the bank.'

'You'd planned it well.'

'I had gone over it a million times in my head but it was nothing like I imagined. I thought everyone was looking at me, just because my heart was beating so loudly. I felt so sick.

Chapter Eighteen

Once we were outside and over the bank I kept thinking he would see us, follow us, catch up.

'Anyway we got to the van and then we drove across country, picked up the motorway. I dropped Katya off at Swansea Railway Station so she could get home. And then I went on to Anglesey to catch *The Swift* over to Dublin.'

I took a long pull on my tea. 'What about the coat in the boot, and the phone and handbag in Norfolk? What was all that about? Was it just to muddy the waters? You could have just slipped away.'

Leah's expression hardened; her gaze meeting mine. 'I didn't want to just slip away. I wanted you to look at Chris. I knew that there was something not right. I've known for a long time. Or at least guessed, but I didn't know what to do about it.' She stopped, as if trying to compose herself.

'When I first met him I was barely seventeen and he was nearly thirty. I was looking for someone to take care of me, to look after me. I know that now but it wasn't so clear to me back then. And it was flattering to think someone like Chris was interested in me. It felt special to be with someone older, sophisticated.

'He'd got money, his own house and he really seemed to care about me, and I'd only got my mum and she couldn't look after herself let alone me. It was so different to be with someone who wanted to know where you were and what you'd been doing, who bought you clothes. I was seventeen, totally naïve, never had a boyfriend, never been kissed. Chris made me feel like a princess.

'Anyway we were out having a meal. It was Valentine's Day and he had made a big thing of it – and taken me out to this really nice pub. We were just about to leave when he got into a row with a woman. I was really shocked, up until then he had always been really calm and easy going. I didn't realise then that it was his ex-wife, Linda, but anyway she must have found out who I was and when I was coming out of work a couple of days later there she was.'

'That must have been a shock.'

Leah nodded. 'To be honest I was terrified of her, Chris had told me she was crazy and was stalking him – but there she was, and she was really nice to me. And calm but certainly not taking any prisoners. She told me that she knew I was going out with Chris and had come to warn me, said I shouldn't see Chris again, that I should keep away from him – that he was trouble, bad news, and that it had taken her years to get away from him.' Leah's voice trembled with the telling. 'God, I wish I'd listened to her.'

In the basket by the stove the dog looked up anxiously and padded over to rest his head on her lap. Without looking she began to stroke him, tugging gently at his ears, her fingers working over his thick silky coat.

'I was so naïve, just a kid, I didn't believe her. I thought she wanted him back, that she was jealous, trying to ruin what Chris and I had.' Leah paused, struggling to keep it together.

'Linda said that she would come and see me again and gave me her telephone number just in case I ever needed it. And then she told me that I had to get away from Chris while I still could. Told me to ring her any time, day or night, anytime at all.

'Anyway when Chris came to pick me up, I don't know why but I told him. I told him everything she had said to me. God, he was furious. I mean really, really, angry. I don't think up until then I'd ever seen anyone so angry in all my life. He told me I wasn't to take notice of what she had said. I was stunned by the way he was about it. He made me give him the piece of paper she'd given me, ripped it up and told me there was no way I was to ever speak to her again, and that I wasn't to worry, that he would go see her and sort it out.' Leah took a deep breath.

'The thing is, after that I never saw her again,' Leah said, setting her mug down on the kitchen table. 'She didn't come to see me and Chris never mentioned her again.' Leah looked up, her gaze holding mine. 'Not once.'

'Every year we would go to Wales in the spring, in February every year without fail. He says it's lovely there at that time of the year – a week or so after Valentine's Day – but it's not lovely. You've been, haven't you? I saw you on the news on the internet. It's cold and bleak, damp and grey. I asked him once why we had to go – and he said because he liked to see the snowdrops in the garden. They made him think about new lives, fresh starts–'

Leah's eyes were full of tears. 'There's a part of me that's always known that they were there, Linda and the children, buried in the garden by the conifers because she had the nerve to cross him, the nerve to leave him. And I was certain that that's what he had planned for me when we got to Wales on that last trip. He knew I was unhappy. I think he suspected I was planning to leave him, and he couldn't have coped with that.'

I waited, thinking about the depressions in the grass beside the river at the cottage in Wales, that I had taken for flower beds, and the snowdrops growing at the head of every one, and the sheet of polythene carefully taped down on the floor in the secret room at the back of the garage, the freezer, the smell of bleach, but most of all the tub of snowdrops, waiting in the sunshine, and I said nothing.

'But you know about them now, don't you?' said Leah, back handing the tears away.

I nodded. 'We found them because of the snowdrops,' I said softly.

'It was my fault,' said Leah.

I shook my head. 'You can't blame yourself for what he did. You were a child, Leah and he was –'

'A monster,' said Leah.

The dog got up, padded over to the door and looked up expectantly.

Leah glanced at me. 'Do you want to go for a walk?' she asked. 'Get the kinks out?'

*

The tide was out. The sand, rippled and carved by earlier tides and the breeze, stretched across unbroken to Omey Island, the roadway across the glittering white-gold surface picked out by poles. Above us, the sky, peppered by gulls, was as blue as I had ever seen it.

'Nice dog,' I said, stuffing my hand into my jacket pockets. The dog skipped and ran around us, not straying more than twenty yards ahead.

Leah nodded. 'He's lovely, isn't he? He found me, first week I moved in he kept turning up on my doorstep every morning.

I've asked around but no one seems to know where he came from. The people at the shop think he maybe came with some people who camped up around the point there.'

'And abandoned him?'

'Seems like it. He hadn't got a collar, wasn't chipped. You know, I've always wanted a dog. And a family.'

I said nothing.

'I thought it was me, you know, after all Chris had three kids, so when I didn't get pregnant I went to see our GP. And Chris let me go through all the tests. Some of them he sat in with me at the hospital and held my hand. Held my bloody hand. And then one day I ran into his sister in town and was saying we were having problems. I told her I felt guilty and she said, "Oh has Chris had his vasectomy reversed?"'

Leah picked up the dog's ball and threw it across the sand. He obliged by retrieving it and bringing it back, dropping it at her feet.

'I would like to have been a mother,' said Leah. 'Sometimes I imagine what they would look like – a boy and girl. They'd be all grown up by now. I might even be a grandmother. But then in some ways I'm glad that I didn't. I wouldn't want to risk them turning out like him.'

'Did you tell Chris that you knew?'

Leah shook her head. 'No, what was the point. I'd seen what he was like when he lost his temper, what it was like by then when I crossed him, and it explained everything, but I think his sister must have said something, because he told me he'd been to see her and then he waited, like he was expecting me to say something.'

'But you didn't?'

'No, I wouldn't give him the satisfaction. But after that we didn't go and see her again, didn't speak to her or about her.'

Leah picked the ball up again and threw it out towards the water's edge. The dog bounded after it, full of life.

'The thing is,' she said in an undertone, looking back to meet my eye. 'I don't think Linda and the children were the only ones.'

I stared at her. 'What do you mean? '

She stood stock still. 'Chris often went away on business. I don't know if you went down there but in the spring the far end of the orchard is full of snowdrops, there are clumps under every tree,' said Leah, as the dog came back again with the ball. 'And there were more every year.'

Coming soon

The next case for Mel Daley…

After Alice
by Sue Welfare

DS Mel Daley is settling into her new life in Norfolk working with the regional murder squad, until one night her brother in law, Jimmy, shows up on her doorstep. Their history is why she left her last job and moved five hours drive across country, but it seems she didn't move far enough.

When the next day the body of a young woman is found at a local farm Mel realises with a growing sense of horror that the victim looks like her sister, the sister who has just thrown Jimmy out.

As she starts to investigate the murder, Mel begins to see that this victim is part of a larger pattern, the victim of a serial killer who has ranged the length and breadth of the country.

Has Mel unwittingly brought a murderer to her door?

And will she be able to stop him killing again?

Also by Mirror Books

1963 - A Slice of Bread and Jam
Tommy Rhattigan

Tommy lives at the heart of a large Irish family in derelict Hulme in Manchester, ruled by an abusive, alcoholic father and a negligent mother. Alongside his siblings he begs (or steals) a few pennies to bring home to avoid a beating, while looking for a little adventure of his own along the way.

His foul-mouthed and chaotic family may be deeply flawed, but amongst the violence, grinding poverty and distinct lack of hygiene and morality lies a strong sense of loyalty and, above all, survival.

During this single year – before his family implodes and his world changes for ever – Tommy almost falls foul of the welfare officers, nuns, police – and Myra Hindley and Ian Brady.

An adventurous, fun, dark and moving true story of the only life young Tommy knew.

Also by Mirror Books

Death at Wolf's Nick
Diane Janes

In January 1931, on a lonely stretch of Northumberland moorland known as Wolf's Nick, flames rose up into the night sky. Evelyn Foster, a young taxi driver, lay near her burning car, engulfed in flames, praying for a passing vehicle.

With her last breath, she described her attacker: a mysterious man with a bowler hat who had asked her to drive him to the next village, then attacked her and left her to die. Local police attempted to track down Evelyn's killer – while others questioned the circumstances, Evelyn's character and if there was even a man at all…

Professional crime writer and lecturer Diane Janes gained unprecedented access to Evelyn's case files. Through her evocative description, gift for storytelling and detailed factual narrative, Diane takes the reader back to the scene of the crime, painting a vivid description of village life in the 1930s.

Central to this tragic tale, is a daughter, sister and friend who lost her life in an horrific way – and the name of her murderer, revealed for the first time…

Mirror Books

Also by Mirror Books

The Hunt for the 60s Ripper
Robin Jarossi

While 60s London was being hailed as the world's most fashionably vibrant capital, a darker, more terrifying reality was unfolding on the streets. During the early hours a serial killer was stalking prostitutes then dumping their naked bodies. When London was famed for its music, groundbreaking movies and Carnaby Street vibe, the reality included a huge street prostitution scene, a violent world that filled the magistrate's courts.

Seven, possibly eight, women fell victim – making this killer more prolific than Jack the Ripper, 77 years previously. His grim spree sparked the biggest police manhunt in history. But why did such a massive hunt fail? And why has such a traumatic case been largely forgotten today?

With shocking conclusions, one detective makes an astonishing new claim. Including secret police papers, crime reconstructions, links to figures from the vicious world of the Kray twins and the Profumo Affair, this case exposes the depraved underbelly of British society in the Swinging Sixties. An evocative and thought-provoking reinvestigation into perhaps the most shocking unsolved mass murder in modern British history.

Also by Mirror Books

Murder in Belgravia
A MAYFAIR 100 MURDER MYSTERY

Lynn Brittney

London, 1915. Just 10 months into the First World War, and the City is flooded with women taking over the work vacated by men in the Armed Services.

Chief Inspector Peter Beech, a young man invalided out of the war in one of the first battles, is investigating the murder of an aristocrat and the man's wife, a key witness and suspect, will only speak to a woman about the unpleasant details of the case. Beech persuades the Chief Commissioner to allow him to set up a clandestine team to deal with this case and other such situations, and pulls together a small crew of hand-picked women and professional policemen. Their telephone number: Mayfair 100.

When Beech, Victoria, Caroline, Rigsby and Tollman investigate the murder, they delve into the seedier parts of WWI London, taking them from brothels and criminal gangs to underground drug rings that supply heroin to the upper classes. Will the Mayfair 100 gang solve the murder? And if they do, will they be allowed to continue working as a team?

Also by Mirror Books

Motherland
G.D. Abson

The first in a gripping series of contemporary crime novels
set in St Petersburg, featuring the brilliant and principled policewoman,
Captain Natalya Ivanova.

Student Zena Dahl, the daughter of a Swedish millionaire, has gone missing
in St Petersburg (or Piter as the city is known locally) after a night out with
a friend. Captain Natalya Ivanova is assigned to the case. It makes a change
from her usual fare of domestic violence work, however, because of the
family's wealth and profile, there's a lot of pressure on her for a quick result.

But as Natalya investigates, she discovers that the case is not as
straightforward as it first seemed. Dark, evocative, violent and insightful,
MOTHERLAND twists and turns to a satisfyingly dramatic conclusion.